Author's note

In order to convey modern-day communication in China this book contains dialogue in the form of WeChat exchanges. These exchanges have been indented differently to the normal dialogue sections to allow the reader to easily identity them.

Love in a Forbidden City

Paul C. R. Monk

A BLOOMTREE PRESS Book

First published in 2021 by BLOOMTREE PRESS

ISBN 978-1-9196486-0-6

www.paulcrmonk.com

Formatting by Polgarus Studio

Cover design by David Ter-Avanesyan/Ter33Design

For Amii

1

Lin Cheng had been looking forward to a prosperous start to this coming Year of the Rat.

Another senior exec all but placed, which meant a 10 percent takeaway on the candidate's yearly salary. A nice catch, though by no means an easy one to land. The spec had been challenging: senior level but under forty, having worked for international companies but available for the polluted skies of Beijing. And yet she had found him, that rare pearl, that five-legged ram. So it was with utter dismay that she reread the WeChat message she had received from Mr. Yang while having lunch on floor minus one with her colleagues. It read: 'Apologies, no longer able to come to Beijing due to personal reasons.'

She had cut short her meal break, slipped into her black wrap-collar coat, and had skipped back through the glossy basement to the elevator. Lin's eyes now singled out "personal reasons" as she strode sure-footed in her stiletto heel ankle boots into the lobby of TalentPlus HQ. It was located on the thirtieth floor of the gleaming office building in the Guomao business district of Beijing. Deep in thought, she continued past the reception desk, pushed the door into the chic, plant-filled open-plan office, and made a beeline for her work station by the window. If Mr Yang's present company had made a better offer, she could deal with it within reason, she said to herself. But *personal,* what could that mean? Why such mystery? He was free and single, and even if he was dating the woman of his dreams, who lived on the other side of the universe, it was no reason to turn down a dream job that others could not even aspire to before they turned forty, especially in the automotive industry.

Reaching her soft leather armchair, she tucked her mid-long hair delicately behind her ears. Then she hit the space bar on her PC and punched in her password, made up of her pet's name and her date of birth. She would have to change it, she thought to herself, wipe away that constant reminder that time was escaping her.

Five years ago, she thought nothing of it; she was twenty-nine back then and seeing someone. But they split because of her career choice, a better opportunity in a new headhunting firm where she now worked and earned twice as much as in her previous job in Singapore. She had met another man, wealthy, a passionless divorcee but from a good family. After a year of her agonising whether or not he would pop the question, he dropped her like a stale dumpling. He had cut her loose, and it was all her fault, she had thought, for going on a weeklong sulk. Just the pretext he apparently needed to call off their relationship without so much as a goodbye. And now, here she was, about to turn thirty-five.

She maximized the WeChat panel on her screen, then drummed her fingers deftly over the pinyin keyboard. She typed: 'Mr Yang, I do not understand. The contract is ready for your signature. Please explain your reasons then maybe we can sort it out.'

She clicked the send button while secretly saying to herself: *Come on, man, what the heck's wrong with you? I mean, you haven't found out you've got a secret child in America, have you?* She knew he had worked there for three years after leaving Wuhan, which was why he was so hot on the market, and not just on the job market either.

The answer came back in a flash. It read: 'My mother has taken ill with a new virus. I have to go back to Wuhan. Thank you in advance for your understanding.'

Lin had earlier stumbled upon some news about a mysterious virus affecting Wuhan that had gone viral on WeChat. But as one colleague over lunch had put it, there had been just a few cases so far, whereas the common flu carried away tens of thousands of elderly people every year.

Then the thought came to her that Mr Yang's mother would probably be no older than her own parents, who lived and worked in her hometown near Qintao along the east coast. What would she do if they caught this virus and died? They would have passed away without seeing their grandchild. The mere thought was unbearable, and she could empathize now with Mr Yang, who was also without children.

She drummed out another message on her keyboard. She wrote: 'I am so sorry to hear that. I sincerely hope she makes a quick recovery.'

Nevertheless, on hitting the send button, she could not help guiltily thinking to herself that the case might not be lost after all. All he perhaps needed was a little time so he could see his mother through her illness. Lin could explain the situation to the employer and probably buy some time, even though it would mean postponing her commission, which was nonetheless better than getting no commission at all.

But the next day brought more news of a similar nature of another candidate from Wuhan. She perused the dwindling list of candidates she was trying to place. This new Year of the Rat might not turn out to be that prosperous after all, she thought to herself. But then, she had a lightbulb moment that could redeem her: she recalled a potential foreign candidate she had been trying to match with one of her mobile game clients. She pulled up his profile picture: short mouse-brown hair swept back, a quietly confident smile, sensual brow, and nice lips. She knew from previous meetings with him that he had good teeth, green eyes, and that he was forty-two. She typed in her message.

2

Standing in line before gate 45 terminal 5 at Heathrow, Colin pulled out his phone from his parka pocket.

He pressed the fingerprint sensor, then thumbed to the WeChat app — that quintessential app for life in China today. It opened on last week's message from Lin, the headhuntress he had met during his previous stay in the Chinese capital, and who was recruiting for a competing mobile game company. He scrolled through the thread as he read:

'Hey Colin, when u due back in Beijing?'

'Hi Lin, next week, still waiting for confirmation. Maybe we can catch up?'

'Sure. BTW can u send me the address of that service apartment you stay at? Have a new recruit coming from Russia.'

'Igor, the concept artist I mentioned?'

'No, a creative director. Worked on same project though'

'Ah, right. Nearest underground station is Wudaokou, Haiden district, here's a pic of the card.'

'thx, good day'

'u too, talk soon'

She must be anxious for him to jump ship, he thought. Why else would she find a pretext to text him? At any rate, the fact he was being headhunted gave him, if not negotiating power, at least a confidence shot to ask for a raise from PlayZone, the mobile game company on the rise and his present employer. He opened the WeChat interface again to check out her profile picture. Chic, mid-thirties, subtly made up, and dark mid-long hair with highlights. He gazed at her pretty oriental eyes, her dainty nose, and her half-parted lips that gave a glimpse of her white teeth. From previous meetings with her, he distinctly recalled her smile against her glowing complexion; he remembered thinking it was nothing short of illuminating.

As the queue shuffled forward, he thumbed back a screen and hit another face. It belonged to Max, a young Russian-Asian: thirty, forthright and proud of his person. He read:

'Same hotel, driver will pick you up.'

'Ok'

'He will take you to the hotel first, then you can come to the office when you are ready.'

'Roger that. See you Friday'

'Ok'

Straight to the point, Max, thought Colin. No fluff. No fanfare, just the bare essentials. Max was the killer HR guy who had headhunted him in the first place, and Colin had seized the opportunity to check out China for better or for worse. But never in a thousand years could he have predicted how radical a life-changing experience it would turn out to be.

3

Ever feel like a strange force is holding you back? read Colin to himself as he perused his little black notebook.

In it he collected scribblings, stray thoughts, and stolen bits of overheard conversations. It was his habit to nail everything down on paper. He continued reading back to himself as he stood waiting at the baggage carousel at the new Beijing airport.

Since the dawn of time when Adam embraced Eve, everyone's life has been intrinsically linked to one other life somewhere in the world, could be anywhere. A recurrent bad dream unrelated to your own sphere of existence is a sure sign that your counterpart is having a bad time, which knocks your stars out of line. And you can only fix them if you can reach out to that person, who of course is none other than your soulmate. This book is about finding that person and setting them right, so that you, too, can live a happier life with your stars all aligned and the positive vibes of the cosmos driving you to where you want to go. Colin rolled his eyes and wondered why he still jotted down such ramblings. There again, you never knew when they could come in handy, especially in the vast and varied world of video games.

Glancing up again, this time he caught sight of his leather travel bag emerging onto the baggage reclaim carousel. He pocketed his notebook, shouldered his laptop backpack, and strode to a clearing at the conveyor belt.

As he grabbed the large brown bag, his eyes fell upon the little brass padlock that fastened the zips together. Then he recalled an earlier feeling of missing something from his jeans pocket. He suddenly realised now what it was. The little brass key. Searching through his memory, he came to the conclusion that he must have left it in the customs tray at Heathrow after he had emptied his pockets. He would just have to find a luggage shop and ask someone to break the padlock open.

He looked around at the calm and sparkling area of Beijing Daxing International Airport to find the way out. So this was the 'starfish' airport that the in-flight magazine had told him was the newest and largest airport on the planet. As his gaze panned around the futuristic forms and sober hues, he could not help noticing a larger number of people than usual wearing face masks. He had learnt during his last work visit that it was a cultural thing, and part and parcel of office etiquette to keep your germs to yourself, not to mention protect yourself from the high peaks of Beijing city pollution. Then he recalled browsing through a news item sent by one of his colleagues as he disembarked from the plane. Something about a new virus reported in a city a few hundred miles south of the capital. Were these people actually protecting themselves against potential infection? Slightly over the top, thought Colin as he passed two customs officers, and then the thought left him.

'*Ni hao* . . . Do you speak English?' he said to the lady guard, thinking it more polite to ask than to just go steamrolling in using English.

'No,' said the woman, vigorously shaking her head. Her coworker shook his head with her as he pointed to the way out.

'I just wanted to know if I could break this lock, lost key . . . no key,' he insisted. But the officers pointed more insistently toward the exit, just content to get him off their patch.

Walking through customs into the arrivals area, he noticed an array of held-up cards and A4 sheets of paper until he saw his name in large capital letters: COLIN FRIAR. He tried to explain to the burly chauffeur that before leaving the airport, he needed to find a place where he could break the lock. There was, of course, no way in the undecipherable world outside the airport that he could even identify the right shop, given that everything was in Chinese characters — characters that had absolutely nothing in common with any European language. It was utterly alienating, like being illiterate. The driver took him to an airport official who must have said it was not possible to break into someone's suitcase, because the driver then swiftly took up the bag himself and beckoned Colin to follow him toward the multi-storey car park.

It was annoying. How was he supposed to open his case now? he wondered as he watched the landscape go by through the car window, his face taut with frustration. He looked at his vibrating phone and stabbed Max's head.

> 'Hey man, you in the taxi yet?'
>
> 'Yeah'
>
> 'Good, driver will take you to same place as usual. Then when you're ready, come here to the studio. We can sort out your registration with the local police later.'
>
> 'Roger that'

Colin put the phone back down on the seat next to him. Grey clusters of high-storey apartment blocks soon replaced the open fields and smooth new motorway. The driver slowed down after they came into a street of residential compounds and ground-floor shops. Recalling the multitude of roadside moped mechanics, Colin cottoned onto the driver's idea.

'You stay here,' said the driver in a staccato fashion after pulling over, and then went to talk with a wispy-haired mechanic. He was one of the multitude who repair the thousands of electric mopeds whose riders will deliver anything to your door, from a packet of aspirin to a four-course meal, and as Colin had previously found out, even an all-in-one HP printer. Online delivery had opened up a whole service industry in conjunction with WeChat, and had given employment to legions of men with electric mopeds and customized three-wheel carriers. The driver returned to retrieve Colin's luggage bag from the boot so the mechanic could break the padlock.

Half an hour later, they were pulling up at the service apartment compound, set in a quiet street in the Haiden district of northwest Beijing. Colin was familiar with the area now: the Lotus mall, the first-storey restaurant windows, and the street-level shop façades. It had not changed in the last couple of months except that winter clothing had replaced the shorts and summer T-shirts. And the beautiful lean legs of Chinese women were no longer on display.

The taxi was paid for, but Colin looked in his wallet, and left a tip of one hundred RMB, ridiculously high, but he was glad to be able to open his bag. He could hardly go to the studio after a twenty-four-hour trip, reeking of red wine and travel sweat.

Using a translation app, he checked in and soon found himself in his room, this time on the seventh floor; not as nicely decorated as the previous one, but this one had a microwave oven, and a larger TV screen. It was a $33m^2$ self-contained service apartment with a double bed on the far end by the floor-to-ceiling window. In the midsection, there was a sofa in front of a low glass table, and a TV with a work table and lamp to one side of it. At the near end leading from the entrance, a short passage led to the bathroom and then, a few steps further on, to a kitchenette with a dividing bar.

Feeling better after a hot shower, he dressed, slipped on his ankle boots, and threaded his arms through his parka sleeves. Three minutes later, he was downstairs in the biting cold and found himself slipping into the same routine he had adopted every workweek morning back in the hazy summer. He quickly found what he was looking for near the fruit and veg stands in a neighbouring compound: a bike, the best means of transport in Beijing by far for anything below five miles in distance, and cheap, too, at 15p for a half-hour ride.

He pedalled along the cycle paths next to the main dual carriageway, wheeled across the fourth ring-road crossing with a hoard of other cyclists and mopeds, and pushed on through a university campus — a shortcut and a much calmer ride away from the polluted highway. Fingers chilled by the mid-morning cold, Colin arrived in front of the modern office tower where now only the most fervent smokers stood huddled and puffing on their nicotine dose. Colin did not smoke and prided himself on his excellent erectile functions, concluding that there was nothing to clog up the flow of blood to the instrument of his manhood. It was something he was thankful for, because it had played an important role in his life thus far and had been the source of unending pleasures that a million cigarettes could never equal.

He slapped his plastic pass on the entrance post and caught the lift to the twentieth floor. So far so good, he thought to himself.

One thing about being in China is that it was still rare to walk about the perimeters of the capital with a Caucasian face. It acted as a ticket for indulgence in most cases so that you were given a wider berth than the average Chinese man. So when Colin signalled to the guard to trip the eye recognition system because he still hadn't registered, there were no questions asked.

Now for the moment to make everyone cringe, he

thought to himself. Giving a wave left and right, he made his way to his work station. *'Hei, zao!'* he called out, then gave a hug to his closest coworkers, who reacted shyly, the Chinese not ones to show overt affection. But he was a Westerner, so they played along, and awkward hugs were exchanged. After a meeting with the producer, he switched on his PC, then headed for the coffee machine. Before the coffee had filtered into his PlayZone mug, he heard a familiar Russian accent.

'Hey, man, you look awful!'

'Thanks for the welcome!' laughed Colin, clasping the outstretched hand.

'You didn't sleep on the plane, right?'

'No . . .'

'Come, let's sit and catch up.' This was Maxim. The Russian-Asian, lean and of average height, made a sign to follow.

'Can't, not right now, Max, I need to meet with Kai.'

Max halted and turned. Scratching his head of short-cropped hair, he said: 'Let's catch up tonight then.'

'All right, but nothing heroic,' returned Colin, wagging a warning finger.

'Relax, man, it's Friday, you can rest all weekend.'

'All right, WeChat me later then.'

Max gave half a nod, then made off, rolling his shoulders like the cock of the walk.

4

For his first ten years of building narratives into video games, Colin used to get a recurring nightmare: going to work only to find he had forgotten to put his trousers on.

It got better after that, though: instead, he would dream of turning up looking like Spock or any other space opera character, which to Colin probably meant that he no longer felt like an impostor. The side effect of this was a warped sense of dress which, since first landing in China, he had endeavoured to tone down to the classic polo, jeans, and hoodie.

Working in games had taught him the importance of creating conflict, setting up obstacles, and putting square things into round holes, all in the name of that supreme video game goddess that goes by the name of *Fun*. But *Fun* also had her moments of inflicting torture. On the Tuesday before leaving to spend Christmas back home, he was adding the final edits to his fifty-thousand-word lore bible when a coder crept up and boldly said: 'Colin, I have fun job for you.'

‘Cool, go on,’ said Colin, already trembling in his ankle boots, because he knew that the day a coder came up to you angelically trying to radiate beatitude, *Fun* was about to crack her whip.

‘We need to make tattoos for player so they can personify their characters,’ said the coder, still trying to fight against the stiffness caused by his natural tendency to geekism, which Colin had long since learnt transcends nationality, race, religion, and even gender. He once thought that the condition must even exist in snowbound Eskimos, and that it would come out when someone decided one day to set up a video game company in the North Pole.

‘Sounds good. How many?’ said Colin on the edge of his seat, trying to sound enthused.

‘Yeah, we will need a few.’

‘Like how many, five, ten, fifteen?’

‘Something like that . . . but per race, per type, and per region.’ Colin’s mind started to reel as the impact of the request forced him to sit back in his office chair. The friendly coder continued: ‘Yes, we need four hundred and forty-four tattoo names.’

‘Wow!’ said Colin, scratching the back of his head that was already beginning to throb.

‘For Thursday!’

‘Oh, really?’ Colin’s hand passed from his crown to his forehead.

‘It’s a priority. We need something to feed to the community because our event is put off: we have big bug.’ Colin flinched at that other three-letter word: *Bug*, the nemesis of *Fun*. 'It is easy,' continued the coder. 'I can think of at least five or ten right now!'

Colin went through various stages of brain shredding, trying to fill in 444 Excel cells by creating families pertaining to factions, zones, and race. But he pulled it off, even including original alliterations such as Kami Caster, which Xiao Long, one of the few designers with a good grasp of English, had something to say about. 'Don't look cool,' he said.

'Then Kami Kaster, with two Ks.'

'Does it mean anything?'

'It does now. And now it has its own etymology. How cool it that?'

But being a narrative designer and writer can get lonely, though, caught as he often was between two opposite personality types: programmers and artists. Not only that, the bare truth was, no one had read the narrative bible he had sent through the DingTalk group while working remotely from his flat in London. The fact that it wasn't in Chinese probably did nothing to help promote it. So that morning, Colin had decided to organise a short presentation of the story outline, which meant spending much of the day being a narrative fleabag hopping here and there, trying to bring the two distinct species together. Once he had finished his thirty-minute PowerPoint presentation, the lead artist said: 'I think I get it, but what we need is Fun!'

'Yeah,' said Xiao Long, 'and by the way, the players loved the tats!'

'Ah yes, so we've decided to create power-ups,' said Kai,

the lead artist, in Chinese, which Xiao Long translated into English.

Colin's face slowly migrated into his boots. But back against the wall, that's when he was sometimes visited by the video game goddess. 'I got it, guys,' he said in a burst of imagination. 'Let's make them different colours: purple for the prime roots, green for the verdant heights, orange for the desert lands, and blue for the great lakes.'

'Yeah, that means more tats, yummy yummy,' said Xiao Long cheerily as the programmers were already peeling away and sneaking back to their own little worlds of code.

Colin had drawn a rough map to show the locations of the different places of the game world. Kai, who was a laugh a minute, picked up on a part of it that looked inadvertently like a small erect cock and two large balls.

'Like Little Dragon!' he said, translating Xiao Long's name into English, and burst out laughing.

Little Dragon smiled along, content to be the butt end of the joke. So, Colin turned it upside down and said: 'And this is yours!' It showed the supposed small male shaft on a distinct downer. 'That's what happens when a smoker reaches forty, ha ha!' said Colin. Everyone including Kai, a heavy smoker, exploded into joyous laughter.

Colin had long since observed that the Chinese will laugh out loud heartily at anything with an ounce of humour. It didn't take much, and Colin was enjoying exercising his flair for innocent silliness, albeit often in mime, and it was helping him become part of the team. As he was nonetheless realising that nobody gave a monkey's ass about the story, he received a WeChat ping. It was Lin, the headhuntress he had forgotten to message. He read: 'Hey Colin, so did you make it back to Beijing yet?'

Too busy trying to humour his colleagues, he pocketed his phone. He would message Lin later.

5

After a wholly dissatisfying afternoon at the office, Lin was glad to join her sword fencing session down in the basement gym.

January was always a difficult time, but why did this feeling of the ground being swiped from beneath her feet seem to be pursuing her more and more often these days? Was she losing her charms? After the session, as she headed for her black SUV Benz, she checked her WeChat feed again. Nothing. At least, nothing but a message from Yuping, her best friend from her university days. She wanted to put off tomorrow's lunchtime catch-up because of a sick child. Lin slipped into the Benz, placed her effects on the passenger seat, and slid her phone into the dashboard holder. As she pulled out of the car park she hit the call button.

Yuping had been a successful modern woman in new China until she married, fell pregnant, and decided to devote her time and fine intellect to her new family. Lin never did understand why such a bright star would hide her light behind a mother's apron. But Yuping was adamant; she admitted it was what she had always wanted, to catch a highly qualified suitor with diplomas as good as hers; a man who could rise with her good self behind him and earn a good salary. She had achieved that goal seven years ago. Now the kids were boisterous lads of eight and six, and she was enjoying motherhood and having a real house with a garden in a suburb of Beijing.

After getting an update on Yuping's son and rescheduling their catch-up, Lin let Yuping continue on the topic of their previous conversation. 'So what about Wei Leng? He is from a good family and works for Renault,' said Yupin. 'Good job. Good salary. Good prospects. And his family is loaded.'

'So why doesn't he have a wife?' said Lin as she joined the steady stream of traffic on the third ring road.

'He did, once. Besides, he could say the same about you: Why don't you have a husband?'

'True,' said Lin, then after a moment's pause while one of Yupin's children was asking his mother something about food, she said: 'All right, I will go.'

'Good, then I will fix it up,' said Yuping, businesslike. 'You might as well skip the coffee at your ages. I can vouch for him and so can Liang. Your mum will be pleased; I think she even knew Wei's mother once. Go straight for the dinner: more intimate, more time, and you'll be able to see immediately how the ground lies.'

'All right, so where do we meet?'

'I was thinking of the restaurant in the Grand Hyatt, nice place, expensive too. You'll be able to check out his face when it comes to paying for the champagne.' Yuping gave a merry little laugh.

‘OK, but not tomorrow though. I’ve an interview with an exec from Italy and a flyer to prepare for our next campaign.’

‘All right, I’ll get back to you with Wei’s availability. Better go, the tigers are hungry. Talk to you later, darling.’

6

That evening found Colin with Max.

They were sitting in the posh whisky bar in the basement of a floral café, a hidden gem unbeknownst to the non-savvy onlooker from the sidewalk. For once inside, a man activated a switch behind the counter, and a segment of a fake bookcase opened onto some stairs which led down into the chic basement venue. It was crowded with students whose parents could afford it, and well-heeled millennials in small groups, talking and laughing out loud.

'The thing about Chinese girls,' said Max in front of his fine whisky, 'is they need to be told!' Colin laughed out loud. It was typical Max talk. The Russian pursued, stabbing the air with his forefinger as he spoke. 'And they are all the same. Why are they all the same?'

'No idea,' replied Colin, sitting opposite with his back against the soft-backed bench, 'but I've a feeling you're gonna light my lantern.'

Max gave a squint, then said: 'It's because they are all born under the same fucking star sign, man!' Colin chuckled.

'I'm not kidding, man; they are all Scorpios! And I don't match with Scorpios!' continued Max, pouring another drink from the bottle of whisky. It was usual practice for them to buy a sealed bottle rather than getting it by the tumbler; this was the best way to avoid any cheap substitute that drove a stake through the brain come morning.

'Don't know what you're griping about,' returned Colin. 'You don't seem to be doing so bad.'

'Oh, I get my end in, but that's it . . . They don't make my heart miss a beat . . .'

'Well, buddy, maybe you're sending out the wrong signals. Maybe you ought to try being more . . . you know, caring.'

'Bah, I tried that, but then they just become demanding. Nah, the best way with Chinese girls is to take 'em firmly, and give it to 'em good. Then, when you're done, they will do anything for you, man. Because Chinese women only respond to male dominance!'

'You wouldn't get far with Western girls,' said Colin, who wondered about the veracity of Max's diagnostic on dating in China.

'Bah, plenty of 'em over here, and they all wanna get laid. And they don't give a shit. Girls today don't give a shit! It's like they've discovered they've got a pussy, man.'

'Come on!' said Colin, chuckling indulgently now.

'No, no, listen to me. Act like a family man, you get shat on. Girls. Like. Dominance! All of them, and they marry through calculation: they catch their pigeon of a husband, then they fuck elsewhere when they can, man.'

'So you don't believe in marriage. I sympathize there.'

'I'm telling you, man, every married woman I've met says she don't love her fucking husband.'

'Maybe it's the way you put the question.'

'You're just thinking like a Westerner . . . Watch out, you will get caught, man. Mark my words: you will get caught!'

Colin laughed, telling himself that this was typical Max, a smart guy but in need of love. Maybe this was his way of venting his frustration. Colin said: 'Perhaps it's because some Chinese husbands are about as tender as a tomb that some women cheat; women have their needs too. Women need tenderness.'

'Bah, that's shit. You're sounding like a family man, like Guanyu.'

Colin nodded with as condescending a smile as he could muster, then looked up as none other than Guanyu came into view and placed his glass on the table.

'Hey, man!' said Max, turning in his seat. 'We thought you'd gone.'

Late thirties, dressed more casually than a twenty-year-old rapper, Guanyu took a seat on the soft, red-cushioned bench next to Colin. Guanyu was in marketing. 'I was interviewing,' he said. 'This is where I like to bring my interviewees . . . Let's get another bottle.'

'Did he get the job?' said Colin.

'I think he did well,' said the marketer. Colin noticed the twinkle in his eye, and knew exactly what it meant. It meant the interviewee turned on his lights, because in spite of being married with a kid, he was attracted to men, which was helped by the fact that his wife lived in Shanghai: convenient, discreet. He had let it slip out the first time Max had introduced him in the same basement bar. A bottle of whisky later, he had announced he was gay, like it was something he desperately wanted get off his chest. Colin wondered at the time how gay men must live in China, where homosexuality was never talked about. Colin recalled thinking that Max had not even noticed the confession, given that they were sitting in a loud corner, and Colin, seated directly opposite, was the only one listening in his native tongue. 'You're talking to an Englishman,' he remembered saying on a *so what* kind of tone, and had added: 'Whatever works best for you, it's all right by me, although I should say, I'm just into the ladies myself.'

Colin recalled all this seeing Guanyu's twinkle of an eye. 'Hey, waiter, bring another bottle!' called the marketer. Then turning back to Colin, he said: 'So, writer, how's life been treating you?'

'Good.'

'He just got in,' said Max, and as a passing comment he added: 'He's buying a house in France.'

Colin smiled as Guanyu emptied the last drams of the whisky bottle equally into the three glasses. The Englishman smiled at Max's surprising retention of his plans for buying a holiday home. It had been his last attempt at trying to inject some mutual spirit of togetherness into his marriage before the unavoidable divorce. But his wife had not shown as much enthusiasm as he had hoped, and it had dawned on him that she, too, must have already realised that their marriage was over by then. In fact, it had been over for a number of years — years of sulks and cold wars interspersed with good times after make-ups. But these had become few and far between, and now with the youngest at senior school, the time had come to free them both from an impossible relationship. If they could not speak to each other while their children were still at home, how could they ever expect to live a fulfilling life together when their fledglings had left the nest?

Colin raised his glass but said nothing of the place in France. He had been stupid to evoke the idea of buying the house last year, but it had made him feel less unsuccessful. 'Can't stay too long, guys, haven't slept for two days,' he said half-heartedly.

'Catch up this weekend, man,' said Max.

'Come on, let's drink!' cheered Guanyu. The waiter brought another bottle of fine single malt as each emptied their glass. There were not many of his Chinese colleagues who drank so hard, and in truth, Colin was past the age of wanting to get a soaking and then hanging over. But these guys were great buddies and pulled their weight in the company. So he raised his glass again, and again…

Guanyu was a frustrated poet, a gentle man with an artist's soul. There could not be two greater extremes than he and Max. Colin was in the middle. Max, sure of himself, commanding. Guanyu searching for meaning in others, craving affection. In fact, it was dawning on Colin that all three of them were craving affection in one way or another.

Guanyu asked Colin how the game was coming along, and the three of them played at making up names for it, before moving onto wider issues. Glancing round, Colin noticed there were just a few masked people, but most of the population were drinking and chatting like on any other Friday night. He felt reassured, for it had been alarming to see so many people at the airport wearing face masks, perhaps they were just part of the same very cautious group.

'I studied literature, you know,' said Guanyu. 'Did Max tell you?'

'Yeah, yeah,' seconded Max, obviously trying to make up for not mentioning it, which was entirely in character because Max only spoke about things that interested him, and literature did not. 'Yeah, he used to write some clever shit . . .'

'Tell me as an author,' continued Guanyu, impervious to Max's short but evocative word picture. 'What do you think of this poem I came across the other day?' Then turning to Max, he said: 'You've heard it, haven't you, Max?'

'Yeah, man, you told me. You go ahead, tell it. It's good, man.'

'OK, hit me,' said Colin, bracing himself for the experience.

Guanyu, with a poetic flourish of the hand, recited a poem about the sun god trying to seduce the elusive dark side of the moon. 'So what do you think?' he concluded once he had finished, unmoved by Max's bored gaze.

'Yeah, err, well, I can't judge it on one hearing in a crowded whisky parlour,' said Colin, careful to tread lightly, figuring that the author was probably sitting in front of him. 'But it sounds like a student wrote it, something people write when they've studied literature and their head's still full of Shakespeare, Cervantes, and Racine. But I do like the recurring themes through the imagery. Something naïve and fresh, but nice, I guess . . . not something I'd write nowadays, though.'

'Just tell him it's shit, man, and drink up!' said Max, becoming impatient. 'I mean all that shit about a pink sun . . . it don't mean nothing in the real world. There's no point to it, right? I mean, it won't make anyone feel any better about themselves, or make anyone rich, so what's the point?'

'I wouldn't say that,' said Colin in a conciliating tone of voice. 'That would be like saying there's no point in creating art. And even that there's no point in making mobile games, which is probably true, but it's culture. It's what makes us human.'

'Nah, mobile games is what makes us money; pink suns make us wanna puke. Anyway, you guys gonna get into this book stuff all night?'

'Well, let me tell you,' said Guanyu, raising a finger, as imperturbable as ever. 'It won a prize. And the writer was me! When I was younger.'

'Just out of university?' said Colin.

'During, actually.'

Colin had expected no less, and was glad he had trodden lightly. He had met would-be writers before in marketing and publicity; it was where they often ended up when they realised they could not go the distance with a novel. That way, they got to spend hours coming up with the copy for an ad and call it a masterpiece. And of course, the like-minded people in the office believed it because it meant they could create a masterpiece too. There again, was Colin any better writing video games and now a mobile game? But at least he had published a few thrillers, which had the benefit of making him feel better about himself.

'What counts, man, is eat, shit, fuck!' said Max, stabbing the air above the table.

'Hah, you are young; you know nothing about life,' said Guanyu gently. 'You talk big about women, and you've never been married. You don't have a kid, and you tell me how to bring mine up.'

'And you talk like an old man. I'll show you how to talk to women. Watch and learn,' said Max.

Two girls, early twenties, had sat down at the next table but one, the group at the table in between having just left.

'No, hang on,' said Colin. 'I'm not into high school girls.'

'Relax and just watch,' said Max with an aura of authority.

Sure of himself, he called out to the girls in English. 'Hey, you two ladies!' They looked once, then looked at each other. Colin thought they must have seen two guys in early middle age and a youngish buck with a lot of front. But then the more assertive one looked again as Max said something in Chinese that must have meant *Come join us for a drink*, while indicating the free space with a nonchalant finger. 'Come on,' he insisted with a smile that was both gracious and condescending. Guanyu smiled politely and encouragingly. The girls glanced at each other again, and to Colin's surprise, they got to their feet, stepped over, and slid themselves into the vacant seats opposite each other. 'There, easy!' said Max, as much to the boys as to the girls. Colin remarked that they had seated themselves closer to Guanyu than to Max.

Guanyu turned to the girls, who apparently spoke no English, and he translated Colin's small talk. They were second-year students, not knowing yet what they wanted to do. Their answers were brief, coy, and unbecoming. Max looked on as they huddled in their seats like lost sheep before the wolf. But he quickly lost interest like a poker veteran drawing cards with a rookie.

'Pwah, they don't know anything,' he said in disappointment across the table to Colin. 'They can't even do banter.' Colin realised that for Max they were too easy; they were not in his league. The group quickly split between Max and Colin, and the girls with Guanyu, with the latter talking about marketing and Colin chipping in at times.

'You need to find out what you really want to do and then drill down,' he said at one stage. But it sounded even more condescending than he had intended and, realising how overbearing he must sound, he resorted to nodding his head in convenient places until the bar staff called time.

After some remonstrance with the waiter, Max swiped the whisky bottle from the table, and they all lumbered up the stairs. They promptly found themselves in the bitter-cold night air, waiting for Guanyu's taxi which he had ordered through Didi, the taxi app that Colin was keen to learn how to use. Otherwise, if you did not speak Chinese, then it was a sure sign for the cabby to charge triple the rate, the tourist rate. Colin had quickly concluded during his previous stays that WeChat and Didi, along with the food delivery app — symbolised by a kangaroo riding a moped — were part of the expat Beijinger's survival bundle that made life so much easier and cheaper in the Chinese capital.

The girls said goodbye timidly and headed back to wherever they had come from.

Stamping his feet to chase out the cold, Guanyu said: 'I asked them what they thought of you two.'

'Stupid females, couldn't even hold an adult conversation,' retorted Max, with his cigarette in the corner of his beak.

'Well,' said Guanyu in his calming way, 'they said I was nice and friendly, but that you looked like you just wanted one thing.' Then turning to the Englishman, he said: 'And you, Colin, they said you were OK.'

'Thanks for the OK,' said Colin, as if it were the worst kind of comment of all, but suspecting Guanyu of sweetening the verdict to his own advantage.

'They always say that, man, but I still always end up fucking them,' said Max with finality. Guanyu looked at his phone screen to match the number plate of the arriving taxi, then he dashed his cigarette to the ground and bundled himself drunkenly into the rear of the cab.

'Let's finish this at your place,' said Max, lifting the whisky bottle.

Colin was wide awake now. It was just past 4 p.m. in the UK. And he wanted to set something straight with Max, because at PlayZone, not everything was set down in the contract. So when they pushed the door into his service apartment, he said: 'How do I stand here? I mean, am I safe?'

'You're here, right? Don't worry, man, you're safe. The way I see it, the project can't go on without you. You represent fifty percent of it.'

Colin wondered if this was Max talking or the whisky. He opted for the latter. Nevertheless, he said: 'OK, and I'm included in the bonus scheme, right?'

'Yeah, told you, you just talk to the producer if you want,' said Max, pouring whisky into the two mugs he found on the bar next to the kettle.

'All right,' said Colin, plumping himself down on the couch. 'By the way, why did Guanyu insist about the name of the game?'

'It's his job, marketing, right?'

'Ah, yeah, guess so, and I'll need to write up a world view doc.'

Max placed the mugs and the bottle on the low table and joined Colin on the sofa. 'He got smashed tonight with his poem shit.'

'Well, it means he has a gentle soul.'

'Nah.'

'Besides, he likes you, you sure he wasn't hitting on you?'

'What? What the fuck!'

'Well, after all, he is gay, right?' said Colin, scrolling through the films on VIP TV with the remote control. 'And he did ask you for a drink, didn't he?'

'Ain't had no experience with a guy before, and I wasn't planning to,' said Max, which came as a surprise to Colin because it seemed to mean that it could be an option.

'Buddy, you really need a proper girlfriend!'

'But he's not gay, man; we've been out a few times.'

'Exactly! And he said he was gay last time I saw him, didn't you hear? That night he passed out on the table, last summer.'

'Ah man, I didn't know that, had no idea, you guys talking shit about literature and stuff.'

'Well, that's what he said, and hey, makes no difference to me.' They chinked mugs and drank.

'Yeah, but keep it to yourself, man,' said Max, looking into his mug. 'He's a married man, and no one must know in the office, delicate here in China.'

'I won't tell.'

'I don't want him getting hurt.'

'Don't worry,' said Colin, perceiving that Max did have a heart beneath that macho carapace. 'If no one else knows, then no one else will know, except you, hah. Anyway, those girls looked like they were fifteen. It was embarrassing.'

'Nah, early twenties, just don't know how to talk to proper guys, that's why I only hit on older girls.'

After chatting and drinking through the film that featured short-arse Tom Cruise playing big-guy Jack Reacher, Max made for the door to pick up his taxi waiting downstairs. 'Hey, man, can't shut the door, lock thing's stuck out,' he said, standing in the door frame.

Colin staggered over to the door and took a blurry-eyed look at the blocked latch, but quickly gave up on it. 'Leave it,' he said in a slurred voice. 'I'll get it sorted in the morning.'

'You sure, man?'

'Nothing else I can do. You head off for your taxi. I need some sleep.'

'OK, man.'

'Take care, and drink a pint of water when you get home.'

As the day began to pale outside the window, Colin fell onto his bed and thought to himself, 'Who said people were not free in China?'

*

Late morning, from the depths of drunken slumber, Colin heard an insistent knocking and a high-pitched voice. *'Ni hao, ni hao . . .'*

He was about to show a leg when two middle-aged cleaning ladies entered the room, bold as brass, the door having been left ajar. *'Ni hao,'* repeated the first one, then sang out something else in Chinese. Colin waved to them to carry on, and the two ladies set about wiping the sideboards, the floors, and the bathroom, to what end he knew not as he had only just arrived.

The next thing he knew, the door was being snugly pulled flush with the frame and clicked shut. Still fully clothed, he fell into a deep, snoring snooze.

*

Late afternoon he awoke, feeling like his head was cleaved asunder.

He had missed the day. He stumbled, still fully clothed, to a couple of water bottles standing on the counter. He ripped off the top of one of them and sank it down. But it was too late; he should have done it before he fell onto the bed. He hated these hangovers. He thought he had seen the last of them. It occurred to him that maybe he should learn to say no. But his principle was to usually say yes to new adventure, for the sake of the writer in him, with the exception of the most extreme.

A short while later, he slipped on his parka and headed unsteadily down to the reception office before it closed. Armed with his translation app, he asked the janitor where he could buy some aspirin. There was a pharmacy around the block. Colin adjusted his direction on his Amap app and followed the little blue arrow on it.

He passed a few people on the way, many of whom were masked. As he continued walking, he pulled up his BBC news app and read:

> ***China pneumonia outbreak: Mystery virus probed in Wuhan***
>
> *Chinese authorities have launched an investigation into a mysterious viral pneumonia which has infected dozens of people in the central city of Wuhan.*
>
> *A total of 44 cases have been confirmed so far, 11 of which are considered 'severe,' officials said on Friday.*
>
> *The outbreak has prompted Singapore and Hong Kong to bring in screening processes for travellers from the city.*
>
> *It comes amid online fears the virus could be linked to SARS, or severe acute respiratory syndrome.*

Before he could fully process the information, a notification interrupted his thoughts and he suddenly remembered yesterday's message from Lin. He would have to at least answer this one, which read:

'Hey, Colin, you back in Beijing? If you are not, you know it's dangerous to come to China now, right?'

7

Lin was feeling restless after another meeting with her team.

Another Westerner on her list was having second thoughts about coming to China because of the new virus. Another one had resigned from a mobile game company before the guarantee time period was over because of a disagreement with a producer. It enraged her whenever this producer's name was mentioned now. An arrogant, self-righteous, big-headed lead who treated his team like underlings. The Russian had come with excellent credentials; she had hunted him down and had managed to convince him that coming to China was an opportunity not to pass over, and now he was on a plane back to Moscow. All right, not quite Western in the Western sense of the word, she reminded herself, but white, not Asian, and having worked on a hit game in the West, so she had labelled him in her mind like her Chinese colleagues as a European. But Lin had travelled, had lived in Europe, America, Singapore; she knew full well that Dimitri was certainly not a Westerner, and even she could see that his art style was much darker.

Why wouldn't the true Westerners come? she wondered. She had been given the go-ahead from her client to extend the pay package to a more attractive level.

She hit the WeChat send button, she knew she was poaching, but that was what she was paid for, she said to herself, to hunt heads. Her message read:

> 'Hey Colin, so what's it like being back in Beijing?'

A minute later, the WeChat icon on her taskbar lit up. He wrote:

> 'Hi Lin, busy busy, sorry, been meaning to get in touch . . .'
>
> 'same here, so much on at the moment'
>
> 'we must catch up, go for a drink someplace, when are you free?'
>
> 'yes, sure, we can meet halfway someplace.'

Lin wondered why she felt a secret smile curl the corners of her mouth. But she enjoyed the thrill of the baiting, and then hooking her fish, and Colin would be a nice catch. A Western lead narrative, an English one who had a fine track record. But how much would he cost? She typed another message that read:

'Or we can meet for dinner, I know
a nice place where they do healthy
food. What about Thursday?'

'sounds good'

'great, I'll ping you'

'righto, see you Thursday then'

Lin did not send another sign-off remark; it would sound too needy, so she reduced the WeChat panel on her PC and opened the report she had been longing to send about the producer who was ruining all her hard work. Luckily, this Brit would be recruited for a different team.

8

'People have big noses in the West,' said Xiao Long, aka Little Dragon, to Colin one early evening. 'Big noses, big eyes, and double chins.'

They were discussing a new character in a side alcove of the large open space where breakfast was offered every morning by the company. In each alcove, a large poster of a game character looked down on those sitting on the benches either side of a fixed table. 'Not everyone has a big nose,' said Colin, slightly amused.

'Compared to Chinese people, they do. That's why you all look the same,' returned Little Dragon, turning his face to show his own profile. 'Look, my nose is flatter against the face. Yours sticks right out.'

Colin jerked back his head and laughed out loud. 'I never thought of it like that,' he said. 'I guess from your point of view, you're right.'

'I study and draw faces all the time,' said Xiao Long with his usual disarming smile, 'and I can tell when someone's been under the knife.'

'Under the knife?'

'Yeah, surgery, that's how you say it, right?' Colin responded with a nod. Xiao Long continued: 'All the girls do it here. Haven't you noticed?'

'No.'

'They all want double eyelids, bigger eyes, and bigger titties.' Little Dragon then turned his head in the direction of a pretty woman in her early thirties. She was leading a flock of HR colleagues at a large round table near the window. 'See that girl over there? She's had her eyes done, she had single eyelids before, and she's had a face-lift.'

'How can you tell?'

'Around the cheeks. Chinese girls have tight skin, so when it's lifted it's even tighter, and when she smiles there's no movement in her cheeks. It's like they are frozen.'

'I can't tell, and even if I could, so what? It's not a crime,' said Colin indulgently. 'You wait till you get older!'

'Nah, I've got a baby face, and I'm fat, and there's nothing you can do about being fat.'

'Eat less?'

'Hey, that's fat-shaming, man. They do it all the time here.'

'Can't say I've noticed.'

'Why would you? You ain't fat!'

'True,' said Colin, turning back to his character bio sheet. 'So what about this fat sultan then?'

'Personally, I like it more realistic.'

'That's good, because so does our audience. Your average Western male biped, twenty, thirty-five, wouldn't play a mobile game that makes him look like a paedophile. Lolitas with frilly panties don't look good in the subway, get it?' said Colin, making the effort to use American words.

'Gotcha, but you'll have to tell Kai.'

Colin had spent his first three months in China getting the crew to trust him by simply acknowledging their viewpoint and laying down his own reasoning, softly, softly, without trying to sell it to them. Otherwise, he knew from past experience of working abroad that the team would clam up. And he would be shut out and would become unhappy. In China, this phenomenon was accentuated by the difference in culture, the difference between Western individualism and Chinese collectivism, and ultimately by the Chinese distrust of the outsider. But once he had secured their trust, he could slowly steer the game to a more Western feel through calm and rational argumentation, no table-thumping here. He did not win them over every time, but little by little his influence was being felt. He said: 'Sure, he'll understand when I tell him about *Shadow Storm*, the last game I worked on.'

'What about it?'

'It's a carbon copy of *Summoner's War*.'

'Looks very different, though.'

'That's exactly my point. *Summoner's War* is a big hit in Asia, so they detected a gap in the market in the West. And you know what they did?'

'They changed the style.'

'Yeah, they copied the gameplay, dropped the Lolitas for realistic-looking characters, gave it a story with a proper voiceover, and did 3D animation for combats. Result: for a mobile game that cost one million dollars to produce, it now brings in over ten million dollars . . . per month! That's why we need a more realistic style, to suit the market.'

'Suits me; I prefer doing big-nose people anyway,' said Little Dragon. Then he glanced at someone in his line of sight approaching the alcove.

'Colin,' said a calm and measured, almost Hawkingsian voice. 'I am going down to get a donkey burger. Do you want to come?' Colin turned to face Yang, now standing beside the alcove table in his bright yellow overcoat. Being an Englishman, eating donkey meat might have come as a culture shock, even worse than the first time he had been served sheep's balls in France. When he told his mother about it over the phone, she was appalled because, unlike hens and cows, donkeys are cute, petable creatures. But Colin had long since shed his cultural culinary prejudices and had been keen to try. From his previous stays in China, he had concluded that the Chinese, like the French, will eat anything under the sun, and he had found that so would he, once at least. Wasn't it part of the author's mind-set? Besides, it made no difference to the animal; it was already dead. Colin had once wondered if he would eat human meat if push came to shove. The thought of it had made him shudder inside. He nodded to Little Dragon. 'You coming?' he said.

'Nah, you guys go ahead. I'm on a diet.'

Colin and Yang looked at each other dubiously. 'What did you say?' said Yang in false surprise.

'Hey,' returned Xiao Long with a smile. 'Just because I'm fat doesn't mean I eat donkeys!'

*

A short elevator ride and a three-minute stroll later, Yang and Colin were approaching the donkey burger place on the other side of the street.

On this side, the low buildings had not yet been replaced by modern high-rise office blocks. These scruffy two-storey edifices, with their garish neon signs and dozens of cables strung between them like noodles, stood like a relic of a suburb now engulfed by the sprawling city. They threaded their way between bikes, electric mopeds, and tricycles that cluttered the kerb and pavement. They pushed on through wrought iron gates, and down an inner corridor that led to the rear of a building. Despite its tackiness and the failed attempts at masonry, Colin always liked walking down this corridor, lit by a single nude bulb and laid with a muddy red carpet as if it once led to someplace special. A generation ago, someone had gone to the trouble of painting the supporting wall with a scene of a French café terrace on the nearside going in, and a red British telephone box on the far end. They were connected by blooming summer flowers. Real bells and dusty baubles adorned the wall here and there and enhanced the feeling that this corridor must lead to some magical place, magical, that is, for the connoisseur of the donkey burger.

They pushed the sticking, glazed wooden doors, then waved a transparent strip of the thick plastic curtain aside before emerging into the rudimentary eating room. Simple wooden tables matched simple stools upon which sat clusters of men noisily noshing, slurping, and chatting. On the far side of the wall a three-metre-wide enamelled illustration gave details in Chinese characters of the recipe, and the virtues and provenance of the donkey meat. The place may have lacked the modern design of a chain restaurant — the chairs, stools, and foldable tables looked like they had been bought at a used furniture school sale — but Yang vowed that the burgers were the best in Beijing, made as they were from a traditional family recipe.

'Same as usual,' replied Colin to Yang's question. 'I'll grab a table.' It was their routine. Yang headed for the counter to place the order while Colin secured a table. Then he forwarded his part of the bill to Yang by WeChat: the grand sum of thirty-one yuan, half the price of a whisky in the basement whisky bar, or the price of a pint of beer at Weatherspoon's.

Five minutes later, they were each served piping hot donkey and herb soup, two donkey meat burgers, and a large bottle of Tsingtao beer. It was not really a burger in the Western sense of the word. It consisted of a roasted rectangular *huoshao* bread pouch filled with the tasty mauve meat, which to Colin was much more tender than beef.

The pair of them said nothing until they had each taken a ravenous bite, a slurp of soup, and a chug of beer.

'I will learn to speak Chinese just to say to the lady at the counter *I love your donkey burgers*!' said Colin before taking another bite.

'Ah, you always say that,' said Yang between slurps of broth. 'And I think you could learn.'

'You've changed your tune. You used to ask me why on earth I should bother.'

'Did I?'

'Yes, and I did try at first, but I just can't seem to get a foothold. It's so alien. Speaking Chinese compared to speaking any European language is like eating noodles with chopsticks compared to eating them with a fork.'

'You use chopsticks very well,' said Yang as Colin took another chug of beer.

'I try, but the noodles slip through them before I can slurp them up, and I can't for the life of me eat fried chicken with them.'

'It will come,' said Yang, who had taken his typical philosophical pose, scratched his goatee, and now said: 'In Chinese culture, we say: *Patience is power; with time and patience, the mulberry leaf becomes a silk gown.*'

It was typical Yang. He had previously told Colin that he had tried his hand at being a teacher after leaving university, but being more gifted at user-centric design, he soon turned to a more artistic occupation and had worked as a designer in the automobile industry in Wuhan. Now he designed interfaces for the mobile game they were working on.

'I will try again then,' said Colin.

'Your teacher will open the door, but you must enter by yourself,' said Yang, turning his head thoughtfully to one side.

'And how did you learn English then if you've never been

to an English-speaking country?' said Colin, refilling the glasses from the beer bottle.

'Songs,' said Yang, clenching his glass of beer. 'I used to listen to songs.'

They clinked glasses. Colin joined Yang in humming chorus sections of a few eighties hits and then asked: 'Is that how you met your wife?'

'We met at university. We talked a lot, we talked and talked and then we realised we both had a strong feeling of togetherness for each other. And so we got married and had a baby. I am happy. I think in a relationship togetherness is the most important thing, don't you think so? In China we say: *It is easy to break one chopstick, but they become unbreakable when we put them all together.*'

'Nice,' said Colin, who gave a fleeting thought to his own situation. He had loved his wife more than anything and, in many ways, still did. But their natures had torn them apart. It made sense when he found out that, according to Chinese tradition, he was of the water element and she of fire. Their relationship had got the better of their marriage. For, although opposite poles usually attract, theirs created a divide, a mound of misunderstandings that built up over the years until it became an insurmountable mountain. It was sad. It had been hard on his wife, too, and yet, whether they put it down to the forces of the cosmos on their own changing persons, or the loss of mutual understanding, they had been obliged to let go. Let go or, once the children had flown, face a life in bitter conflict interspersed with too rare moments of love.

‘Well, I admire that,’ said Colin, ‘that togetherness. It is often something we overlook when caught in the passion of love and romance.’

They finished their meal in song and beer and soup slurps, softly humming parts of songs when the words escaped them. The lady at the counter hailed a *men zao* with a burgeoning smile as they ambled across the tiled floor to the sticking glazed door behind the PVC strip curtain. In the red-carpeted passageway that took them back into the ordained chaos of the Beijing suburb, Yang explained that *men zao* literally meant *walk easy.*

‘So, like *take it easy,*’ said Colin.

‘Yes,’ returned Yang who seemed to connect with the translation. ‘Take. It. Easy.’

9

Since Colin's return, Little Dragon — who spoke with an impressive US accent from a misspent youth fed on eight hours a day of YouTube and porn — had been harping on about a foray into a karaoke lounge. But it was not just a song-and-dance one: it was one with girls.

After a late day at work, the jolly-faced Chinese lad walked with Colin back to the Wudaokou neighbourhood where they stopped at a street food counter. 'Try these, they're good; they'll warm you up,' he said, inviting Colin to dip into his open bag of fried somethings.

Colin peeked into the mixed bag dubiously. 'What are they?' he asked.

'It's a surprise,' said Xiao Long, 'and you have to guess.'

'Frog legs,' said Colin, pulling out his Y-shaped surprise from the lucky dip and examining every angle.

'Nope. But try it, I'll tell you after.'

Colin took a nibble at the crispy deep-fried offering while Xiao Long picked up the thread of their conversation. 'The girls are the most beautiful, and it's a really nice place, top class; you'll love it. So, you wanna come? Kai's coming, and so is Yang.'

'Yang? Doesn't seem the type.'

'That's what he said. But his wife's in Nanjing,' returned Xiao Long, as if that sufficed for an explanation.

'So how does it work, by the hour?' said Colin, reviewing the middle part of his snack which he assumed must be the bit he was about to chomp into.

'Nah, it's one fee. We pay up front, and we can party all night as long as we want.'

'Aha,' Colin returned, crunching into the very edible crispy snack. 'So what happens?'

'We gotta get there early or all the best-looking chicks will be taken . . . So, you just choose which one you want from the line-up, and then she stays with you all night.'

'Oh, like an escort.'

'Nah, it's not like that, but you'll see. We call them hostesses.' Then Little Dragon nodded at his bag of fried somethings. 'So, what do you think? You like it?'

'Quite good actually,' said Colin, taking another crunch.

'What do you think it is?'

'No idea.'

'Have a guess.'

Colin took another and examined it to figure out what part of an animal's anatomy it could be. 'Err, a cat's cock?'

'No, man, that's a Western cliché. We don't eat cats, not in Beijing. In another province, they do, and it's condemned.'

'Really then, no idea.'

'I'll give you a clue. It's part of a duck.'

'A duck's cock?'

'Nah.'

'Duck's balls?'

'Nope. Look at the shape.'

Colin pulled out another piece of another duck. 'Err,' he said while holding it by the two struts which resembled soft bones. 'I can't see.'

'All right,' Little Dragon said, pointing to his own mouth. 'It's a duck's tongue!' he continued with an expectant look on his face.

But Colin, after many years of travelling the world, was no longer surprised at what people could put between their teeth. He said: 'Oh, I would never have guessed. Quite nice, though, really.' Then, playing up to Xiao Long's expectations, he added: 'Weird though, right?'

'We eat everything on the duck. Look, here's another part,' said the fat Chinese lad, pulling out a duck's foot from his mixed bag of fried goodies. This, of course, would not have gone unrecognised had Little Dragon played the same guessing game as with the duck's tongue.

'No thanks,' returned Colin. 'Besides, there's nothing on it!'

'No, but you can crunch it; it's good. Anyway, so you're coming then, right?'

'Where?'

'With me, Kai, and Yang, this Thursday.'

*

The lads had been looking forward to the event all week.

On the following Thursday, Xiao Long caught Colin's eye behind his desk. 'So tonight's the night!' he said, with a lascivious leer. Colin acknowledged with a nod as the WeChat icon on his PC screen flashed. It suddenly came to him that he was supposed to be catching up with the headhuntress from TalentPlus this evening.

It turned out not to be Lin but a meetup member of a language exchange group he had joined during a previous stay. But thankfully, the prompt now reminded him of his meeting that evening with her. She was a senior headhunter, no less, so a worthy as well as an attractive contact to nurture. Stroking his chin with one hand, he clicked on her headshot with the other. Then he typed:

'Hey Lin, really sorry but can't make it tonight unfortunately, I have a late meeting, what about tomorrow or this weekend?'

Barely thirty seconds later a notification came through.

'No problem, quite busy myself at work so it turns out good. Can't friday, saturday would be fine. There's a mexican place in sanlitun we can go to'

'sounds good'

'will let you know later, have to rush, busy busy'

'ok ok'

Colin switched back to his work in progress while reflecting how much life was made simpler with the easy and casual use of WeChat. You could interrupt someone's working day and get an instant reply. As long as you cut out the fluff, people did not find it intrusive. It was more like picking up the thread of an ongoing conversation, which Colin was realising was in perfect adequation with the Chinese language, this mysterious tonal language where the way you pronounced the written word could lead to a completely different meaning when spoken out loud. The grammar seemed simple enough; it had no articles like *a* or *the*, no gender like *she* or *he*, and no tenses like the past and future. So cutting to the linguistic bone made the language short and to the point, just like a WeChat exchange. But there were drawbacks.

Where a Chinese might find Westerners overly polite to the point of not speaking their mind, a Westerner might find an exchange with a Chinese person brash, abrupt, and curt, even to the point of being outraged. But Colin knew better than to be galled by the seeming abruptness of exchanges, and WeChat was a good illustration of how Chinese social interaction worked. Compared to, say, the French, who loved the sound of their own voices, Colin had come to appreciate the directness of the Chinese: no chaff and straight to the point. But there again, that did not mean that they always spoke their minds either. He was finding that more often than not, they went around a problem instead of confronting it, in the same way that moped riders manoeuvred around any pedestrians who got in their way without making any fuss.

Thinking back to his WeChat exchange with Lin, he wondered if these meet-ups with her were moving out of the realm of work-related relations. He had already met with her a number of times last summer when she had tried to woo him to join a competing company. So, had they become pals? Was this catch-up a work-related one? Or were they moving toward a nascent friendship? As he was contemplating her pretty headshot, another notification sent the WeChat icon blinking. He hit the profile of Little Dragon. 'Like this,' it said, followed by a colon and then another message containing the photo of a beautiful twenty-something Mongolian woman showing considerably more flesh than clothing.

10

What do Chinese people think of Westerners? Colin sometimes asked himself this question whenever he found himself travelling in the underground in Beijing or on the MRT in Singapore.

Were they attracted by big eyes, feet, and hands? he wondered. But there again, Chinese women were so slim, curved, and tight-skinned, their features well defined and dainty as living dolls. At least, that is how he saw them in his mind now as he made his way into a plush building with Yang.

Colin had been caught up in a last-minute meeting, and Yang had agreed to wait for him while the others went ahead. Xiao Long would reserve the female company for the latecomers.

'He says we should wait here,' said Yang, having just received a return message from Little Dragon. 'He says he will be down to meet us.'

'Is this some kind of hotel?' said Colin, looking around at the venue, a stylish modern office building with uniformed doormen.

'No, they are offices. I think it's on the top floor,' said Yang, then added a little nervously: 'Do you know what to expect?'

'No more than you do,' said Colin, but it was clear that Yang really did have no idea what to expect as he watched the right-hand elevator display counting down to ground zero. A few moments later, the elevator doors opened.

'Hey! Been waiting for you guys, where you been?' said Xiao Long, jumping out with his usual big round-faced smile — a smile that could win anyone over no matter what came out of its mouth, and sometimes what came out was not very pleasant. Like the time he pretended to be a Jap in search of a one-night stand and brought out the worst in an old gentleman's distrust of the foreigner. Or the time he video-streamed himself asking a couple of girls why they did face surgery because it was wrong in his eyes. So when he complained about them being late, Colin just gave a wry grin. 'Never mind, it doesn't matter,' said Little Dragon, beckoning them into the lift with an alluring smile. 'Come on up to the palace of forbidden treasures!'

It was an unexpected view when the doors opened on the top floor, for Colin found himself walking into an elegant lobby with faux French panelling. They could have been standing in a scene from Flaubert's *L'Éducation sentimentale* or in a painting by Toulouse-Lautrec, thought Colin as they were ushered down the long, carpeted corridor with a high, painted ceiling. It was intermittently lined with padded doors, each one leading into a karaoke parlour where he could hear false notes being belted out in Chinese as he passed by.

'We chose a girl for each of you. Hope you like them, but if not, you can change them if you like,' said Xiao Long. Then, turning to Colin, he said: 'And by the way, yours might be shy at first. She's never entertained a white guy before, so don't be put off, but I think you'll like her.'

Podgy Little Dragon paused at a door and let the usher open it before bounding inside.

'You go,' said Colin to Yang. 'No, no, after you,' returned Yang, visibly perturbed. Colin suddenly felt a pang of guilt for his part in talking Yang out of backing out. Yang was married with a daughter, though he did admit he enjoyed being at liberty in the capital, leaving wife, child, parents, and parents-in-law behind in the provincial town where they lived more cheaply than in Beijing. Besides that, with four grandparents to care of his daughter while his wife was at work, the child would not lack affection. Such was often the way in China, which Colin accepted and almost admired: their capacity to let the grandparents take an active role in bringing up the offspring, whereas in the West, they went on cruises before ending up waylaid in nursing homes. But Yang was not averse to taking some fun, and Colin sometimes took his overt naivety as play-acting.

'Come on, you guys, what are you waiting for?' called out Little Dragon from inside the boudoir-like chamber. He was already nestled in the arms of his chosen one.

Colin took a leap of faith and tried to make a dramatic entrance. But when he announced himself with an English 'Ta-da . . . hi folks! 'he was met by four sets of female eyes agog with curiosity. Did Colin detect a furrow of disappointment, or worse, pity? Then it hit home. A quick flash around at the girls told him he was old enough to be their father. Colin got the inkling that the age detail might have escaped Little Dragon. He was thankfully quickly relieved of an agonising moment as Yang followed on behind.

'That one's yours,' said Little Dragon, pointing to his right. Colin was looking at an elaborately cut melon on a fruit platter on the low table. Then he realised that Xiao Long was pointing to an attractive young lady, coquettish and spirited, in hot pants and a short-sleeved shirt, sitting with her legs tightly crossed on the sofa behind it. 'Do you like her?' said Little Dragon in his usual brash way. 'If you don't, you can just trade her in for another.'

Colin gave an awkward smile. 'No, no, she's fine,' he said.

'You don't have to worry, man,' insisted Little Dragon. 'They get paid for this, and besides, she don't speak English.'

'Oh,' said Colin, who wondered how an evening with a Chinese beauty would pass without verbal communication.

'And anyway,' said Little Dragon, 'we're gonna bring in the leftovers so you can properly choose for yourselves.'

Yang, being the gentleman he was, said something nice in Chinese. It no doubt meant his hostess was fine too.

Ten minutes later, Colin was being served beer in a small glass by his hostess and listening to his Chinese pals wailing out their restrained emotions in a sad ballad into a karaoke mike. It was becoming evident to Colin that this was the Chinese favourite genre of song, and he wondered if it was because they were ordinarily so reserved with their feelings.

Not only that, it suddenly dawned on him that a vast majority of his team were only children, which surely must have stunted their emotional development. In the West, Colin had never liked working with an only child, yet now he was working with a whole team of them. Coming from a large family himself, he found it difficult to accept the exclusivity that an only child experienced throughout their formative years. But now he was beginning to understand the other side of the coin. In a word: loneliness. It perhaps partly explained why at work his colleagues often called each other Sister Wang Li or Brother Zhang Yong. Not through a sense of party comradeship, but perhaps rather through a need to feel part of a bigger family. The one-child policy had allowed young people to access higher education, but it also deprived them of an inner balance. So Colin was changing his mind about only children.

'You can touch her, you know,' said Xiao Long craftily, insisting Colin should feel more at ease. But he was not. Here was a girl half his age, who understood not a single word of English and who had looked upon him aghast. 'Don't worry, she won't bite. You're her first white guy; she's intimidated, that's all.' The girl flashed a spirited look at Xiao Long and fired off a string of words in Chinese.

'What did she say?' said Colin.

'Oh, she just wanted me to tell her what I said!'

Some minutes later, Colin felt the girl relax, and so he put his hand around her waist. But he felt nothing. It was all fake love, and he felt not an ounce of burgeoning passion. Instead he pretended to listen to Xiao Long doing a rendition of some US rapper hit, and then watched jovial Kai pull a serious face for once and do a popping dance routine, the one he had no doubt learnt as a fourteen-year-old kid. Colin pictured him as the centre of attention and applauded by parents and grandparents alike, no competition, an outright winner. Colin for his part offered a rendition of 'Creep.'

More drinks were served, more sad songs were sung, and there was some groping from the audacious Little Dragon, followed by a slap. Holding his cheek, Little Dragon walked back to Colin and surreptitiously said: 'Not the titties, don't go for the titties!'

'OK, OK,' said Colin, 'copy that . . . or rather, I won't copy that!'

There were parlour games of a suggestive nature, one of which entailed the losing couple being told to perform sexual positions fully clothed, which made everyone laugh. It was all innocent fun for the boys to indulge in while getting just a hint of fake romance from the girls, who agreed to laugh at their games and to be hugged like teddy bears. Even Yang was feeling relaxed now that clothes were staying on. Maybe this was the way Chinese men practiced their courting skills, thought Colin. It was perhaps no coincidence that the place certainly resembled a nineteenth-century Parisian *maison close*. Except, of course, that here the clothes stayed on.

It was past 3 a.m. when the boys said their goodbyes to the tired-out girls at the lobby lift. Ten minutes later in the taxi, turning to face the others in the rear, Xiao Long said: 'Did you get their WeChat?'

‘I did,’ declared Kai with a jovial laugh.

‘No,’ said Yang, and Colin answered likewise. This was a relief for Yang, but for Colin, it came as a disappointment. The lack of complicity left him with a void filled by feelings of failure and loneliness. He could have used the 5000RMB to pay an escort, he thought to himself. But there again, wouldn’t he have been left with the same hollow feeling of fake love?

11

How many chances had she missed? How many times had she placed her career above love? thought Lin to herself.

But it was not too late, she kept telling herself, and besides that, she wanted a child. She did not want to end up like all those modern-day Chinese spinsters who had forsaken love because they needed all their energy to blaze their trails in a male-dominated society — a society where everything fell upon the only child's shoulders. And so, like so many of her generation, she had put love on the back burner. She would have married the 'right' partner and adhered to a marriage of convenience, had the opportunity arisen. But she had failed, and now a potential suitor would wonder why she was still single, thinking that there must be something wrong with her.

One afternoon, she paused at an article in her WeChat feed. *Chinese women hire remote anonymous male to send romantic messages.* 'Wow, is this what it has come to?' she thought to herself before actually considering what it would feel like to receive such tailored messages before bedtime for the price of a few yuan. A few days later, she hit the WeChat icon of a lady divinatory practitioner instead.

She had been toying with the notion ever since Yuping had mentioned it to her. Yuping had told her some of her fortune teller's uncanny results. So Lin got to thinking there was no harm in giving it a try. It was better than paying an anonymous student to send her romantic messages. Heavens, if it came to needing to pay to receive packets of fake love on the Lunar New Year, then she was lost. She would rather let her mother match her up with a suitor at one of those mothers' match-meetings in front of the Temple of Heaven. So, she had transferred the fee, sent the numbers when asked, and received the fortune teller's prognostic. But nothing concrete had come of it. Even Wei Leng hadn't come up with a slot in his agenda yet. So she decided to follow up. At the least, it would allow her to vent some of her frustration.

She hit the icon and typed: *Hello Madam Yaxian, I am getting back to let you know nothing has happened yet. I haven't had a single date. You said I would meet someone by the end of the year, and yet the year has been and gone. What should I do?* Lin felt her stomach muscles contract as she hit the send button.

During their previous exchange through WeChat, Lin had sent the divinatory practitioner two random numbers which would reflect her state of mind and connect her with the cosmos. All Madam Yaxian had to do was to consult the corresponding numbers in I Ching, otherwise known as the Book of Changes, an ancient divination manual that made the prophecies of Nostradamus look like a modern saga in comparison. It is said to have been passed down through the ages from around 1000 BC. The ancient Chinese oracle allowed the learned reader to foresee the potential events and encounters in a person's life, or rather, to give the person a heads-up to future windows of opportunity so that they would not be missed. Lin wanted to believe in it, for it would give meaning to existence in that everything was linked together, interwoven between the physical space and the spiritual one. It was the mystery of China, of the ancients.

She glanced back to the WeChat thread as a notification came up. She read the message from Madam Yaxian: 'Give me two random letters.'

Lin typed *n* and *z* and waited for Madam Yaxian to read in the Book of Changes. Some minutes later came the message from the universe. Lin read: 'The man you were waiting for was possibly on a trip, maybe abroad. What you must do is put two dolls, male and female, on the side of the bed you do not sleep on.'

Lin thanked the divinatory practitioner and got back to her PowerPoint presentation on the meaning of passion and how to discern it in a candidate.

*

That evening, Lin looked around her bedroom to view her cuddly toys; she disliked dolls.

'You will do,' she said, picking up a white rabbit. 'And you too,' she said. Then she sat the rabbit and a little cuddly panda upon the headboard on the side she did not sleep on.

12

Shoes, thought Colin, perched on a cold bollard outside a Mexican restaurant in the Sanlitun district, shoes of every style and no two pairs the same.

The freezing January day was dimming into twilight; his eyes had fallen to watching people's feet for the past twenty minutes. Remembering what his gran used to say about catching piles on cold surfaces, he shifted from one buttock to the other as he continued to note that no two people's shoes were the same. It was like a parade of the individual's right to be different — that individuality being expressed more discreetly at ground level.

The fashion from the feet up was certainly tamer than in any London street. As for the footwear, however, to Colin it was as though people were tentatively daring to express their desire to be unique through their shoes. Shoes conveyed perhaps a grain of folly that, in a bizarre way, enabled them to remain unique, especially the younger generation who had learnt to be exclusive, being as they often were only children, doted on and over-loved.

He continued his watch: big shoes, classy shoes, shoes with big bumpers, bear-feet shoes, hiking boots, retro trainers, Converse creepers . . . was this their way to stay in touch with their true selves? he wondered as he looked down at his own feet, shod in Timberland bumper boots that enhanced his person by three centimetres. This, to his delight, made him taller than the average male biped in his new habitat. Still with a contented grin on his face, he looked up to find, clicking toward him, a pair of mid-heeled shoes that married well with snazzy stonewashed jeans and a stylish thigh-length black puffer coat with faux fur trim and elasticated stretch belt cinched in at the waist. 'Hey, good to see you!' said Colin, who, just coming out of his introspection, struggled for a moment to recall her name. But then he remembered as the petite lady approached with a disarming smile.

'Colin, so sorry,' said Lin in her usual surprisingly powerful voice, while pushing back her thick shock of dark hair. 'Had to go back for my gloves, then got held up at the elevator.'

Colin waved it off, made some polite talk, and followed her into the Mexican restaurant. It was set in a district of Western-style bars and ugly malls that was still commonly known as Sanlitun Village. He admired the way she spoke to the waitress in the no-nonsense, confident voice of a woman used to wielding authority. Not that Colin could understand what she was saying, for Mandarin seemed to offer no linguistic foothold. He could, however, ascertain when a customer was the boss, and he liked being led by Lin for that reason. He was in good hands.

'You must have been freezing out there,' she said with a smile of concern as soon as the waitress had shown them to a table and handed them each a menu. 'You should have waited inside.' Colin did not want to own up to the fact that he did not enjoy waiting for ladies in a restaurant and suffer the possibility of being stood up. He said: 'No, I'm a radiator, actually, and I was having a good time watching people's feet.'

'Feet?' Lin retorted with a little laugh, half wondering if she had understood correctly through the ambient din. The group table next to them was celebrating a birthday with sparklers and giving a rendition of 'Happy Birthday to You' in Chinese.

'Yes, feet, I've found out that in Beijing, no two people wear the same pair of shoes.'

'No,' laughed Lin, who had placed her menu flat on the table before her, 'that would be impossible, at least for them to wear them at the same time, ha!'

He smiled at her repartee; it always kept him alert and reminded him that she was a smart cookie, one who had studied at a fine university and had an academic brain. Not only that, but it came with the distinct advantage of also being grounded in common sense. She had been raised by an entrepreneur father and an ambitious mother, he recalled her saying once. 'Ha ha, you know what I mean,' he said. 'I was wondering whether it had anything to do with the one-child policy. You know, once having left the cocoon of their exclusive home habitat for the workplace, maybe it's a way of keeping hold of something of their singularity.'

'Hmm,' said Lin dubiously. 'Well, in fact, when I was growing up in the '80s and '90s, there were only a few types of shoes people could wear. My sister and I both wore the same.'

'Not at the same time, though, right?' said Colin, who regretted the irresistible counter-quip. But she let him have a ha-ha-clever-clogs smile for the effort. He continued. 'So, in some ways it might be true then. People crave to be different, which is the contrary to Chinese culture and teachings, isn't it?'

'It used to be, maybe, but China has moved on,' she said, browsing through the menu, visibly conceding to pass onto something else.

'I didn't know you had a sister, though, didn't know it was allowed,' he said a few moments later, sensing the shoe story had run its course. And after all, he had come to meet Lin, not talk about China's shoes.

Looking up, she said: 'Yes, we were in a small town, so my parents were allowed to have a second baby.'

'So, you're the eldest then.'

'Yes.'

'Is she married?'

'No, we're both merrily single,' she said, pursing her lips.

Did he detect a faint note of exasperation in her voice? He dropped the subject, a difficult one, he figured, for a Chinese woman past traditional marrying age. And after all, he had come to catch up with Lin, not talk about her younger sister.

He asked how she had been since the last time he was in

Beijing. A different season back then, end of summer when the leaves began to turn a bright shade of orange. They had gone out for the day to visit a grey-bricked traditional residential area known as *hutong* with one of her female colleagues. The colleague had left them in the evening, and they had gone for a drink and a bite to eat in a music café by a lake. He recalled her wearing a jean skirt and a chaste top, which did not prevent him from remarking on her body shape. This evening she was dressed in snugly fitting jeans and a knitted sweater that showed the curves of her generous bust.

They ordered their meal of tacos, cheese corn, avocado, onion rings, and mini wraps, which soon populated the table in the Chinese fashion so that they could both dip in willy-nilly as they chatted away.

Colin told her he had been thinking of writing a book set in Beijing. 'What will it be about?' she said in an eager voice.

'No idea yet. A colleague, Max, said I should write a romance,' returned Colin in all seriousness.

'Why not? Beijing from a Westerner's point of view. Might even interest a Chinese publisher.'

'Yeah, that would be great!' he said on a lighter tone of voice. 'If it became a big seller, I would never have to write another video game again.' But in the same instant, remembering her job title, he added with more gravitas: 'Although, I must admit it's not such a bad job really.'

He reached for a wrap while she told him that writing a book had been on her things-to-do-at-thirty list. 'That list is still only half-ticked,' she added with a playful little laugh.

'It would have been a self-help book, maybe.'

'One thing about writing a book is it's never too late to start,' said Colin. He suggested she check out what was selling on Amazon China. 'Then you can check out the contents page, and there you have a ready-made template for a structure which you can adapt to your needs.'

'Good idea,' she said, covering her beef wrap in avocado. 'Then I fill in the blanks, right?'

'Yes.'

'Do you really think anyone can write a book, though?'

'You can. You're smart. You have expert knowledge in your field, and you have a ready market to sell to.'

That was nice of him, she thought to herself; then she said: 'Must be exciting to write books.'

'Yeah, and it can give meaning to everything you do, everything you see, and everything you visit, because in fiction, everything is potential material for a book . . . right?'

'Excellent, we must work on this Beijing book,' she said spontaneously.

The conversation flowed agreeably from writing to passions: fencing, scuba diving, and then travelling abroad, like her friends who were about to set off to New York in a couple of days. But to Colin's surprise, she said nothing of a potential role. Was she deliberately making him wait?

As they chatted away, Lin wondered why she felt drawn to this married man. But she let the thought go so she could just enjoy the night out, because she didn't want to tell him yet that the role she had intended for him was closed. But there was no harm in establishing a friendly footing.

Moreover, there would be other roles, she said to herself. Besides, he hadn't mentioned it either. And what's more, she noted he kept his marital situation to himself. For she had not failed to notice he only ever spoke of his children, never about his wife. Was he divorced? Or was he just in an unhappy marriage? Anyway, she was glad to vent her English, too, to a native speaker instead of stumbling along with a grim-faced East European or an agitated Italian.

Before they had exhausted their conversation capital, the waitress came and asked them if they would pay the bill. Surprised, Lin looked to her left to find the birthday table empty and already cleared away. She had not noticed. So why did she feel drawn to this man, this talkative thinker? she wondered. And why did she allow him to pay for the meal without any objection?

Ten minutes later found them standing before the restaurant, the last customers to leave, with the waitress bolting the door behind them. 'Bloody cold,' puffed Colin, burying his hands into his pocket as he looked into her face, snugly cocooned in her faux fur-lined hood. The chill made her dark eyes glisten like glass orbs as she looked up at him, standing with a metre between them.

'How did you get here, by the way?' she said, her puff of air filling the cold space between them.

'Underground. Easiest way. Can't speak Chinese, remember?'

'It'll be closed at this hour, closes at eleven. Better get a cab. Have you got Didi on your phone?'

'Yes, but it's all in Chinese.'

'Oh, let me set it up for you,' she said spontaneously, and

he handed her his phone that was linked to his Chinese bank account.

A few moments later, moving closer so she could show him the screen, she said: 'Look, I've entered the address of where you're staying as "Home," here. All you need to do from now on is let the app enter your present location, and then, tap the destination and choose "Home." Then you can access a choice of messages in English that you can send to the driver. Easy, right?'

'That's grand, thanks!' he said; then while she was still holding the phone, he tapped one of the prewritten messages which said he was at the GPS location. 'Like that?' he said.

'Yes,' she said, handing him back his phone. 'Now the driver won't need to call you.' She had taken off her glove, and his hand brushed against the tips of her slender fingers that he had been watching dance deftly over his phone screen. They resembled those of a female light elf, he thought: long and slender and beautifully tapered. He could swear her touch sent little magic sparks through his fibre. But, feeling the cold, she pulled her hand away, slipping it back into her leather glove.

'So, what are you doing tomorrow?' she said in a poised tone of voice.

Colin wondered if this was an invitation to make a proposition. He had not been expecting it, so he latched onto the first thing that popped into his head, having recalled the attractions on the wall map while standing in the underground train. 'Thinking of going to the zoo, actually,' he said.

Lin gave a little amused laugh. He had evidently picked the wrong venue, and now he realised there wasn't much that was romantic about watching monkeys and felines going stir crazy in their winter cages. 'What for?' she said.

'Always good to visit local attractions. Could be an accidental meeting place for characters,' he said, trying to look earnest.

She gave another little laugh and said: 'At the zoo?'

'Yes, why don't you come along?' he said, determined to pursue his initial intention.

'Oh, no, thanks, I have some friends over tomorrow, the ones who are going to New York next week.'

He noted that she gave a straight *no* for an answer, not a *no, I can't*, which might have left the door open for him to propose another day. He insisted anyway, like a man compelled on an onward march by the spirit of stubbornness into an abyss. 'Just going for research purposes . . . always good to observe the locals at leisure!'

'Ah, right, nice,' she returned, noting the serious look on his face, a serious look that made her smile inside. It was the look of a little boy taking his roleplaying seriously, that of a nine-year-old who had mounted a broomstick steed and commanded it to giddy-up. 'Well,' she said, mirroring his sobriety, 'have a nice time at the zoo then.'

There followed an awkward pause which was curtailed by the ring of her phone. 'That's my taxi,' she said, before taking the call. After a quick exchange with the driver, she turned to Colin. 'He should be in the next street, must be over there,' she said, pointing toward the street behind them.

Colin followed her to the corner as a white Buick pulled up. Then he advanced his chin to plant a kiss on her smooth, cold cheek. Having lived in France for a number of years had left its mark on him. It was a quick goodbye kiss, nothing tender, and somewhat awkward. For though the French, like the Chinese, will eat anything under the sun, unlike the French, the Chinese do not often hug, let alone kiss.

'Your car should be here soon. Will you be all right?' said Lin, one foot in the cab.

'Don't worry,' he said reassuringly, 'I can read a number plate, ha. You'd better get off!' Even though he was unable to see her through the tinted windows, he gave a quick wave as the taxi pulled away.

Ten minutes later found him travelling in his own cab back to his service apartment, quite content, having spent a pleasant evening with an attractive lady. He no longer thought of her as the headhuntress. And he had gotten Didi configured on his phone out of the night. It would mean a future saving. And this was an express taxi he was travelling in, which meant the service was prepaid so he had nothing to do on arrival. While he watched the little silver car move through the Didi street map, a WeChat message came up. He touched Lin's face. Her message read:

'Your taxi arrived?'

'I'm in it'

'good!'

'freezing out!'

'could be snow in the morning'

Thirty minutes later, he was back at his apartment. His phone blinked and he pulled up another message from Lin.

'Home now, thanks for the dinner!'

'Pleasure, lovely evening!'

'yes, and good talk too. Interesting about the book'

'next time maybe we can work out the plot, ha!'

'hahaha sure, would love to, now to sleep . . . night'

'night'

13

Some famous Chinese names have more of a resonance in the West than others.

The name that most resounded with Colin was *Ming*. As a lad, he would watch *Antiques Roadshow* with his gran, who fed him wine gums for his assiduity, especially if he sat as still as her two King Charles spaniels at her feet, waiting for their chocolate buttons. He recalled hearing an account of a lost-and-found vase from the Ming dynasty going for a fortune. This in turn was an invitation to climb the bare wooden steps of the old Victorian terraced house to rummage through the spooky attic. But what most reminded him of the namesake was that it belonged to the villain in *Flash Gordon*. Ming the Merciless of Planet Mongo, whose looks to a backstreet kid from Ponders End North London were something reminiscent of a Chinese man.

A Bing search had informed him that Beijing Zoo was built on a traditional Chinese garden from the Ming dynasty. The name having struck a chord in his memory, he had read on to find that some of these gardens had been recreated and would be a pleasant option for passing an afternoon away from the bleak high-rise buildings of the metropolis.

So, in part, thanks to Lin for provoking the visit, to his foible for wine gums while watching *Antiques Roadshow*, and to his boyhood passion for Ming the Merciless, Colin had ended up at the Beijing zoo. Perhaps such was the unknown order of things in the universe, thought Colin. And perhaps what would happen next was part of that intricate order, a set of earthly meetings and cosmic collisions that put Colin where he was now, and was pushing him inexorably into whatever it was he was about to step into.

Not having the linguistic capacity to cherry-pick, he bought an all-in ticket, then walked through the turnstile amid a light stream of Chinese families. In a few moments, he was standing before the large direction panel. He always liked the big cats and the elephants, so that was what he intended to visit first.

As he stood there, trying to get his bearings with the winter sun warming his face, he felt a buzz in his pocket. It was just a news notification, but it made him think of Lin. She had sent him a cheeky message earlier in the day asking if he had been to the zoo yet. He had told her that he had taken a late coffee at June's Garden Café downstairs and that he was planning to go that afternoon. In some mysterious, cosmic way, she was inadvertently compelling him to go see the animals or face being taken for someone who spoke lightly, and who had only mentioned the day out at the zoo in the hope that she would go along too, which would look clumsy. So, he had felt obliged to haul his body to the place where, in his singular world, a Chinese emperor rubbed shoulders with Ming of Mongo.

However, gazing over the wall map, he now saw why he really should visit the zoo of Beijing. This was the zoo of the giant panda, the animal that was as much an emblem of China as the thunder dragon. Moments later, he was walking past the little monkeys and birds in their cages without pausing until the asphalt pathway took him to the outdoor panda den. Here, wisps of snow had accumulated among the rocks, and a thin layer of frost surrounded the emptied pool. Before it, between a swing and an old tyre, sat old-man panda. He was gazing, his legs leisurely spread apart, at the gallery of onlookers peering through the Perspex screen and the wire fencing. Colin couldn't resist a furtive smirk as he considered why it was called a giant panda. He pinched the smile away from his lips and then moved to the wire fencing to take a more dignified side profile shot. 'This will get her,' he thought to himself with a secret smile as he sent the photo onto Lin's WeChat feed. 'I'm at the zoo!' he wrote before smugly pocketing his phone. He followed the smooth path into the cosier panda house, where specimens old and young were performing their various activities. One was munching bamboo, another was retreating through its trap for some peace and quiet, and another one was power-napping spread-eagled on a wide tree trunk. As one female panda gazed back at Colin while stripping another bamboo stem of its leaves, Lin made his pocket buzz.

'Determined! So you go to see the panda!' She punctuated

her message with a poked-out tongue sticker.

'Yeah, cute!' replied Colin, thinking to himself that this lady didn't miss a beat. He watched the bears eat, snooze, lethargically climb, eat again, and lounge blissfully as if they hadn't a care in the world. This, of course, was true, born and raised as they were in captivity, and sometimes sent on holiday overseas where they were treated like royalty. Another Bing search told him that Tian Tian, the panda on loan at Edenborough Zoo, was actually born in Beijing.

It was past four by the time he drew away from the panda house with souvenir coins for his coin-collecting son. He then climbed to the top of the zoo to see the big cats in their pungent winter quarters. The great white tiger's killer rage was palpable through the thick glass screen as it beat the concrete floor round and round between its den and the corridor. There was, of course, certainly a big difference between keeping a cuddly panda in a comfy den and a three-metre-long cat in a cage. He wondered if he was more the cat type or the panda type, maybe somewhere between the predator and the peaceful loner, he thought as he pitied the cat going stir-crazy.

The elephants' quarters were no kinder. So he walked at a brisk pace around the flowerless Ming gardens edged with snow until the sun grew cold. He looked over his head to see the ravens beginning to cluster in the bare birch trees for another long and frosty night. Their chatting reminded him of the previous evening sitting at table with Lin, never a silence between them.

He took the underground back to Wudaokou station as

evening began to fall. From there, he scanned a bike QR code and rode to the MacDonald's joint near his service apartment for a takeaway.

A little later, as he sat in his self-contained bedsitter biting into the double cheeseburger, Lin sent him a picture of her culinary creation. She wrote:

> 'Today is home cooking day for my friends, lamb chop and hotpot!'

Sitting on the edge of his sofa in front of the low table and the TV, Colin contemplated his burger, too salty, too filling. He wondered what she was really trying to say. What subliminal message was packed into her portrait of her dish? Was she trying to lure him by his stomach? He prodded his phone keyboard.

> 'Looks delish!'

The WeChat string came back as he finished the last cold chip dipped in ketchup which he washed down with some cold Coke. It read:

> 'So good advice about the book, thanks for the talk.'

She was referring to their discussion over dinner at the Mexican restaurant. How intriguing, he thought, that she had brought it up now instead of letting it float into the past.

He cast his mind back to their nonstop chatting. And now she picked up the thread of it as naturally as a piece of stitching. Were they sewing together some kind of a fabric? He punched in his reply.

'My pleasure, for me a very enjoyable evening. BTW, didn't tell you, but last night was the cheapest taxi ride I've had in BJ!'

'haha, normal price, before you paid the tourist price! So writing a book is a great idea and a good reason to do research to create something new. I like that idea.'

She was decidedly focussed, thought Colin, which was probably normal given that she was a headhunter. It was as if she was sounding him out, plumbing his depths and by consequence enabling him to plumb hers as she circled back to books, and he joined her wholeheartedly. He typed:

'Yeah writing a book gives meaning to everything. It means that when you visit something or feel something, you take note. And ultimately it results in an intimate expression in the form of something you can hold!'

'yes, and travel with a purpose!'

'you got it!'

'a bit scary, though, whether it will succeed'

'it takes a leap of faith!'

'yeah, I get it. Do you think I can learn the process and work on this? So maybe I can help you with your Beijing book'

'why not, although I don't know what it's about yet . . .'

'so how do I start?'

'first, get a notebook so you can jot down ideas on the fly . . . then start throwing down the ideas on A4 paper until a broad plan starts to form'

'ok, doesn't sound too difficult.'

'next, bunch them together . . . then create a timeline, story arcs, characterisation'

'oh, this must be where it gets complex'

'Haha, yeah, best if I tell you the rest face to face'

'Yes, yes, let's discuss it over a coffee sometime'

'You're on!'

14

The following Monday, Lin was trying to work out a slogan in English.

It was an approximate translation of a well-known Chinese four-syllable phrase. These idioms, called chengyu, contained wisdom passed down through the ages. But how do you translate them into English that often uses more words to express the same concept? she wondered. Her gaze paused on a familiar face in her WeChat contacts: the odd Englishman who had a thing for people's shoes and went to the zoo on his own. The thought brought a smile to her face: imagine a grown man watching pandas. It was cute, though; he must have a soft spot. She typed:

'Ok, I have to find a slogan. Which one do u like as a native Englishman? 1. Our dream, our fearless journey. 2. For our dream, fear of nothing. 3. Dream on, fearless journey.'

The message came back a minute later. It read:

> 'None of them. You need alliteration or something with your three concepts of journey, without fear, and dream.'

He must be busy, she thought, but to show she was unmoved by the brashness of his reply, she pursued:

'it's a slogan for a campaign. So translation from Chinese haha'

'what campaign?'

'recruitment'

'ah, right'

'dream fearlessly – our dream, our journey to fearless – coz the Chinese version mentions the dream. Anyway, how is your work?'

'busy, actually I'm working on a campaign too, a story campaign! I'll get back to you in a while.'

'yes, yes, no hurry.'

Lin went back to her flyer. It was late in the day, and her thoughts turned to the previous weekend, her Western cooking success, and the evening spent with the English panda lover. Then she thought about Wei Leng, the blind date that Yuping had fixed her up with the coming Friday. He had a good profile and a great resume, he was intelligent, and he had a good income. But how come he no longer had a wife? Maybe she ran off with his best friend, or even more dramatic, maybe she had died and he had spent ten years getting over her. Enter Lin . . . She was roused from her daydreaming by the WeChat icon flashing on her taskbar. It read:

> 'Back again. Off the top of my head you can do something like – turning bold dreams into brave journeys. So with "bold dreams" and "brave journeys" you get the notion of fearlessness and you get the alliteration for the rhythm . . . get it?'
>
> 'yeah, so: bold dreams ~ brave journeys!'
>
> 'actually, I didn't mean to shorten it, but that works too'
>
> 'good, I will ask the design team to work on it. Was about to leave. You?'
>
> 'still at work, important beta test coming up'
>
> 'oh, ok'

Was this panda guy dumb or what? Lin thought to herself. So she added:

> 'thought maybe go for a drink. Never mind, though.'

She couldn't be any clearer than that, could she? He replied:

‘good idea, what about Thursday? tomorrow is test night’

‘yes, let’s check back later then’

‘ok’

‘good luck with ur test!’

‘thx’

15

How do you drive your imagination so that it obeys when you want it to perform? thought Colin, gazing out at the bleak winter sky.

He had taken refuge in his usual spot, near a window in the open area where breakfast was served in the morning. But at this hour, the breakfast table had been cleared and tidied, the hotplates were turned off, and the central space and alcoves were made free for meetings. He had just edited some dialogue to take into account gameplay changes. It was the only way to get away from the constant hum of the PC, and away from that dastardly DingTalk, the professional app that worked similarly to WeChat. It totally replaced emails that were now considered to be too slow, and it was impossible to know if a person had opened a message or not. But Colin also knew that it was the all-seeing eye that allowed the company to see what was going on at every level.

Colin suddenly felt a shadow over him. He looked up, pulled out his noise-cancelling earphones and said: 'Hey, how goes it?'

'Good, man,' said Max, 'getting shit done before it hits the fan! Coffee?'

'Yeah, let's,' said Colin, putting down his pen.

'What's your shit, man?' said Max two minutes later as he sat down at a small round table opposite Colin. Colin did not like everything being designated as 'shit.' He even took offense when one level designer told him once that he would have to fill in all the 'shit.' By shit the level designer had meant 'story content' in the same way that Max now meant 'news.' Or maybe the Russian had just forgotten the word and used 'shit' as a placeholder, except that Max used it as a placeholder for everything. But it sometimes made Colin laugh out loud, like the time he needed a plane ticket and one of Max's assistants was busy with the Friday afternoon beer theme. 'Hey man, she's busy, it's Thanksgiving and she's been doing all the turkey shit, man, and now she's doing the corn and pumpkin shit and getting shit everywhere . . .' Max really did have a language tic, or maybe an attitude problem.

'Oh, things are better,' said Colin, after another sip from his PlayZone mug. 'The style is getting a lot more Westernized, more realistic. Semi-realistic to be precise, somewhere between *Fortnite* and *Lord of the Rings*.'

'Yeah, man, but soon as your back is turned they'll be putting Lolitas with big boobs everywhere again!'

'Well, not anymore,' said Colin, smiling. 'The art team seems to be nailing it.' This had come as no great surprise to Colin, given the Chinese reputation as copyists, although putting an eighteenth-century female pirate in a medieval fantasy world reminded him that culturally, they were indeed worlds apart. He continued: 'And they seem to be trusting me more.'

'Let me give you some advice, man,' said Max, who squinted twice and then fidgeted from buttock to buttock which, Colin noted, usually preluded a condescending lecture. 'Don't look for friendship in China; you won't get any. The Chinese always keep to themselves, man.'

'I don't agree. I've been to a few places, made a few friends,' said Colin, with a thought for Lin.

'You just listen to me, man,' said Max, getting worked up, 'I've lived here ten years: they don't give a shit. I've been working in this company over a year already, and has anybody in my team ever asked me how I am doing? Never!'

'Maybe you're too brash, Max,' reasoned Colin.

'Nah, man,' said Max, squinting and pressing his forefinger to his thumb to help hammer home his meaning. 'They. Do. Not. Care.'

'Sounds like you're thinking of changing jobs,' joked Colin, who secretly wondered why Max insisted on staying if he did not like it. 'Let me know in advance when you do, won't you? You're the only one in HR who speaks bloody English!'

'Nah, you're safe,' said the Russian, 'and I'm too busy making connections, building up my network.'

But Colin knew Max was one to watch and that he would spare no feelings if it came to curtailing his contract. And right now, he needed a fixed salary, and this was the best place to be, far from home, far from a painful divorce. 'You need to show some empathy!' he recalled his ex-wife yelling at him once as he now said the same words to Max.

'In my job, that's hard, man. I have had to fire friends, and that ain't easy.'

'Oh, just let me know well in advance if you plan on giving me the shove.'

'Bah, told you, you're safe, man. They need you.'

After such a confession, Colin suddenly found it difficult to take Max's words at face value. Did Max have a sadistic side? he wondered. But then he dismissed the idea, preferring to stay with his initial diagnosis, that this man just needed love like all the rest.

16

How do you justify writing video games at forty-something? thought Lin to herself as she stood before her bathroom mirror.

It was Wednesday evening. She was putting the finishing touches of cream around her eyes to moisten the skin. She had noticed with horror a few weeks earlier that it had begun to tighten into fine little wrinkles whenever she was tired. Tiny little lines magnified five times in her magnifying mirror that made them look ten times worse. What would she be doing, where would she be at forty? she wondered. Forty was in five years' time, the same distance she had travelled from thirty which seemed like yesterday — yesterday when she had everything planned, all sorted in her mind. She would be with her husband and have two kids and a well-established career by the time she reached thirty-five.

But that was yesterday, and true, she had carved out a successful career, although it had taken some hard decisions along the way. But she had a good salary, had seen the world, had bought a flat when Beijing was still affordable, and she drove a nice car. Compared to many others, she had few concerns. Life had treated her well, and she loved her parents, who were financially comfortable enough to take care of themselves. But there was one thing missing in her parents' lives too. They had no grandchildren, no child to mollycoddle and worry about. Had she failed them? No, of course not; she was not yet forty, only thirty-five, and she was about to go on a blind date with a man with a seriously good job. A sensible man with sensible ambitions, a man who probably did not play video games, let alone write them. So, although the Book of Changes might not be something she would confide in for life's big decisions, maybe the divinatory practitioner had paid dividends after all.

There. She was done. Made-up, powdered, and pretty. Should she take the car? she wondered as she made her way into the kitchen. No, a taxi would be better in case she had a cocktail. She had already shifted two penalty points onto her sister's licence. She could not risk having to do it again, not for another twelve months, at least. And besides, her sister had such expensive taste in shoes.

Picking up her phone from the kitchen table, she instinctively pressed the WeChat icon. She could not help feeling a pang of self-reproach on typing a message to the Englishman. Was she not guilty of leading him on? She sent her message anyway. It would leave her open for a follow-up meeting with Wei should he ask; you never knew, and she knew he was flying to Shanghai on Friday as he had brought forward their date to this evening. Then she pulled up Didi to order a cab.

Sometime later, Colin would read: 'Hello, I think I won't be able to meet up tomorrow, so maybe Friday is better?'

*

She arrived at the rendezvous fifteen minutes late, but Wei, dressed in conventional business attire, gave a polite smile as she approached him. She was relieved. It was not an open smile, just a slight glad twitch at the corners of the mouth as he showed her to her seat.

The meal was pleasant enough, interspersed with appropriate conversation on the subjects of work, family, friends, and hobbies. Nothing deep for the first date, and he proved to be attentive enough, though on a number of occasions, he took refuge in his phone that he left on the table throughout the duration of the meal. And at times she found herself trying to pull threads of conversation from him while trying very hard not to make it sound like she was interviewing a candidate.

They drank honey pear tea with their Beijing duck and platters of fish and vegetables. At the end of it, Wei politely proposed to see her again, but not this week or the next as he had some business to see to. But he would let her know his availability. Then she ordered a cab.

Sitting in the back of the taxi, she reflected on the evening. Why was she left with a feeling of dissatisfaction? Then she realised what it was. She had been burning to ask why he was still single. But if she had done so, it would only have drawn attention to her being not just single but a spinster at thirty-five. How horrid, so she had let the burning question grow cold and had kept to niceties. Hardly a passionate way to begin a relationship, she thought to herself. But thinking back, she had detected that Wei was a one-step-at-a-time kind of guy, so she had been right to wait for the next date to dig deeper. Wise move, she thought to herself as she scrolled through her messages in the back seat of the cab. She had always been a clever planner. She opened a new message.

'Hi Lin, no worries, I'm working late again today and tomorrow, so what about Saturday?'

Lin was glad; two dates. Decidedly, the stars were in her favour, she thought. She wrote back.

'yes, yes, ok understand. Let's do Saturday afternoon then, shall we?'

17

The following Saturday morning, Colin lay in his bed past his usual alarm call.

Having come to the end of a scene in the novel he was reading, he now sprawled out between the crisp cotton sheets changed the previous day by the service lady. It was one perk of living in a service apartment: sheets and towels were changed and the cleaning was taken care of. He felt calm, appeased, relaxed, like life was suspended. Everything he had been concerned about, had striven to secure for the past seventeen years, no longer mattered. Upon the signature of the terms of a divorce, everything that had cluttered his mind day and night had shrivelled into a tiny ball, easy to clasp. And the barriers to the world had fizzled away upon the end of that relationship. He was a freed man.

He felt like the English patient in the book he was reading of the same name, indolently waiting and breathing, life having lost its tiresomeness. All the plans of a decade and a half had been flushed away now, all water under the bridge. Thank goodness he had his kids, though, and with them a manifestation of times past and memories shared that photographs recaptured — photographs that both parties had copied and kept as the evidence of their own identities and past love. Yes, the kids made it all worthwhile. They meant that the river would nonetheless continue to bring Poohsticks under that bridge, little barques of happiness that made all those years of trying to keep the marriage together worth it.

Stretching out like a bodega cat, he decided he would have an expensive coffee and a panini down at June's Garden Café. He would treat himself to a relaxing moment in the snug basement out of the cold, his big Western nose sunk between the pages of his book, a studious eye on the text, a roving one on the pretty career ladies, mid-thirties, modern women of means.

Still feeling placid, he reached for his phone. 10:46 already. Ah, there was something else he had to do, he recalled now: a meet-up. There again, people sometimes said things just to be polite. But the next moment, he sat up on singling out a message from Lin.

Funny, he thought to himself, he never really liked recruiters. He disliked their false affability, juggling as they did with every candidate with the same well-honed friendly patter. While all they really cared about was for any one of them to land the job and bring in the cash. So what did this Lin want, really?

Her message carried on from their exchange of the previous Wednesday. She had messaged him to call off their Thursday-night meet-up. Colin had replied to suggest they meet Saturday as he was working late Friday on the beta version of the game. Her message read:

> 'So, any plans for experiencing Beijing for your book?'
>
> 'No plans. You free? If so, let's go somewhere if you like'
>
> 'sure'
>
> 'what about we meet first at a café with a notebook and pencil and see what comes out?'

Colin was thinking of a late-afternoon coffee, but her next message changed his plans. It was accompanied by a pic of a map. It read:

> 'are you ready to go out yet? If so maybe we can go to the Guomao district, there's a big Starbucks in Kerry Center line 10. Nearer to my place, takes a lady longer to get ready haha'
>
> 'haha, not ready yet either but can be there in an hour or so'

As he hit the send button he wondered why he didn't put it back to a later time, but his thought was interrupted by Lin's response.

> 'ok, that's fine. Same time for me to get out, I think. Then we can go anywhere from there.'

'will ping you when I'm out the door.'

'ok'

After another moment's pause, Colin hauled himself out of bed, half wishing he had given himself the morning to chill out. But as he shot a glance out of the window at the leafless trees below, he could not help feeling a zest of excitement. He watched a man, bundled up for the cold, scurrying along the opposite side of the street below. Along the wall that flanked the man, Colin could make out the twenty-four spells of the Chinese calendar. Twenty-four simple illustrations accompanied by Chinese characters translated into English, no doubt a relic from the Olympic year when China invited in the world. Today was two days before *Major Cold* which led into *Start of Spring*. A spell lasted two weeks, which meant he had been in Beijing between two spells already, given that he arrived at the end of *Winter Solstice*. He had promised his boys he would hop back to the UK during the Chinese spring holiday, which would begin in just over a week.

The previous spells had stripped the trees of any obstinate leaves. He could clearly make out the plywood roofs of the little market stalls on the other side of the wall. Here, a couple of market venders sold fruit and veg to the people of the neighbouring compounds.

Having showered and dressed, he pulled up Didi to situate how far he was from the central district that Lin had suggested. Moments later, the app let out a ring and said something in Chinese as Colin eyed a little car on the map heading toward his compound. Its number plate was shown in the interface, and Colin realised he had just ordered an express taxi that would be downstairs in fewer than six minutes. With no time to figure out how to cancel the cab, he dashed into the bathroom, where he quickly lathered his face and began scraping around his mouth, careful not to nick the mole between his left nostril and mouth. It had become an automatism, and he frankly no longer even saw it.

He managed the mole bristles without any bloodletting, and ten minutes later, he was boarding the waiting taxi. From the back seat, he punched in a message to Lin: 'Accidentally called the cab early so I'm on the way.' Then, as an afterthought, he added: 'but no worries, I'll just hang out somewhere till you arrive.'

As the taxi travelled from the fourth ring road through the inner city, he noticed that the streets seemed more deserted than before and that more people were wearing face masks. It reminded him of the increasing speculation that the new virus from Wuhan could be spreading from human to human. For otherwise, how could it have spread from Wuhan to Thailand? Until then, he had dismissed the disease as of little consequence. It seemed such a trifle compared to the common flu which, he knew from his time in Paris, killed twenty thousand people every winter in France alone. And in 2003, he recalled, the heatwave bumped off twelve thousand elderly Parisians, their bodies left to lie in refrigerated trucks for want of space, until families had returned from their sacred summer holiday to reclaim them. So the coronavirus in Wuhan, with its second death reported during the week, had made little impact on his imagination. And besides that, he had been working through the game narrative, so it was rather the encroaching darkness of the Dark Lord of Morah that occupied his ponderings these days more than any encroaching real-world disease.

18

An hour later, Colin was sitting opposite Lin at a window table in a Starbucks café in the Guomao business district.

It was an area Lin knew well. Important networking galas were held in the chic hotel complexes where once poor *hutong* neighbourhoods stood. 'Have you heard the latest about the virus?' she said, delicately drawing back her hair over her right ear as per her habit.

'I saw. Second death,' said Colin with his hands held over his goblet of latte.

'Yes, people are saying it could turn really bad, like in 2003, when hundreds of people died from SARS.' Satisfied he had taken note of the news that was on every Beijinger's lips, Lin decided to steer the conversation onto something more fitting for the occasion. On every subject, she noted they seemed to share the same viewpoint. Yes, the interior design was Western but impersonal, unlike the comfy armchairs in New Oxford Street in London; yes, the China Central Television building that stood outside the window looked like a giant *n*; and how intrepid was Carlos Ghosn, the former boss of Nissan-Renault-Mitsubishi turned fugitive, having escaped from Japan in a double bass case. But this was not a job interview, she kept telling herself as they each sipped their *ná tiě*. She was not testing to see if he was a right fit. But then, why had they met? 'So, what about the novel?' she said.

'I was thinking we could cook up a character,' said Colin, who then touched the side of his coat that he had placed over the back of his chair. 'I've brought a notebook.'

'Great, so let's move to across the road, shall we?' said Lin, who felt a pressing need to step into the wintry air to freshen up her neurons after an hour of talking and listening in Brit English. At least she was getting used to the weak rhotic *r* sound. Ten minutes later, they had taken a table at a tearoom in the chic and glossy China World Mall downstairs from the cinema.

'Let's start with the female character, shall we?' said Colin, once their pot of black tea was served. Lin agreed. 'So how old is she?' he pursued as he opened the teapot lid and stirred the brew.

'Hmm, thirty-five-ish,' said Lin, her chin resting on her thumb.

'Her profession?'

'Lawyer's good, would appeal to the audience.'

'Sounds good, but I don't know anything about lawyers. What about HR? You know about that.'

'Too dull, no one dreams of working in HR.'

'What then?'

'War correspondent? That's what I wanted to be when I was growing up.'

'All right,' said Colin as he poured the tea. 'So, one Chinese lady, cosmopolitan but from small town . . .'

Lin gave a nod and said: 'Good.'

'Lawyer stroke war correspondent stroke headhunter,' said Colin, passing Lin her tea.

'Could also be in finance or banking or internet,' said Lin, with a little shrug of a shoulder.

After another half hour of character-building, they had listed the cosmopolitan lady's family background, her date of birth, and that she was a Scorpio, as well as a series of potential names that would not alienate a Western reader. These included Na as in Chi-*na* that they could extend to Nana, which Colin recalled was the name of a heroine by French author Emile Zola. Reading back the character details to her, Colin registered the vacant look of someone struggling to listen. 'You must be tired of me gabbling on,' he said.

Lin twitched her mouth into a nascent smile, then gave up trying to put on a show and said: 'Been working late, it's nothing.'

'You need a power nap,' said Colin, popping the lid on his black fineliner pen. 'Come on, let's dive into the cinema upstairs. They're showing *Downton Abbey* in English!'

Lin laughed and agreed, and Colin called over the waitress and scanned the QR code on the bill to make the payment.

The cinema was the ideal refuge where, lights down, they could be together side by side without having to fuel a conversation. The film was already halfway through, and Colin estimated it meant there was still another hour's respite from solid talking. It was the perfect place where he could run the filmstrip of their conversation through his mind. What a narcissist he must have looked, he thought to himself. He had imposed his passion on an innocent bystander again, one who did not even read fiction.

Had it not been this boundless passion that had been partly responsible for the breakdown of his marriage? All those nights — nights spent giving himself freely to his vice, his one, absolute, all-consuming mistress, that ravisher of time — time stolen from his wife. And what had she gained in return? Had he written that big seller he had always talked about? No, and in truth, apart from two beautiful children, all she had gained out of their union was a house in need of repair and dwindling love in a mediocre neighbourhood. The boys would leave the nest one day and live their own lives, become too preoccupied to have concerns over their parents, and the house would become hollow. He hoped she would sell it, start over, and find new love. It would perhaps attenuate the guilt he felt over his indomitable passion. These were the ponderings that played through the film inside his head as he watched the Crawleys play out their Christmas drama. And he promised himself he would not subject his pretty companion to his passion anymore.

'You OK?' he heard Lin say and caught the flash of her tallow-coloured face in the dark room. He bowed his head toward her only to catch her silky hair swishing away, leaving a light perfume on his nose.

'Yes,' he whispered, and moved his hand toward the shared armrest where she had placed hers. But he felt only the displacement of air around it as it flew toward her face, where she now pushed her hair from her eye. So he settled into the trials and tribulations of the Crawleys and their intrepid downstairs people.

When the lights went up during the credits' roll, Colin was surprised to see not a room packed full of homesick expats from England, but only Chinese faces. Were they attracted by the Englishness of it all? he wondered while feeling a slight pinch of pride.

'Enjoy your nap?' said Colin, turning to Lin.

Lin laughed and said: 'No, I didn't sleep, actually. Beautiful country house, though.' Again, Colin could not help feeling that pinch of pride to be an Englishman, at least on his father's side. But then he heard the scowl of a little voice inside his head that reminded him that this English heritage was not his. None of his ancestors would ever have lived in such a stately home. Places like those were reserved for a minute part of the British population, of which his forebears were not a part. And besides, his mother was American. So why would he feel a pinch of pride at a symbol that could only represent oppression of the working people and the docking of their talents? But maybe that was something to do with being English, too, he thought; then he let it go. Moreover, Lin said nothing of the heritage of that certain Great Britain. After all, this was China, the People's Republic; why would she care about upstairs people? Instead, she looked around the room as the viewers shuffled from their seats. So, quite spontaneously, before she could say she would head home, he said: 'Let's go someplace.'

'All right,' said Lin, raising her chin to him. 'There's a

place called Atmosphere, top floor of the China World Tower, great view over the city. I work close by actually.'

She wondered why he had suggested extending the evening. But it did not matter; no one was waiting for her at home. Besides, she enjoyed his company: he listened well. Wasn't that what every woman wanted, someone to listen to her, to encourage her? He could have dismissed her idea to write a book about HR, but instead he had thoughtfully come up with a simple, practical solution to help her bridge her lack of know-how of structuring a book. But why did he even bother? Why should he care? And why were they going to the top of the China World Tower for an evening drink?

On the way out of the cinema, having freshened up in the ladies' room, Lin suggested they grab a bite to eat first. She would not be able to sit through the evening with a growling stomach. So they first made a detour to the upper floors of restaurants and went for Thai.

An hour later, in the swanky, top-floor bar of the China World Tower, they continued conversing over cocktails, neither of them feeling they had used up their days' capital of spoken words. Both being single, maybe they were making up for months of being unable to just talk out their thoughts. Maybe they simply got mutual satisfaction from advancing and talking, then retreating and listening, like in a nuptial dance, as the soft and sweet alcohol brought down any previous inhibitions. But there had to come a pause where they mutually edged back into their seats. Feeling relaxed and playful, Colin looked around the large, sumptuous room from their table, located two rows back from the more expensive window seats.

'See that woman in the red dress?' he said in an intimate voice while pulling forward again, his big Western eyes flitting toward the bar. 'I bet she's an escort.'

'Oh, you mean?' said Lin, leaning forward to meet him on a private level. 'No . . . really?' she said, playing along, although secretly wondering why he had shifted the conversation to sexual innuendo through the observation of a high-class hooker. Touching her right jawbone as if to guard her mouth, she said: 'How can you tell?'

'Put it this way, why would a pretty young woman be dating an overweight middle-aged man?'

'Security, wisdom . . .'

'Money.'

'Hah.' Lin turned her head furtively to her left, toward the expensive window table. With a saucy smile, she said: 'And what about them?' Colin followed her eyes and saw an American talking big and loud in the company of two young women.

'Not so sure,' said Colin in an equally playful voice, 'because he's young and not bad-looking.'

But Lin was becoming drunk on words and alcohol, and frustrated at not venting her pent-up desires. What was he playing at? Why was he beating about the bush? The thought suddenly seemed to sap all her energy.

'You all right?' said Colin, noticing her glazed-over eyes and a thin layer of sweat beginning to glisten on her smooth ivory forehead.

'I'm fine, just have a bit of a headache, must be the drink. I think I need some air.'

'I have some paracetamol,' said Colin, recalling the packet he had purchased after his first night back in Beijing and which he kept in his coat pocket.

'I'd better not, but let's go, shall we?' said Lin, who was finished with the ambiance of the snazzy expat bar. Five minutes later, they were exiting the lobby into the fresh air that revived her spirits. So when Colin asked if there was anywhere else they could go for a drink, she suggested Beer Smith's. 'That's if it's still open at this time of night,' she added, realising it must be close to 1 a.m. 'If not, then I'd better get back home.' Home to her rabbit and panda, she thought secretly as they turned a corner into another modern compound to find the pub in question on the ground floor. The band was sliding back behind their instruments as Lin and Colin entered.

It was a spacious expat pub where locals mixed with outsiders. Upbeat music, beer, jeans, and shirts. The band played hits from the '80s and '90s, which made conversation impossible. Colin noticed Lin had revived as he asked in her ear what she wanted to drink. Moving closer, she asked him to repeat the question. He asked again, his nose this time brushing her scented hair as she drew it back with a slender finger to hear him better.

In place of the flow of words, they swayed and seat-danced to a tune by Bon Jovi, a stark favourite among the locals and one of the first Western bands to crack the land of the panda. The interlude from talk allowed Lin to recharge her batteries and consider her options.

An hour later, after another blast of 'It's My Life' that

found a resonance with the crowd, it was time to call it a night.

'I'll walk you back to your car,' said Colin, holding the door into the cold night air.

'Would you?' she said. 'I should never have brought it.' Colin sensed a new nervousness in her voice. 'I wasn't expecting to drink alcohol, and so late . . .'

'You'll be able to drive all right, though, won't you?'

'No, mustn't. It's strict in China. I'll order a driver to come.'

Soon after, as they approached the modern office building under which she had parked her car, she got a call from the driver, who had just arrived. They found him shortly after with his foldable electric bike, in the building lobby where a security guard was dozing. Lin entered into conversation with the middle-aged driver. Then she turned to Colin, who was prodding his Didi app. 'We can get you a cab after,' she said, 'but first, would you just stay with the bike so the driver can follow me to my car in the basement?'

Colin agreed. Ten minutes later, he found himself watching Lin's black SUV Benz pulling up outside with Lin in the front passenger seat. Could he sneak a kiss before leaving her? Was it acceptable in the presence of the driver?

Lin had been wondering why the Englishman had been dithering with the taxi app. So when she got out of the car, she suggested they sort out the cab from her place.

Wasn't that an invitation for 'coffee'? thought Colin, who was not sure yet how to interpret a woman's intentions in China. But women in China were surely the same as women in Singapore or Montreal, weren't they? Surely if a woman offered to take a guy back to her place after a night out, there could only be one intention, couldn't there?

It was not far from the city centre, twenty-five minutes at most, time for Colin to become both eager and slightly anxious at the prospect of the night ahead. After all, you never knew if you truly had a spark for a woman until you kissed her, he thought to himself alone on the rear seat as Lin gave instructions to the driver up front. If there was no spark, there could be an embarrassing moment, he thought to himself.

The car was artfully driven and carefully parked by the driver. He then recovered his electric bike from the trunk before heading off to another alcohol-impaired client. Lin had paid 100 yuan, which Colin roughly equated to around a tenner. Decidedly, this petite lady had the world about her sussed and knew how to leverage all its benefits, which were numerous, it being a service society.

Lin wondered why she had taken the car in the first place. But how could she have suspected that the afternoon would lead into an evening dinner and cocktails, cocktails that would bring her guard down? Yet, thinking about it, wasn't it rather his talking that had disarmed her? For she had already felt tipsy even before going to the top-floor lounge. But most of all, what compelled her to take him back with her? Nevertheless, there they were. She beckoned him to follow her through the basement car park and the half-lit compound complex. Then they passed into a wide and shabby lobby of a high-rise, where they took the elevator to the twelfth floor.

During the short walk and elevator ride, they talked about the driver experience that left Colin wondering if such services could exist in cities back home. He said: 'You go out for an evening in your status symbol, get merry like everyone else, and at the end of the party, instead of calling a cab, you call a driver to chauffeur you and the extension of your personality safely to your door. How cool is that?'

'But how much would people pay for the service in the UK?' said Lin. 'In China, the disparity between the classes is wide enough to make this kind of service work both ways.' Colin agreed as the lift came to a shuddering halt.

They silently followed the freezing cold corridor to the end, where she pushed her key into the last door. Colin stepped into her world. He had been half expecting to find low tables and cushions on the floor in a tiny room in the ancient Chinese fashion. But the flat was spacious and modern, simple yet stylish, like millions of apartments around the Western world. He found a warm open-plan room with a fitted kitchen at one end and a lounge at the other.

Lin was not smiling. She felt anxious. What was she doing? What did she expect? She had not had sex for over a year. She had never before even brought a man back to her apartment, not even her ex, who had once refused her invitation anyway. But at least she had a backup plan. She had a spare room, and if it did not go beyond conversation, then he could sleep there, saving face all round.

She switched on the big white lounge ceiling light, leaving Colin to remove his shoes by the door, and then discover the ornaments and photographs of friends and family neatly stuck on the fridge to his right. He scanned the lounge to his left and stepped over to the sofa, where he found the button of the overhead lamp that gave out a more romantic glow. Next, he walked back to the main light switch and flicked it off just before Lin came out of the bathroom.

Lin did not smile, and Colin suddenly realized that for all her self-assurance, she must be feeling nervous. So, he gave her a coy smile as she brushed by him and sat down on the sofa beneath the overhead lamp.

He sat down beside her in front of the low glass table, where there was a basket of assorted sweets and an array of fragrant candles still unused. As she was about to say something, he turned his chin toward hers. Their eyes locked momentarily. Colin paused an instant, then they mutually moved closer until their lips came together.

Upon their touch, Lin felt an electric sensation as Colin pushed his lips into hers, their hands holding each other for balance, before their torsos met, leaving their palms to touch and their fingers to entwine. In a frantic bout of discovery, they then frisked each other's bodies until he softly cupped her breast. Lin breathed a sigh of deep pleasure, a profound, almost orgasmic pleasure that her body had been craving for so long. As she swayed and sighed with waves of desire, he kissed the smooth crook of her neck, his warm hands now under her pullover and feeling her bare ribcage, her soft belly, her sides, and, cupped in her bra, her breasts, full and firm.

Her body seemed to react with an intensity he had never encountered before as she moved in spasms with each caress. Her slender hands ran under his shirt from his chest to his waist until both he and she were groping in a frenzied desire. Hardly unlocking lips, they half undressed one another. He pushed her back onto the length of the sofa while he gently pressed his thigh between her thighs, his right leg trailing off the sofa.

'Come up, you are falling,' she murmured, holding his head in her two hands like she would drink from his mouth. But then she eased herself from beneath him and, slipping her fingers around his wrist, she led him into her bedroom.

19

Dressed in an oversized nightshirt in the K-pop style, Lin drew back the thick garnet-rose curtain to peer through the tall bay window. 'Hey, it's snowing!' she exclaimed with a note of excitement.

Colin, his hair still damp from his shower, reached out and pulled her onto the warm bed, where he covered her neck in soft kisses. She smacked his lips with a kiss and then brought her hand to her chin. 'Ouch, you have bristles,' she said.

'Sorry, if I'd known I'd have brought a razor,' he said jokingly. 'And maybe I should have brought something else too.' Lin knew what he was referring to. They had taken no precautions. But it wasn't as if they were complete strangers; they knew each other well enough to trust each other, didn't they? 'What if you fell pregnant?' asked Colin frankly as she lay resting her head upon his chest.

'Don't worry, it's highly unlikely,' she said, raising her face to see the expression in his eyes, 'but would you be mad?'

Colin cast his mind back to an afternoon the previous

summer. It was their first get-together after their initial meeting, and Lin had invited him to visit a *hutong*. She had explained it was a traditional neighbourhood of old courtyard homes and narrow lanes that once made up most of Beijing, back in the days before skyscrapers and pollution, when the Forbidden City was the tallest building in the land and city smog did not obscure the view to the Fragrant Hills. She had decided to go with one of her colleagues. The three had met for lunch at a Georgian restaurant between the calm and leafy Embassy district and the Liangma River. The conversation had turned to the changing place of women in China. The colleague affirmed that she was quite happy without the yoke of marriage and exclaimed adamantly that she wanted to remain free, no kids. Colin had asked Lin if she felt the same, which would have made sense given that she was still single and without children. According to their table talk, he had discovered that in China it was commonplace for women to wed and have their children young. Their mothers often took care of their daughters' offspring in the hometown so the daughter, often an only child, could earn a living like the son that the law forbade them from having. Colin's female company, both in their mid-thirties, had explained to him that older women were mostly undesirable for Chinese men, not least because women of Lin's calibre and generation were tough cookies. They were hard-thinking, Benz-driving, headstrong fillies who at thirty-five were no longer malleable. These were career women who had set out to stake their claim in the male-driven society as trailblazers, entrepreneurs, and leaders, and they had won their place. But often they had won it at the expense of their private lives. For once a woman was over the thirty-five threshold, most men wondered what had gone wrong. Did they have a defect, a personality disorder, a bad temperament? But during that meal, contrary to her colleague, Lin had affirmed her desire to have a child, and then had reiterated it when Colin had at first understood the contrary.

Back in the bedroom, Colin said at last: 'Well, I wouldn't mind so much if it were a girl, I haven't got any of those,' he joked. It had seemed strange and yet natural to be literally telling her he was OK about making a baby after their first night together. Or maybe it was because he had just received confirmation that she would probably not get pregnant. 'But why do you say it's highly unlikely?' he said, guessing by the tone of her voice that it was not for the obvious reason.

'Because my tubes are blocked; that's why I had some of my eggs frozen.'

'For IVF?'

'Yes.'

'I know a couple who had it done. They ended up having twins.'

'Yes, that's possible too,' she said, her cheek still resting on his beating chest. 'I've thought about it, two birds, one stone.' Then, stroking the side of his face with the backs of her fingers, she said: 'I'm hungry. I will get us some breakfast.' She pushed herself up from his chest and swung out her legs. He let her wrist slip from his grasp as she escaped from the bed and watched her straighten her nightshirt. Then she danced across the high-ceilinged room into the intersection that linked the two bedrooms, the bathroom, and the kitchen-dining area.

'I'll do the coffee,' he called out and lay languidly for a few extra moments on the soft, oversized bed, his body now relaxed after a night of lovemaking. He reminisced. Upon first meeting her in that coffee bar for a potential job offer the previous summer, never in a thousand years would he have imaged that her body would be so receptive to his every touch. He heaved himself up from the bed. Half-dressed, he stepped to the window and looked down at the white blanket of snow that covered the road forty metres below, and then at the purple-coloured sky and the opposite Soviet-style tower blocks that stood there, shabby and austere.

There was hardly a soul out there in the cold and frosty Sunday morning, just the odd car ploughing slowly through the shallow snowfall. But then, feeling slightly uncomfortable in the bedroom alone, he picked up the quilt by two corners and flung it squarely over the bed before joining Lin in the kitchen area, where she was making eggs and toast.

*

After a night spending her pent-up passion, Lin needed food.

Never in a million years did she imagine that lovemaking could be so intense. Again and again, after bouts of slumber — each sleeping on top of the other as if they would become one, one mass, one body — they had found each other's lips, and again fell into another bout of soft, exquisite, all-empowering lovemaking.

'Did you know, no man has ever come here, let alone

slept in my bed?' she said, glad to share a secret with him as he wrapped his arms around her and snuggled his face into the crook of her neck.

'Nice,' he said as she turned to face him and, on the tips of her toes, smacked him on the face with another kiss. She slipped away, not yet entirely used to the attention of a lover. 'So where d'you keep the coffee?' he continued.

'I already boiled the water,' she said, and told him where to find the coffee bags.

'So, you've never ever brought a man back to your place,' he said, playfully dubious a minute later.

'No, never,' returned Lin in all innocence, and getting a liberating buzz out of not needing to hide anything. 'Not even my ex.'

'How does it feel?'

'Strange. Good. I don't mind it at all, actually.'

'Good,' he said, pouring water from the kettle into a mug.

'I . . . I didn't even mind your snoring,' she pursued, glancing at him with a cheeky smile.

Colin was jarred at the thought, almost scalding his hand that was holding a mug handle. 'Oh, really? I don't usually snore, must have been the alcohol . . .'

'No, but I didn't mind it at all,' she returned in a cute voice. 'In fact, it made me feel good, don't know why.' They laughed coyly together.

A few minutes later found them sitting either side of the kitchen table, tucking into their eggs on toast and drinking coffee.

Colin went off on a tangent about the power of passion. It somehow led to the subject of pastimes and how people in the West like to chill out or vegetate in front of the TV. Lin, sitting opposite, had that vacant smile of someone having dropped a stitch and completely lost the thread. He was about to change the topic when she unexpectedly leapt up from her chair, skipped over to his side of the table, and jumped astride his lap.

How cute he looked when he had that serious look on his face, and she stopped his mouth with a kiss before he could get another word out.

'I ought to go maybe,' he said at last.

'Have you anything urgent to do?'

'I did tell Xiao Long I might go with them to the Great Wall,' he said, 'but there again, it wasn't confirmed.' Yielding to an irresistible urge, he then placed his forehead flat against hers and, like two lodestones of opposite poles, they stuck together.

'Then stay,' she said, his mouth now brushing against her lips as she spoke.

Scooping her up, he pushed back the chair from the table and got to his feet, her arms wrapped around his neck, and her legs clamped onto his waist. He almost tripped on the small step of the intersection before continuing into the bedroom, where they toppled over in laughter onto the big bed, much too big for just one person.

Colin's phone buzzed in his pocket. It was a message from Xiao Long. Did he still want to go to the Wall?

*

Late afternoon, again Lin found herself peering out of the bay window at the flurry of snow in the dimming light.

It all contrasted with the yellow glow from the lamplight and the comforting clicks from the radiators of the collective heating system. Inside it was warm, like in her heart, a fuzzy comfort that she had not felt in a long time, if ever. But the planner in her wondered how long it would last before it grew cold. There again, did it really matter? Right now she was just enjoying the moment and the warm glow within. They had made love on the reading divan in front of the window; she had felt an urge to share a fantasy come true with the outside world, and show that she now had a share of that elusive human emotion called love. She smiled to herself as she moved across the room, glad to be heading to another living presence. She had been living here alone for so long. And yet, the presence of this man from another world seemed so natural as she entered the bathroom again without knocking. He was standing before the sink mirror with a towel tucked around his waist. She brandished the object she had gone to fetch. 'One toothbrush,' she said. 'I knew I had one in my travel bag, got it from a hotel.' Then, touching her chafed chin, she said: 'I wish I had taken the razor too; your beard is so hard.'

'Oh sorry, was that really me?'

'Your kisses, our kissing,' returned Lin like an accomplice. 'It's OK.'

'Your skin is so soft and smooth,' he said. It was the kind of thing any woman liked to hear.

'Chinese men don't have such hard whiskers, and you are

hairy too,' she continued, now holding him by the waist and inspecting his chest hair. Colin let himself be touched. Her slender fingers seemed charged with an appeasing current.

'So I've been told, like a bear,' he said.

'Like a panda bear,' said Lin with a musical peal of laughter. The thought of the divinatory practitioner flashed through her mind as she said: 'And they are so long!'

'Well, I haven't trimmed them in a while,' he said jokingly.

With a look that meant business, Lin told him not to move. She returned moments later with a pair of scissors. 'Let me,' she said, reaching up to kiss him.

'Have you done it before?'

'Never,' she said in her musical laugh. But trimming the chest hair of this man she hardly knew seemed like the most natural thing to do in the world. So she began shearing away the hairs against the back of his comb. 'It's long in the middle and then gets soft and silky on the belly,' she said, as though trying to analyse something she wanted to apprehend.

'Yes, don't cut those ones, though!'

'No, just the chest ones. How funny, they are turning white on your chest, and on your belly they are black.'

'Age.'

'Black and white.'

'Like a panda bear,' joked Colin, recalling her previous reference to the emblem of China. He stood there, letting her pass her hand and scissors meticulously over his pectoral muscles, thinking to himself he had never been touched in this way before.

'Yes, it's so strange to have a panda in my bed,' she returned with a coy smile as the towel around his waist came loose and dropped to his feet. Lin continued artfully raking and shearing his chest hair.

'I'll do those ones,' he said, looking down toward his nether regions.

'I can do them too,' said Lin, taking half a step back to admire her work and the man with whom she felt completely at ease. It occurred to her that maybe she should feel embarrassment, but she did not. She said: 'Not bad for a first time, right?' She approached and reached up to kiss his lips again. Then he let her inspect his prickly cheeks and the rest of his face. She already knew what to expect from their previous encounters, but this time she could touch it and take charge.

'Dry skin,' she said. 'You should try this.' She reached for a vial from the bamboo sink unit. 'It's geranium essential oil. Five drops on your palm, then rub your palms together, and spread it over your face from your forehead and down over your nose and cheeks. It will keep you looking young.'

He let her apply it for him. Shouldn't he feel some embarrassment? he wondered. But as she rubbed the essential oil into his skin, any notion of modesty slipped away as he stood there perfectly naked.

'Actually, you've got a handsome face,' she said, stepping back.

'Glad you've just noticed!'

Lin let out another pretty peal of laughter and said: 'Except for your mole.'

‘Mole? Ah, yeah, it’s kinda grown on me, so I don’t even notice it anymore.’

‘It sticks out,’ she said, combing his trimmed chest hair.

‘It does now, never used to, though.’

‘It’s OK, we can get it removed,’ Lin retorted, reassuringly.

‘Removed? What for?’

‘Health and beauty.’

‘Well, now you mention it,’ said Colin, peering into the mirror, ‘it does kind of stick out quite a bit now.’

‘And it’s in a bad place.’

‘Bad place?’

‘Under your left nostril is a bad place.’

‘Really? How do you know?’

‘I already checked. I can show you a picture of moles according to the principles of ancient Chinese face-reading. Yours stops you from living a free life, and from being successful. So you should have it removed.’ Colin let out a short laugh as he looked more closely at his mole in the mirror.

What was she saying? she thought to herself for a moment. But didn’t her mother always tell her that it was the woman who made the man? In that case, was she counting on a long-term relationship? she wondered. It was true, though, that her colleagues often told her it would suit her to go out with a foreigner. Even so, how strange; it was not in her nature to be so free with a man, moreover a man with whom she had spent just one night. And here she was, trimming his chest hair and offering to modify his face as he stood naked with a towel at his feet. ‘OK, you get changed, and I'll order dinner,' she said after another kiss on his mole.

*

They continued their incessant chat over a dinner of chicken and mushroom and pork and green pepper, each layering on phrases and thoughts spontaneously, hardly leaving any silence.

At one point, Lin said: 'Oh, by the way, your HR director resigned Friday; it's big news. Apparently she had an issue with the CEO.'

'Hmm, not that I know her,' said Colin, 'but I hope it doesn't mean the bonuses will be pushed back!' At that moment, a song from his random playlist came up on his phone that he had paired with the Bose Mini speaker sitting behind them on the TV unit. 'Listen,' he said, reaching for the phone and turned up the volume. Then he stood up and offered his hand to dance with the pretty Chinese lady to 'China Girl,' in an apartment in the very heart of China.

As they swayed to the music, it dawned on him how the lyric uncannily matched the situation, how she had shut his mouth with a kiss. What would the twelve-year-old kid from Ponders End think if he knew his older self would one day be living one of his favourite Bowie tracks?

20

A new chance at love, that was what he needed, he thought to himself as he stood holding his phone in the crowded elevator.

He knew now that elemental powers existed not only in video games, and that being romantically involved with someone ultimately meant feeling at one with that person, like opposite poles drawn together. That is what he strove for now, a oneness, and he had found it in the space of a weekend with Lin. Never had he experienced such a magnetic pull, the pull that made him sleep on her, pressed against her, his head squashed on her breasts, her belly, her thighs, her face. It was all very puerile, he thought to himself, even blushing at his thoughts as he stepped into the lobby of the twentieth floor, where decorations were waiting to be hung up for the Spring Festival.

With his ex-wife, oneness had been achieved, but intermittently. Their elemental powers being at odds with each other's, too often their personalities clashed, so inexorably forcing them asunder. They should teach the importance of elemental powers at school, he thought to himself. It is what pulls people into unexpected love affairs and creates unbreakable bonds: Cleopatra and Mark Antony, Edward and Mrs Simpson, John and Yoko. If they taught the importance of body and mind, there would perhaps be fewer unhappily married couples, he thought. Instead of *Don't marry that boy, he has no prospects,* it would be, *Don't marry that boy if your temple lodestones don't attract. To find out, place your forehead against that of your partner. Does it stick? Does it stir something beneath your temples?*

He slipped along the aisle where on either side, eyes were glued to PC screens. A line of mouse-clickers, their minds in another world, so much so that nobody lifted their head to so much as blink a hello. It was a world Colin was used to, and be it in Beijing, Montreal, or Singapore, it was one of the things he disliked about working in games, or rather, working with people in games. They were not that much fun to be around. He recalled having so much more fun when working on set in Toronto with real actors, chatting and larking about while waiting for the next scene to be queued.

As he ambled to his work station, for no particular reason he recalled on one set a Welsh actor playing a Londoner. He could not get rid of the Welshness in his voice when pronouncing 'bottle' and became quite irate when Colin picked up on it. Then there was the French-Canadian director who made a comment on how good was the actor who played Churchill, but let himself down when he said: 'Just one thing, though, the accent did not sound very German, did it?' Colin had turned, speechless, toward the linguist on set with whom he had been chatting. The linguist explained gently to the director that it was normal as Churchill was actually a Brit! True, thought Colin, some of them were uncultivated, uncut diamonds, but at least they always said hello when you arrived, and he by far preferred their company to the mouse-clicking screen-gazers who had lost touch with humanity. But there again, you could not expect everyone to look around to say hello every time someone walked up the aisle, could you?

This morning, there were more mouse-clickers in the aisles than when Colin usually arrived. There was a reason, and that reason was that it was past ten o'clock. Everybody had finished breakfast. 'Hey!' hailed a voice as Colin approached his desk. He could always count on Xiao Long for a greeting.

'Zao,' returned Colin with a two-finger army salute.

'Late, huh, not like you,' continued Little Dragon with a rascally glint in his eye. 'Where were you yesterday then?'

He was referring to their trip to the Great Wall that didn't go ahead. Colin firmed his lips so they could not break into a guilty smile. 'Ah yes, sorry about that, I was doing some research,' he said.

'Research? What was her name?' said Xiao Long, a broad, expectant smile gleaming from ear to ear.

Unable to keep a straight face, Colin let out a false laugh. 'Hah, you have a filthy mind!' he said, grabbing his coffee mug.

'I told ya, I was brought up on porn,' said Little Dragon, who had a keen eye. Colin knew he was a smart observer, and Colin had broken his habit of arriving well before ten when most of the crew were breakfasting in the main hall on dumplings, noodles, and boiled eggs. He put on his business face and headed for the ground-coffee machine. He had to get himself away for fear of letting something slip, his mind being too occupied to focus, entirely taken up as it was with Lin. Besides, he was itching to check his phone.

*

Lin instinctively covered her naughty grin with her free hand as she recalled how insanely at ease she had been with this English guy.

To think, she had given him a face mask, had trimmed his chest hair, and had even made him think about going for face surgery. How she could be so candid was beyond her. It was as if they had been in a relationship for months already. But how could she consider herself to be in a relationship at all after a single weekend? It must be because they had spent so much time incessantly talking during their previous platonic encounters.

Monday being the day her number plate disqualified her from driving into the city centre, they had shared a taxi part of the way. How irresistibly coy he had become when she had edged her hand up his thigh while on the back seat. It only spurred her on more to see how far he would let her go before holding back her hand. Whatever was she thinking?

She was already ten minutes late for the Monday morning meeting, which should normally freak her out. But standing before the meeting-room door in her high heels and designer suit, she only had one thought. She gave a quick glance left and right before looking into her phone. She just had to reach him one more time before she could do anything else.

*

Waiting for his fresh coffee to pour from the coffee machine, Colin hit Lin's WeChat profile pic. She said she had arrived at the office, was about to go into her meeting, and left a line of kisses.

Colin wished her good luck and sent a line of kisses back. He spent the morning in a daze, as though he had been knocked out and was still punch-drunk. He shifted unproductively between one writing task and another — from dialogue to character bios, to some lore text and then back again to dialogue, only to find it impossible to get a handle on any of them. So he played about with some one-liners, his mind unable to focus on anything more than single strings of words. 'Just stay chill, keep your balance like yin and yang!' he wrote for one Kung Fu Panda character.

After lunch of *saming ji shale niurou* — beef and salad sandwich — he joined Max, who was eating his takeout by the window. The light was a dingy purple; it looked like it would snow again, and they were both wearing T-shirts and black hoodies. Colin, who had spoken earlier with the producer, decided to raise the question of salary. He said: 'I spoke to Mingyu earlier; he sent me a 360 evaluation file to fill in.'

Max shovelled the last pincerful of food into his mouth, and then said: 'It's OK, man. It's for the bonus review.'

‘Which means I’m in it, then, right?’

‘Yeah, told you before. It’s a means to mark your performance. It gives A B C D et cetera. The biggest you can get is four times your salary, but that’s quite rare.’

‘I hope not that rare; I need to pay my taxes, remember? If I’d have known it was a contractor contract I’d be signing, I’d have given you a contractor price!’

‘Don’t worry, man,’ said Max, rising to his feet as was his usual method of curtailing a conversation. ‘You want more money? You just say how much within reason, and your request will be taken into consideration in April. That’s when we have the salary review.’

‘Well I heard the HR head just up and left the company. Is that true?’

‘Who told you?’ said Max with a double squint.

‘Nobody you know. Anyway, I’m glad I’m counted in the bonus at least.’

Scooping up his empty takeaway meal container and chopsticks, Max said: ‘Good. Let me just grab a coffee. I wanna talk about the new crea.’

While Max was fetching his PlayZone mug to fill with coffee, Colin couldn’t help pulling up his WeChat app and reaching for the first person on his mind. He wrote:

> ‘Hey Lin, good news, spoke to the producer this morning, I’m in the project bonus.’

Seconds later, her reply came through.

'Nice, more secure to have confirmation.'

'Also HR guy asked how much more money I want, not sure what to say, so I thought I'd ask my favourite headhunter, any idea?'

'Just ask what's on their mind when it comes to it.'

'Right'

'And you should tell them there's at least one headhunter after you with an offer! So he knows he has competition, haha! That way he won't feel safe!'

'Right.'

'And good to have salary increase as bonus is based on it. So all good. Am thinking if they think it goes well with the project the salary can go from 6 to 7 because the feedback so far is good.'

'Noted.'

'So when can you meet with TalentPlus headhunter?'

'TalentPlus headhunter?'

For a moment, Colin wondered if there was a new offer on the table. But the next instant, he was shot back down to earth.

'Come on . . . Headhunter is ME'

'Ah of course, what do you have in mind?'

'Ok not with headhunter, when can you meet China girl?'

'I can meet China girl any time. When you free?'

'Anytime'

He was about to punch in a smile when he glanced up to see Max striding back in his usual way, shoulders back, chest out, proud as a rooster. Instead Colin quickly typed:

'he's back, gotta go'

Colin coolly swiped back to the contacts list and hit the home button as Max sat down opposite him and placed his PlayZone mug of coffee on the table. 'I was saying,' said Max, 'we've found a creative director. Could you talk with him? Might take him for dinner tonight, would be great if you could join us. He's going back to Hong Kong after tomorrow.'

'Ah,' said Colin, with a look of disappointment, 'working late. I can tomorrow, though.'

Max glanced down at Colin's thumb caressing his phone screen. He said: 'So what did you get up to last weekend?' Colin, who was expecting to pick up the subject of his salary, was caught wrong-footed. It was typical of Max, blurring the lines between personal and professional issues: a dangerous mix, a technique that Colin suspected Max of using to deliberately destabilise his counterpart, unless it was just ingrained in his fibre; he was Russian after all. Maybe seventy decades of communism had etched it into the collective DNA, despite Max having lived in post-Soviet Russia since he was eight.

'Oh, nothing to write home about, research, walking around, and guess what?' said Colin, trying to think up something that he might potentially have seen as if to prove his innocence. But still under the influence of Lin's new place in his life, his mind was not as fluid as usual, and a missed neurone connection allowed Max, who was not a patient man, to jump in.

'Don't tell me, man,' he said, glancing at Colin's phone as if he would ask Colin to show it to him. 'You found a girl!'

Colin let out an exaggerated laugh. 'Nothing so dramatic, buddy, hah! I was going to say . . .'

Again the cunning Max jumped in: 'You been seeing that HR girl you told me about. How else would you know about the HR woman who resigned? Because not even your team knows, and I'll ask you to keep it under your hat.'

'Nothing of the sort. Besides, I have a life outside mobile games,' said Colin, shrugging off Max's remark. 'No, I went to a meetup, and by the way, you should check out the Swing Bar 58, great singers!'

'Yeah, man,' said Max, slightly nonchalant, slightly peeved. 'They've been coming here for years, man, Korean.'

'Ah, right,' conceded Colin tamely, having achieved his goal of changing the subject, which was not difficult to do with someone like Max who liked to give the impression that no one could teach him anything in life, because he knew it all.

Slightly impatient and deciding to keep the high ground, Max said: 'How's your Chinese?'

'Trying to string words together,' said Colin, 'not so easy, though, not because of the grammar, but because of the pronunciation . . .'

'Oh, yeah, what you need to do is just write down ten words a day and learn them by heart,' said Max, like a pharmacist dispensing a prescription. He took another sip of his coffee and continued. 'But the best way is to get a Chinese girlfriend. That's how I first learnt. It's twenty-four seven then, man. But you have to choose one that doesn't speak much English.'

'And what if I'm not open to relationships?' said Colin, humoured.

'Well, it's nice to have company.'

'You can talk. You're still single.'

'I am not single, man, I am solo!' said Max, stabbing the air between them. 'Anyway, haven't found the right woman yet, because for me a woman has to be perfect in every way. She has to be feminine, she has to be unselfish, and if she has a car, she has to open the door for me.' Colin laughed out loud. Max continued. 'It's true. I always test them when I first take them to dinner. If she takes a napkin to show she's well brought up, then she has to pass one to me. If she gets one just for herself, then she's cooked; I just fuck her and that's it,' he concluded.

With amused indulgence, Colin said: 'Or maybe she just got what she wanted: a meal and a one-night stand. Because those girls you date are still in that girls-just-wanna-have-fun phase. And besides that, you have no passion, no particular talent, no house, no car, and you're not rich, so what can you offer a woman to make her want to see you again anyway?'

'I have me, I have me to give!' said Max, holding out his palms as if it were obvious.

Colin laughed. 'Maybe you only get one-night stands because they won't stay any longer than one night.'

'Well, I'm having fun, man. And if I wanted to marry a girl, I could do it just like that,' said Max, snapping his fingers to punctuate his point, and then said: 'Anyway, didn't you have a birthday recently?'

The remark made Colin smile. 'You have it on file, don't you?' he said. 'Because I stopped counting at thirty-five.'

Max, remaining straight-faced, said: 'What element are you?'

'Water.'

'My folks are fire, but it's just made them impatient. Anyway, it doesn't mean a thing, all this Zodiacology shit, man.'

'Well, I've been looking into the Chinese Wuxing elements lately, inspiration for the game.'

But Max, having lost interest, drank some more coffee and then said: 'So what's this girl?'

Colin gave a little laugh. 'There is no girl,' he said, playing the innocent.

'What about that HR girl you were seeing?' pursued Max with a squint. 'Her name was Lin.'

Colin tried to hide his surprise behind another chuckle when he said: 'I only went out with her a couple of times last summer to speak about a job, told you.'

'I remember. I don't like people poaching on my patch. Anyway, she don't know the mobile game business that well; in fact, she knows nothing.'

'Ha ha, I told you: I'm not looking for a Chinese girlfriend anyway. And I'm not open to job offers either. Especially now that I know I'm in the project bonus. Although I did get a firm offer of seven thousand. But I repeat, I'm not open to offers . . . yet.'

'Good. The pay review is in April. Anyway, I got a meeting.'

'Yeah, me too.'

'So, let's go out to eat with the crea tomorrow evening.'

*

After an art meeting during which Colin found out that Kai had decided to give a character a gammy leg because it looked cool, Colin pulled up his WeChat interface on his PC.

He reduced the WeChat window, then wrote to Lin:

> 'Let's go to lunch some time, and meet in the evening. Can't say what evening yet because things keep changing . . . but when are you free for lunch?'

Lin was behind her PC. After hitting the WeChat icon, without a second thought she wrote:

‘sure, tomorrow is ok, lunch and dinner. Both. You are my priority this week. Remember I’m leaving soon to go to my hometown for the spring festival. Have to see my mum and dad’

‘Ok, I’ll confirm tomorrow then.’

‘Ok. I did not do too much work today. Keep thinking of the past weekend. Difficult to concentrate.’

‘Hey me too, haven’t thought about anything else.’

‘You do too? I feel better now, missing your kisses. Even though my lips are really dry today, and my colleague asked me what’s wrong with my chin because the skin was red.’

‘Did you tell her?’

‘Of course not. It’s just a small spot I said.’

‘Good’

‘I better leave you to work . . . keep thinking erotic thoughts . . . this is crazy. Speak later when u are home.’

‘Speak later, probably back around 9:30’

‘Ok, wrap up warm, it’s cold out’

‘BTW, you’re my priority too.’

‘Good to know.’

*

Zipped to the chin, gloved, and snugly scarfed, Colin pedalled his hired bike through the wide streets and avenues where lanterns, banners, and decorations now appeared in a profusion of red and gold.

He well knew by now that red was not just associated with the national party. Since the dawn of the Han dynasty empire, it had been associated with good fortune. This was why the Chinese stock market displayed rising stock prices in red and a down market in green. And at no time was this notion of good fortune more apparent than during the Chinese spring festival, a family celebration par excellence, made even more special by an imposed public holiday spanning over a week from Friday. It meant that hundreds of millions of people would be heading to their hometown at the end of the week, using whatever means of transport they could afford.

Colin was becoming used to the garish red-and-gold colour schemes in every retail and restaurant window. At least, being on the payroll, albeit as a contractor, meant that he would get a holiday out of this spring festival, precious time which he planned to spend back home working on his next novel: a welcome change to writing about ghoulish ghouls and a treacherous royal cousin with a gammy leg. After the spring break, he was allowed to work remotely for a few weeks before returning to Beijing.

Pedalling in the cold night through the shallow slush, he wondered what all these people would be doing during their national holiday. Feasting and visiting cousins no doubt, like people do at Christmas in the West. He imagined it must be like Christmas without *The Wizard of Oz*, *The Sound of Music*, *It's a Wonderful Life* and a multitude of glitzy snow-filled romcoms, not to mention the carol singers, the Christmas party, the baby in a manger, and the Christmas mass. And maybe most of all it lacked the Christmas spirit, the Chinese seemingly being more restrained in their wishing goodwill to all men. There again, maybe in their own way they did. Maybe he just didn't get it. For how many times at work had he gotten the wrong end of the stick when trying to guess what two Chinamen were saying to each other? Maybe it was just that this culture was still too alien to him, making him view it from the outer rim.

He knew full well that the only true way to penetrate the mystery would be to learn the language. But learning another language at forty-two would sit somewhere between humbling and humiliating. Besides, how much longer would he be working there before moving on to another project, another game, another country? He had not envisaged staying longer than the duration of the game production. Now, however, maybe he had a reason. As he mingled at the intersection with cyclists, moped riders, and pedestrians waiting to cross the fourth ring road, he wondered if he should take the plunge.

*

There was only one thing on his mind once he had finished his dinner, having stopped off at the convenience store to get a ready-cooked meal of chicken and rice in curry sauce.

He pulled up his favourite profile on his phone, then wrote: 'Beautiful way to spend a weekend – café – cinema – cocktails – restaurant – pub – live music AND making love night and day - missing your kisses!'

He sat for a while, intermittently checking for a return message. When none came, he forced himself to put down the phone on the bedside table. Then he stripped, showered, and slipped into bed, where he responded to comments from his readers on Facebook. He had a weekend's worth to catch up on. But his attention was soon drawn elsewhere. He hit the WeChat icon. The return messages from Lin read:

'Hey same here. Sorry, I was tidying things up here, a bit messy
'I feel my day was really wasted, felt so guilty at work, and I kept laughing to myself . . . hope no one saw me. Must be weird.
'so actually we spent two days and two nights together. Not a one night thing at all . . .
'Are you having your power up session?'

Colin had a smile in his heart when he wrote back:

'I was answering my readers then jumped in the shower . . . thought you'd gone to bed.'

'not yet and my phone was on mute.'

'BTW it's a power nap . . . nap'

'Haha
'O how do your readers like the book?'

'Just a couple of grouches, but all in all, some lovely feedback' 'great, happy for U'

'how is your chin?'

'it will be fine. I will put more cream on later. I have to say I have never had such a wasted weekend . . . loved it though'

'not wasted, living the life!'

'a great way of living it! So your colleagues didn't ask you what you did during the weekend?'

'Of course they did, even Max the Russian guy.'

'haha what did you say?'

'And Yang and Xiao Long'

'Now I'm really laughing out loud!'

'Max said, so you've found a girl!'

'really? no way!'

'yeah, told him I hadn't, though'

'so he guessed you found a girl?'

'and Xiao Long wouldn't believe me when I said I was doing research'

'Hah now I know I'm the research topic!'

'no no, you're not'

'but u did enjoy this research weekend, right? And the subject was nice haha'

'Stop laughing . . .'

'u are funny. Normally u look serious, but can be very funny and cute, especially when you keep talking and talking which makes me wanna kiss you'

'You did, and you made me shut my mouth'

'so we've got to meet, lunch and dinner'

'let's have lunch tomorrow . . . I have to go out tomorrow evening with Max . . .'

'hmm . . .

'Ok'

'and let's try to meet Wednesday evening'

'and when we meet Wednesday, let's see if we can meet Thursday too, Friday I'm leaving, and ur leaving next week. So Friday morning u can leave for work from my place . . . can u?'

'could do'

'great, love it'

'me too'

'oh this maybe too strong a feeling now'

'yes, let's go slowly, take it easy, men zao!'

'I'll arrange a meeting with a client near your district so I won't be far away tomorrow. I miss you'

Suddenly Colin's screen was a shower of what he thought was snow falling, like in a shaken snow globe.

'how did you make it snow?'

'snow? ah, not me, wechat. Look: miss you'

Again his WeChat feed was a shower of snow.

'ah keywords!'

'yes, because the app detects words like "miss u" or "happy birthday"'

'miss you miss you miss you

'did it snow?'

'that makes it romantic, and a lovely surprise'

'yes, like lots of snow'

'in fact, it's stars falling down not snow'

'send me an avalanche of stars then'

'haha miss u miss u miss u miss u

'you get them?'

'yeah!! the stars falling down?'

'u are easy to please'

'like in the China Girl song – saw these stars crashing down'

'Yes, and I will kiss you tomorrow to shut your mouth'

'You bet'

'I have to go wash and sleep

'no more being late to office'

'ok, Miss U, night, sweet dreams'

Tired out and with finger cramp from frantically prodding the keyboard on his phone, Colin turned out the light.

*

In the small hours, he awoke from a restless slumber. He tried repositioning and prodding his pillows to make them more comfortable. But there was nothing he could do to replace the cushion of her body. The short nights and afternoon dozes of just one weekend with Lin had sufficed for his body to let him know that a quintessential piece of his life was now missing beside him.

He felt a constant stirring behind his temples too. And was that not the seat of his soul? he wondered. Whatever it was, he felt it constantly twisting and turning like a newborn twin deprived of its sibling. But Lin was not a sibling, he thought to himself, and it was evident she was more than a lover. Could she be his soulmate?

Now that he had found her, his whole being craved for her, so that he could become complete. No use, he had no choice but to do something about this unbearable yearning. He had to reach out to her. Thank goodness for WeChat, he thought. Even though he knew she would not see his message for another few hours, it might at least act as a vent to relieve that insatiable rustling behind his temples. Without turning on the lamp, he reached for his phone and typed.

> 'Can't sleep, I'll be a wreck in the morning, all your fault, got you stuck in my mind!'

As he scrolled up to peruse the previous conversation, to his surprise came notification of Lin's reply. It read:

'Haha, me too!'

Colin propped himself up on his elbow.

'Hey, it's past 3am, you should be asleep'

'I woke up just now feeling horny, thinking of ur kisses, ur hands and everything, then got your message'

'amazing'

'you are in my mind too'

Colin thus relieved, his mind appeased, his whole body became calmed like the time when he was given morphine to relieve a painful infection that had nearly cost him his life. He lowered his head onto his pillow and fell into the deep rejuvenating valley of sleep.

21

There was good and bad about starting work at 10 a.m., thought Colin. The good thing was that it still left plenty of time for recovery after a sleepless night.

And even if he did oversleep and miss breakfast, it was only two hours to lunchtime. The bad things were that it meant working late into the evening, and that the morning, that high-performance time of the day, was pretty much wasted. But today, Colin was not complaining. He had missed the collective breakfast and was looking forward to lunch. He had made a feeble excuse of having to pick something up from his apartment to get out of a lunch plan with the creative director. Even an invitation to lunch at the donkey burger place could not tempt him away from his rendezvous.

They had agreed to meet outside his compound. She would take a detour and drop him off at the studio on her way back to work. Bicycles were great, but this time, to avoid wheeling through the slush, he told Lin he would take an express taxi. As he sped off in the direction of his service apartment, he wrote:

'Now in taxi – Didi is great!'

Ten minutes later, the taxi arrived at the top of the narrow road, busy at this time of the day with a stream of cars crawling along from the opposite direction. Colin made a sign to stop at the roadside. '*Zhe ge, hao!* — Right there, good!' he said, estimating that it would be quicker to finish the rest of the way on foot. The driver got the picture and pulled over. Didi took care of the payment while Colin sent a WeChat message to Lin.

'Where r u now?'

'just parked, can't believe I'm doing this, it's crazy'

'I'm coming up the road'

He pocketed his phone and found himself breaking into a trot until she came into view. Seconds later, standing in her woollen overcoat, scarfed and gloved, she turned to see him walking toward her with a coy smile.

Their subdued greeting did not compare to their passionate messages. Colin understood, this was not Paris, and he refrained from putting his arms around her as the compound guard stood watching. For it was not appropriate to display one's love in public on the streets of Beijing. So he took her hand, which she had ungloved. It was an ample-enough offering, one which by far outweighed their WeChat intimacy, because there was no interface between them now: this was for real.

'Let's get some food and go back to your place, shall we?' she said.

*

Having someone in your life meant giving up a portion of your freedom, thought Colin. But he had not contemplated giving up anything so soon after his separation, despite the one-night stands that left him feeling hollow. Was he ready to compromise now?

It had only been six months since he had signed the divorce papers. Six months to recover from the demise of a marriage of seventeen years. The moments of happiness in the end were far outweighed by the sulks, frustrations, and fights that neither of them had wanted but were inexorably drawn into. It was something to do with their personalities.

When he discovered Lin's star sign, he remembered thinking that Scorpios were supposed to be the most difficult personalities of the zodiac. And yet, as he pushed the door into his service apartment and put down the food on the low table, not even their lunchtime hunger could prevent their mutual desire to hold one another, to touch, to fall onto the bed locked in a passionate embrace.

No, he had not planned on giving up any freedom so quickly after his divorce. But this was not giving up freedom: it was becoming whole.

Lin had not been expecting to take this man and make him hers, let alone so quickly. Yet, something compelled her to scan the sparse room: his neatly folded clothes in the open cupboard, his razor, toothbrush, shampoo, and deodorant in the bathroom. She felt a thrill at being in this man's private quarters, and she wanted to know everything: how he lived, the manly objects, those differences between the two sexes that in reality she only knew a little about.

She asked him about his colleagues, laughed out loud when he told her about Max and Xiao Long, and she jumped on his lap and pulled off her cashmere pullover when he kept talking on and on.

'Let's keep this to ourselves for now,' she said in a low, excited voice as she placed her forehead on his.

'Yes,' returned Colin. 'It's our secret.'

*

The following evening, Colin stopped off at his service apartment after work to shower and shave so his stubble would not chafe her skin.

He had told her he would be late. Once out of the shower, as he sat on the edge of his bed, wrapped in a towel, his first instinct was to check his phone. Lin had written:

'I was thinking of when I first wanted to kiss u, there were a few moments.'

'Ah, when was that?'

'will tell you later'

'tell me now'

'when you get here, are you out yet?'

'just getting changed, will let you know soon as I'm out'

'ok, I will have a shower and power nap then'

Half an hour later, as the cab was pulling away past the freezing guards at the compound entrance, their hatted heads sunk into their shoulders, his phone blinked. Lin's message read:

'so u are not out yet?'

He typed:

'Just in the taxi now'

'good, can you find my address?'

'I chose the one you put into my list after mine. Didi says I'll be there in 33 mins'

'impressive, call me when you arrive, so I can wake up'

'ok'

*

It was past 10 p.m. and the traffic was fluid on the fourth ring road that took him eastward.

Half an hour later, he found himself standing in front of the convenience store near her compound. He became acutely aware that his presence must be a surprise to the residents: Westerners didn't usually travel so far into their private circle. He sent Lin a message to say where he was, along with a photo of the storefront. He followed her instructions until he recognised the stairs that led into the underground car park, and then the steps opposite that led into the lobby of her high-rise block.

Three minutes later, he sent another message as the front door at the end of the twelfth-floor corridor creaked open. He entered the apartment to find her in a dressing gown and slippers. Any elegance was thrown out of the window. But somehow it felt like they had been together as a couple for enough time not to need to pretend. Somehow it felt natural as he stepped into her warm embrace. He took half a step back. 'What?' she said as he looked her up and down.

'I just love your slippers,' he said cheekily. She let out her melodious laugh, and he realised in that moment that this was not mere physical infatuation. Any remaining shyness slipped away when, after a late dinner, she took him by the hand and led him into her fragranced bedroom.

*

The following morning, while she was sitting on his bare buttocks, daubing his shoulders with essential oils, she said: 'What are you going to do next week before you leave? Your flight isn't until Wednesday, is it?'

'I will do some writing, and I will Zoom my kids,' he replied in all simplicity. He knew that if this liaison was to work, he must include his kids in their conversation, to send a clear message that they meant the world to him, that he would never brush them aside.

'Yes, good,' she said as she continued rubbing his shoulders, while secretly thinking to herself that she had competition. But judging by his candour, she knew she would have to embrace it with grace as part of the package.

After a pause to let it sink in, he said: 'Oh, and I need to find a small padlock for my bag.'

'I have a spare one,' she said, pouring a few more drops of essential oil onto his back. 'You can have that, save you searching.'

'Great, thanks,' he said with a sigh of contentment, his cheeks flat against the pillow. Then, raising his head slightly, he said: 'How long does it take to fly back to your hometown?'

'It takes an hour and a half to get to Qingdao, but it will probably take more time getting to the airport because of all the people getting out of Beijing at the same time for the holiday.'

'Let me know when you get there, won't you?' he said.

She laid her bust flat on his back. 'Oh, by the way,' she said into his ear, 'have you heard about the virus?' It had occurred to her that he was probably unaware of the latest developments of the virus spreading from Wuhan, a virus that had people feeling increasingly anxious with the collective recollection of the SARS epidemic of 2003 that killed hundreds of people. She continued: 'They have locked down Wuhan and the whole of the province of Hubei.' But, enjoying the moment, Colin was no longer paying attention, and he rolled over, catching her in his arms.

22

Colin had lost track of home and international politics, the ongoing Brexit saga, the latest sporting events and world catastrophes.

Living in a foreign land paradoxically makes it easy to forget about the outside world. But it suited the narrative designer in him well enough. In fact, setting aside the real world could be advantageous when your job was to create a new world view and a civilization from scratch. He had come to realise that a good grounding in history, however, helped in that endeavour, more so than the bytes of current affairs from around the world. Whether the genre was alternative history, sci-fi, or fantasy, the same emotional levers applied.

Being bound in the oblivion of the present meant that he could focus on the story world all the more. In terms of language, he had not been away long enough for the linguistic disconnection to have any effect on his capacity to create dialogue using the appropriate registers. Besides, he had brought with him a few books from his bookcase, books whose plots he already knew, which enabled him to revel in the prose, dialogue, and styles.

Among those he had brought were *The 100-Year-Old Man Who Climbed Out of the Window and Disappeared* and *The English Patient*, the former for its structure, wit, and Scandinavian humour, the latter to unlock its prose which, in the same way an orchestra will show more personality after its third night, only yielded its full measure of warmth and brilliance after a second reading.

So, when on Thursday evening, while lying on her bed with her head and shoulders propped up on pillows, Lin said: 'Have you seen the latest? The virus is gaining ground quickly.'

Colin replied: 'What virus?'

'The coronavirus, silly Englishman! It's getting worse every day now.'

Colin, his head on Lin's bare shoulder and peering at her phone screen, raised his head to process the images she had pulled up. There were phone-filmed scenes of officials in hazmat suits dragging supposed carriers of the virus from their homes to force them into isolation. It was out of this world, like something from a dystopian video game. He said: 'But isn't that against civil rights?'

'They say it's the only way to stop it spreading. That's why they've locked down Wuhan and the whole of the province of Hubei. Wuhan alone is eleven million people. It's serious. People on WeChat are suggesting they could be hiding the true numbers.'

'Would they?' said Colin, now propped up beside her on his elbow.

'Maybe,' she said, scrolling through more phone shots, 'so as not to cause a panic.'

Colin looked into her face. Gently, he said: 'Are you sure you ought to be going home?'

'Yes, I have to,' said Lin, putting down her phone beside her on the bed and turning to face him. 'It's the spring festival, very important in China. My family will be expecting me, and besides, there aren't any cases in my hometown yet, and it's outside the city.'

'You be careful,' he said, lightly touching her soft cheek with the backs of his fingers. 'Do you think it will reach Beijing?'

'They will be very cautious here because it's the capital. So don't worry. Anyway, you'll be out of it come next Wednesday!'

'Yes, that's true,' said Colin with a solemn smile, searching Lin's face. They had the same thought. They locked eyes and kissed.

'It's too short,' she said in her sweetest voice. 'We haven't spent enough time together. Why didn't we start this earlier?'

'Because you didn't take me back to your place.'

'You are such a silly Englishman,' she said, gently running her fingers down the stem of his neck.

'There were a few times, though, when I was about to steal a kiss.'

Lin's eyes lit up with curiosity. 'Really?' she said, turning his face to her with an index finger. 'So why didn't you?'

'Because it was too cold for a start.'

'When was it?'

'Well, one time was when we went to the 798 art district.

We came out of the photo exhibition, then we went and had a meal in that new Thai restaurant where you told me you thought the waiter was cute.'

'Did I?'

'Yes, you did,' said Colin softly, kissing behind her ear. 'When we came out, it was so cold that we waited in your car for my taxi to come. Remember?'

'Oh, yes, but then it came too quickly.'

'Would you have let me kiss you then?'

'Yes, yes, I would have,' she said, turning her head to look into his eyes. 'I wondered what you were waiting for actually. And when you kept talking and looking so serious, I just wanted to kiss you. So you see? We could have started earlier, even the last time you came.'

'True, but look on the bright side: we did it, didn't we?' he said as he placed his arm around her torso and with the momentum rolled her under him, his elbows supporting his weight. 'And I will be back next month.'

'Yes, yes, you're right,' she conceded, a thought playing on her smooth brow.

'And I'm in your bed now.'

'Yes, you are. Will you forget me, though, when you're back home?'

'No chance, *baobei,* I've only just found you,' said Colin, using the Chinese word that Lin had taught him. It meant *darling* and sounded like *baby*. 'And I'm not so easy to bed, you know.'

'Ha ha, and do you know what? It feels so natural. Never thought I could be like this with a man.'

'That's because I love kissing you.'

'You do.' Lin sharpened her eyes playfully. 'So maybe I should watch out. Because you love women, don't you!'

'Sure, but that's probably because being married for so long deprives you of them . . . and I have mostly been faithful, you know.'

'Mostly? Tell me when you weren't.'

'Only when overseas. But I told you, never more than one-night stands.'

'Except for the one in Canada who posted a nice message through your front door. "Dear darling," she wrote.'

'Oh, you remember?'

'Of course, and the Indian girl in Singapore, and the Tunisian girl in Paris.'

'Hmm, I'd better watch what I say. Anyway, those were the one-nighters, even the Canadian girl, except there were two one-nights,' said Colin, who then, with his lips puckered, dived into her warm neck.

'So you'd better come back,' she said, holding his head back with her two hands while looking into his eyes.

Colin reduced his grin to a sedate smile and said: 'I have a game to work on; it's not due for release till August. And now I've got a special incentive to finish it. Because, to be honest, I didn't think I was going to; things are just so different here. I mean, coming here is like becoming illiterate. And that's not easy for a writer. But I shall be back.'

'You mean for the game bonus.'

Colin shifted his weight onto one elbow and pulled her onto him with his free hand 'No. I mean for you!'

'So sweet . . . You always say nice things . . .'

'Not to everyone.' They kissed. 'So what time does your plane leave?'

'Eleven fifteen, so we have to be up really early.' Lin yawned and laid her head on his chest.

'Sure,' he said, holding her tight to him.

'What will you do alone in Beijing? Go to the zoo?' she quipped.

Letting out a laugh, Colin said: 'Nah, I'll do some writing, a video call with my kids, then check out on Wednesday. No point rushing back too quickly. The boys will still be at school, and in any case, the company pays to the end of the month, so it makes no difference to them.'

'Wish I could stay longer, but I must go home for the Chinese New Year.' Lin gave a little meow sound; then, drumming her fingers on his chest, she said: 'Oh, remember to wear a mask next week.'

'What for?'

'For when you board the plane, or they won't let you on. I will give you some.'

'OK.'

'Now we have to sleep.'

Colin agreed, but a few moments later, raised up on his elbow, he said: 'What's interesting . . .' Then a few seconds after that, he said: 'What's interesting is . . .'

'Come on, tell me,' said Lin drowsily.

Colin continued with a delicate flourish of the hand. 'What's interesting . . . is keeping people awake by saying *What's interesting*!'

Lin laughed and threw a pillow at him, then turned over to her side, curling her legs beneath her.

'I will let you sleep,' he said as he moved closer to her.

'It's OK, I can sleep on the plane. I'm just glad you are here with me. I think I've been really lonely.'

He latched onto to her, easing his naked body to fit into her semi-foetal shape. She reached for his hand on her hip and pulled his arm around her like a blanket.

*

During and after his divorce, Colin realised he was not that fond of people.

It dawned on him one day when, alone back home in his London flat, a visa photo of himself caught his eye. He had felt compelled to turn it face down, just like he did with the Writers Guild of America magazines that showed writers' faces on the front cover. In this way, he realised that he was not such a people person. And yet, strangely enough, he loved watching them living their everyday lives, as if they were another species, as if he were a cat half napping, half people-watching. Or perhaps he just needed to distance himself from them, which would explain why he now stood gazing out of Lin's bay window at the crisp early morning. He had been wondering what the green outdoor lockers on the far side of the narrow street below were for.

Then a masked delivery guy, late thirties, warmly clad and wearing spectacles, pulled up on his silent electric scooter as proudly as if he were riding a thoroughbred. He dismounted, raised the seat and undid a nut to detach a cable. Then he pulled out the gut of the beast in the form of a very large battery. Next, he lumped out another one from the locker and placed the run-down battery inside it. Colin realised now that the lockers were nothing more than battery chargers for the delivery guys. Next, the delivery guy re-gutted his steed and fastened the cable, did up the nut, closed the seat, and got back on his mount. He pulled out his phone and popped in his earphones, chose his favourite track and rode off to his next delivery, silently, contentedly, along the road flanked with bare trees under a stark blue sky. And so the demystification of the lockers was complete. You just had to sit and watch like a cat, thought Colin, just keep watching from a fence, a café terrace, a family kitchen table, an apartment window. Strangely, he felt like running down and shaking the delivery guy by the hand.

Then he heard a noise: someone was chuckling. He turned back to the room and realised it was himself, and that he was happy, suddenly happy, just like that. He joined Lin under the quilt and snuggled a kiss under her jaw. She woke and smiled contentedly as she turned and pulled him into her embrace, both of them knowing it would be their last before she took her plane to her hometown near Qintao.

23

Lin spent the duration of her flight thinking about the past week.

She was flying away from something she had hardly dared to hope for, but returning to the embrace of her family. It was a tug of war of emotions that wrangled inside her as she sat behind a masked couple whose young child kept popping its head at her over the seat. Should she have forfeited the traditional family get-together so she could spend more time with Colin, to get to know him better? To share his last moments in China that would either bring them closer or make them realise they were in fact miles apart? Would he return even? He had admitted that it had not been his intention to finish the game he was working on. He had insisted that she head back to her hometown to be with her family for the New Year. It was nice of him, but maybe he said it to be rid of her. In the taxi home from the airport, she thought: Wasn't it dubious what he said about what would happen if she fell pregnant? But maybe that was just idle man-talk.

Her doubts and overthinking were soon curtailed by New Year preparations when she arrived in her childhood home. No sooner had Lin set down her luggage than she was roped in by her mother and sister for a last-minute shopping foray. And then there was the house to prepare for the visits of relatives.

That evening after dinner, while watching the *New Year's Eve Gala* on TV — a gala watched by a billion viewers — her phone blinked. Snatching it up, she hit the profile she had been waiting to hear from. She read:

'Hey, baobei, how are you? Busy?'

She wrote:

'It's been nonstop since I got here. Busy cleaning the house and shopping for gifts and wine etc. and helping my mum and sister with the cooking.'

'So this is the night of the big feast!'

'Only with immediate family this evening, dumplings, TV show, fireworks, every year same routine. But it continues over the next few days'

'Sounds like fun . . .'

'Sunday my family will host the feast, so my cousins all come with their family, maybe three tables of guests or more'

'Nice, traditional!'

'Did u write ur book today?'

'yes, a little'

'u are disciplined, some good progress?'

'just organising ideas, but you keep popping into my head'

'Ha, just write something. It's a good way to get rid of invasive thoughts, including me haha'

'So do u wish Happy New Year on the stroke of midnight or the next day?'

'From now to tomorrow. But the official time is at midnight, like for New Year in the west.'

'My team have been opening red packets all evening . . .'

'so the company has a wechat group?'

'no, it's in Dingding, but don't know how it works . . . fun to watch everyone getting excited, though'

'just click on the red packet when one comes up. Might be zero or you might get lucky'

After some moments, a new message popped up in Lin's feed. It read:

'Hey, I just clicked one and got 74 rmb!'

'good for u'

Amused, Lin sent a little red packet of her own. She typed:

'u get my love bag'

'oh yeah, you just sent me 8.80 thxxx! is that lucky?'

'the number 8 is a lucky number in China, because *ban* means *eight* and also *luck*.'

'is there a number for love? In English we can write 143 which corresponds to the number of letters in the words I-love-you'

'We use 143 too. In China there are also some numbers for love like 520 which sounds like wǒ ài nǐ = I love U. But I don't think there's one single number for love though . . .'

'don't think we have one in English either'

'maybe it's because you can't count it'

'Good point, but if there was it should be 0, like a perfect never-ending circle, right?'

'Haha or an 8 for eternity'

'Yes. BTW, do you have New Year's resolutions?'

'Actually I had a plan when I reached 30, to smoke a cigar every year. But haven't done it for years'

'we'll do it together'

'I can never finish them though, get me drunk'

'so we'll share one, and we'd better make a list of all the things we said we'd do, right?'

'now I'm turning u into a planner!'

'Actually, that's what I already do, I plan stories haha!'

'oh today there's a joke on wechat coz now it's suggested to stay home rather than go out because of this virus'

'ah, so people make love and have babies, right?'

'you got it, so they say in November time there will be a baby boom!!'

'Hmm, you got me thinking about how I can create a hook for the book. I could include this virus thing, although not as the main theme.'

'yes, the virus maybe a good theme, along with what happens in this time period and after'

'could be a good hook'

'actually there's a lot of tension now, and panic, because of the rise in deaths to 26 and because they

say even people not showing
symptoms can be spreaders. And
now museums and art galleries
have closed, and even the temple
fairs in Beijing have been cancelled.
I hope ur flight has no issue, maybe
you should check'

'Should be ok, it might be different though if I were coming into China'

'the virus is creating even more
panic on the internet as that's the
main news channel that people use
nowadays.'

'But there are many more deaths each year from the flu'

'yes and car accidents every
day . . .'

'must be because there's no cure yet'

'we had experience of the SARS
virus in 2003 so that's why I think
there's more panic than usual.'

'yes'

'There were a few hundred deaths
and no cure'

'but did you know in France in the summer of that year there were over ten thousand deaths just because of the heat?'

'I was in university that year'

'old people were dropping like flies'

'So a bad year globally'

'In fact, I just checked on wiki, it says in France there were 14,000 heat-related deaths'

'OMG'

'they had to put the bodies in refrigerated trucks because there wasn't enough room in the mortuaries'

'Oh, I just heard the news that the spring festival holiday may be extended if this virus goes on.'

'I hope they don't restrict flights back into China once I'm in the UK'

'hey, me too!

'and BTW they have restricted traffic now in the country to stop it spreading'

'wow, but I guess it makes sense'

'But some patients have recovered and have been discharged from hospitals according to the news, so at least it's possible to recover from it'

'so maybe I have my first chapter: It's a love story on the backdrop of a virus that is trying to close down shops and restaurants and even close the routes into China. And maybe I'll make the virus much worse in the book, scarier too, with Chinese zombies . . . haha just kidding!'

'haha u are so addicted to China now, Chinese food and China girl!'

'Yes, and you're my Chinese muse too!'

'Nice, so China girl off to bed not too late today!'

'Yes, yes, you have a relaxing evening so you'll be on form for the weekend! I'll be working on my book'

'Yes, yes'

'Just give my profile pic a rub when you need me and I will be your genie!'

'all right will do . . . hugs and kisses'

'Hugs and kisses'

An avalanche of stars came crashing down on each of their screens. Content and too fatigued to get up from the family sofa, Lin sat through the rest of the Chinese New Year's Eve show with her parents and her sister. Sitting with her legs curled beneath her, she suddenly had a worrying thought: What would she do if flights back into China really did become suspended?

24

Three days later found Colin reading through their WeChat thread again.

He imaged Lin would be nestled in the bosom of her family now, so he had decided to leave her alone during the weekend. He also spent the whole cold and dingy Monday to himself, perfect weather for staying inside without any regrets, to throw himself into the first chapter of his book. But that constant soft aching behind his temples kept obliterating his focus. He ended up aimlessly checking star signs, something that would never have occurred to him ordinarily, and he checked so-called best matches with some surprise. By the end of the morning, he had produced nothing more than a couple of loose passages, a creation that had neither head nor tail.

So he sat trying to analyse the sensation that had cost him two thousand words: the aching behind the eyes, the tingling pressure behind the temples. Was that the sensorial area of love? The impression was so intense at times that he wondered if he had a tumour growing on the brain.

A Bing search told him about temporal poles, the amygdala that regulates emotions, and the chemicals in the brain that champion the feeling of unity of love and the desire to merge with the recipient of that love.

It was all there, a profusion of organs, regulators, and chemicals that created that pleasant turmoil behind his temples. So, there really was a place where love resided in the mind, and it happened to be exactly where he felt an aching sensation that made him incapable of focussing. 'Love is real,' he said to himself like it was an epiphany. It was a pivotal feel-good moment, like one that gave a person the sudden certitude of the existence of God. For surely it indicated too that there must be a seat of the soul. His life was no longer a lost ship in the ocean: it had a new purpose, a new direction. But there again, wasn't he embarking on this voyage too quickly? For how many lovers crashed onto the rocks, and how much love was not reciprocated in this world? Did the music industry not make billions each year thanks to unrequited love? And what about the cultural divide that could influence mind-set? Would their love be accepted by her family? He knew that in Chinese culture, the family played a critical role in any relationship.

He walked his thoughts to the window. It was already getting dark outside. Flurries of snow were swirling again in the blustery view. He stood for a while, scanning the thousands of dwellings of the neighbouring apartment buildings. How many people were there alone in their rooms out there? he wondered. Alone during the Chinese New Year.

He had managed to resist reaching out to her for three days and three nights. But now the desire was too strong, and as evening encroached, he could not hold back any longer. He had to sense her desire and intentions again, even if it meant reading between the lines, interpreting what was left unsaid. And what if, now in the bosom of her family, she had cooled off? Should he let her go? Or would he make a fool of himself and try to shamelessly cling onto something precious he had thought was his?

He dropped onto the bed, made himself comfortable and then pulled up her profile on his phone. He typed:

'Hi Lin!'

The answer came back in an instant, direct, grammarless, just the naked thought.

'hey thought u were gone . . . like a ghost . . . no message . . . just gone'

The sight of her spontaneous words thrilled and reassured him almost as much as the caress of her slender fingers would have.

'gone?'

'u went to your place . . . we did wechat once and that was it'

'I'm still here'

'Ok, u miss me?'

'you bet, been thinking about you'

'was not sleeping well last night'

'me neither. You ok?'

'thinking of u and sleepless

'that's bad again.'

'glad to hear it

'but sorry about that'

'it's ok. In ur apartment?'

'yeah, where else?'

'well guess where I am?'

'in bed'

'haha'

'where are you then?'

'I am just laughing, u are right . . . am in bed . . . naked . . .'

'Wow! Wish I was there!'

'haha, anyway, feeling better now . . . There was a party today with family and friends'

'Ah, u must have good friends'

'yes, and close ones. Weren't here today, though'

'but sometimes it's just nice to meet likeminded souls'

'true

'Oh I had a traditional Chinese star sign reading by one girl

'interesting one'

Colin smiled as he typed:

'actually I was just about to tell u I checked our star signs, something I never ever do'

'haha'

'so how was your fortune, good or bad?'

'u were suspicious about scorpio, remember?'

'me?'

'yes u said scorpions live in the desert and in western culture are regarded as dark and vicious.

'anyway, didn't know it was so complicated. This girl, she seems good at it, though. She said I have been hard and strict on myself and I should relax and take care of myself more'

'there's a simple rule: if it's good then believe it, if it's not then don't'

'yeah, and strange, she checked my dates and said I met someone sept-oct time'

'well, she's right about that! We first met back in September'

'I was totally shocked.'

'did she say anything about us?'

'well, she said I was seeing someone and it's good, and to just enjoy it

'But what a funny thing, I am so surprised u checked our star signs and I love that u did, regardless of what it says.'

'It's good'

'so u see, even in my hometown, u are not here and I sleep less

'been waiting for ur message'

With a pang of guilt, Colin typed:

'I was waiting for the light to blink on my phone too, didn't want to interrupt your family get-together'

'feel so close to u'

'and I to you.'

'great feeling of intimacy and we match in everything'

'Crazy, I was literally just reading this:

Colin copied some text from the website he had been reading, then pasted it into the WeChat feed.

"'The most fabulous part of a Scorpio/Pisces relationship is the erotic dance that happens in the bedroom. They are romantic, passionate, emotional, sensual, and creative lovers, whose aim is to please one another. There's role-play, mystery, fantasy, and a merging into one another that makes their lovemaking magical."'

'wow'

'And:

'"A Scorpio woman and a Pisces man can share a passion and romantic closeness that's truly rare."'

'it reads so true, and now u are a star sign reader! how crazy!'

'Ha-ha, I'm just so surprised at how much there is that relates to us, it's quite mysterious'

'only those who have ever been in this situation would understand it'

'True'

'It's mysterious and magical'

'Yeah'

'Just imagine, there are people who have never experienced such strong intimacy. And I could have been one of them. So glad I met u . . . I was thinking maybe it was just me being horny that week. But it's not. I continue to be so every time I think of u'

'Maybe it really is written in the stars, right?'

'Oh, by the way, the star sign reader told me I may have been a nun in my past life. That's why I'm kind of still single . . . It's like a habit of being alone passed down to me. So in life it's a challenge for me to be in love and loved. And I just realized that u are a friar – Colin Friar!'

'Wow'

'the nun and the friar!

'Maybe it's bullshit . . . but it makes me happy

'it's too lonely by myself . . . without u here'

'I will try to stay in China as long as possible from March'

'ok, that's nice, hope so, but it seems a long time before we get to March

'wish I were in ur arms now'

'me too - I love holding you'

'u were naughty when keeping me awake . . . last night'

'last night?'

'last night in Beijing'

'couldn't stop kissing you, I was tired too but just couldn't stop'

'u didn't stop at all'

'don't remember how many times we made love'

'nonstop'

'yes'

'do u think maybe it is too good and that we are setting ourselves very high expectations? What if we meet again and it's not as good?'

He felt and shared her anguish, and he thought it clever and forthright of her to manage their expectations at this early stage of their relationship. It was refreshing and he desired the same openness. He typed:

'don't worry'

'I want u all the time'

'But what will happen the first time we disagree?'

'we will be fine . . . we will kiss when we disagree'

'so let's make a pact'

'rule number one'

'we kiss when we disagree'

'thinking the same . . .'

'we're always thinking the same'

'love it and love u . . . maybe too early to say it . . . miss u so much . . .'

Colin was again moved by her openness. He typed:

'I want to say it too, but was thinking of telling you face to face, mouth to ear'

'me too . . . the pillow talk time'

'I want to hold you in my arms and say I love you'

'love it

'a bit scary . . . this is so not me . . .'

'so let's wait until we see each other, make it special'

'ok, make it real . . .'

'yes'

'I need time to adjust to it . . .'

'yes'

'this overwhelming feeling'

'take it easy, one step at a time'

'yes

'I did not expect we would have such a conversation tonight . . .'

'me neither, but I feel much better for it'

'me too . . .'

'to know I have a very special reason to come back'

'ok I think I need to sleep . . . overwhelmed . . . tired out'

'ok, sleep tight, baobei!'

25

Before going to bed, he had a Zoom call with his teenage sons.

Daniel and Francis had taken the divorce in their stride, even embraced it because it had been on the table for so long, and it meant no more cold wars between their parents. They were already independent, free-thinking teenagers, soon on the cusp of manhood, and would need his support and encouragements far less. They would have other issues, more important ones than thinking about their old man. Where would that leave him? he wondered.

So something in the cosmos had compelled him to meet his soulmate. And yet, why was he about to leave her? He had mulled over the question long into the night. Some things just did not tally. You started to believe in something magical and wonderful, and the next minute, the reality of life smacked you in the gob. You were back on planet Earth, back at square one.

The first thing he did on cracking open an eye late next morning was to reach for his phone. Lin had left a message as if a night had not come between them. No greeting, no formality. He read:

> 'the spring festival holiday has been extended. The company sent notice to recommend we go back to Beijing on Feb 2nd and stay home for one week working remotely. For us from outside the province, we need to stay at home for two weeks, so I don't have to start working in the office until Feb 17th!'

Charmed by her sense of continuity, he typed:

'Hey, cool! Guess it's because of the incubation period of 14 days'

'yes'

'where are you now? living room?'

'watching news of the virus with my mum'

'bet she's glad to have u'

'she does all the talking . . . nonstop, so I just need to be present and respond with head nodding'

'haha'

'Imagine if we have to work from home when u come back, we could work together all day. I have two rooms. So work, cook, eat and have coffee breaks'

'would be too tempting to extend the coffee break, though!'

'ha, naughty you! Missing me?'

'Definitely! Why do u think I couldn't get to sleep last night?'

'Good! So when u come back from England bring some masks with u, and wear the ones I gave you in the taxi and everywhere until you get back to England!'

'Yes, sir!'

'seems the virus is getting serious, even on the roads in my hometown now there are municipal agents checking cars and checking people for fever, especially those coming from other cities'

'that's worrying, stay safe!'

'Yes, but no cases in my hometown yet, should be fine.'

'reassuring'

'number of cases have almost doubled in a day, though, and deaths have increased to over 100, yesterday was 80 I think, now 106. But cases have increased from 2800 to 4700!'

'hey that's terrible! What's going on?'

'Yeah worrying, quite big impact on the economy now, on everything . . . first time we've ever experienced this'

'although the number of deaths hasn't increased in proportion, right?'

'seems not'

'hope they can find the vaccine quickly'

'yes, hope so too. They need to work out the genome sequence and find out how it works first, though'

'so you'll be staying longer at your parents', right?'

'plan to go back to Beijing feb 2, my hometown isn't too affected'

'but the enemy is all around!'

'Ha yeah surrounded'

'you could always hop on a boat to North Korea!'

'Haha, North Korea was the first country to close its door to China. They announced it already a couple of days ago!'

'oh'

'just checked news again, seems this virus is worse than SARS. And one person who died in Beijing was a high school kid's father. Seemed strong and healthy, in a good position. It's a top school in Beijing in Haidian, now seriously watched.'

'Beijing? ah right'

'so its concerning, now only my hometown, a few other places and Tibet are clear with no cases, don't know how long it will last though. Gotta go, let u continue with ur work.'

*

Wednesday morning, Colin was packed and waiting to go.

Sitting on the sofa in front of the TV screen, again he checked Max's message that he had received the previous afternoon. It gave instructions about the driver who would arrive at the service apartment at 8:30 to take him to the airport in good time.

Colin turned his attention back to watching CGTN China 24. He had tuned in as a report was showing footage of the ongoing story of a new one-thousand-bed hospital being built in a week. An incredible feat and it was happening in China, in Wuhan, to cope with the imminent influx of coronavirus patients. Seeing the images of a ballet of bulldozers and construction workers working around the clock, the gravity of the situation suddenly hit home to Colin. Elsewhere, people were being forced to remain in their compounds. News came through of an entire family wiped out in Wuhan: mother, father, and child. They had remained locked down in their flat without medical care. Was the Chinese government being overzealous? According to President Trump, this was yet another scandalous example of the Chinese communist party's lack of respect for civil rights.

Despite the American president's lack of diplomacy, Colin wondered if he was right. At least, the images seemed to prove an exaggerated attempt at controlling the populace, didn't they? But for what purpose? Why would an industrious country like China, hyper-focussed on business, shut down everything in the name of public safety? Were they expecting a hecatomb? Yet the figures were still nothing compared to the yearly death toll of the flu.

Ten minutes later, he was downstairs in the empty street, where the apartment guardians were masked now. Colin had been obliged to scurry along from one building to the other down the long corridor, having discovered the exit to his block was chained and padlocked. In this way, the guards only had one entrance to watch. A new law had come into force that equipped them with thermometers with which they scanned the wrists of incoming residents to check they had no fever. It had been quickly ascertained that the virus caused the temperature of those infected to rise to above 37°C. But to Colin, it no longer mattered, for he was on the way out.

Wearing latex gloves, the masked taxi driver placed Colin's backpack with his brown luggage bag in the boot, after Colin had locked the little brass padlock that Lin had given him. He zipped the keys in his wallet. As he took his place in the rear seat, he noticed the Plexiglas dividing screen which allowed passenger and driver to travel in their separate cubicles of air space.

He glanced back at the service apartment compound as they pulled away past the now-closed June's Garden Café. But his headspace was consumed with thoughts about the paradox of his mystical match with Lin. Had he come all this way to repair her soul just so that he could sleep easy and then go back home? Yet so many crazy coincidences made their encounter so much more special than any run-of-the-mill romance in a foreign city. They made it heavenly; they made it soulful. And somehow they made the afterlife more attainable . . . and yet it was all being taken away by his scheduled return to England. He bucked up when his eye caught the flashing LED on his phone. He would be back, he told himself, just as he had told her. He read:

'Hey, where are you now?'

'In the taxi, on the way there'

'Got your mask on?'

'Wearing it now'

'Good, because now it's law, and they won't let you on the plane without it'

'Ok, it's suffocating, though'

'never mind, just hurry back!'

'Oh, forgot to tell you, I checked where love is in the brain'

'u are so funny. Where?'

'Remember I told you I lost my focus?'

'Yes'

'and that I get a constant tingling beneath the temples!'

'Yes'

'that's where love is'

'Hah, congratulations! Officially diagnosed!'

'At any rate, I tick all the boxes, even the star signs match'

'so u were really wondering what's happening? good, makes me happy' 'just understanding, the abstract and physical'

'but what if it was just a one week thing? then ur gone, a shocking possibility'

'not just a one week thing. From the first kiss, suddenly everything changed'

'I have prepared myself to accept it if it's just a week romance before the British guy flies home'

'I know but you need not worry'

'Because if it is, there's nothing I can do anyway, just have to accept it, no expectations'

Sitting in the back of the taxi that had joined the thin stream of traffic on the ice-edged fifth ring road, Colin suddenly sensed her fragility. He knew that a person could take a wrong turn when the mind was fragile; could she shy away from the risk of a bruised heart? He suddenly realised he did not want to lose her, and the imminent separation could well lead her the wrong way if he let doubt and fear of pain slip into their nascent relationship. Or could she be testing him, his intentions? She had been hurt before. Should that be the case, then he would have to come out fighting: she was not the sort of lady to appreciate submissiveness, which was not a role he could play anyway. He took a few extra beats to gaze out of the window at the lone masked drivers. Then, in an attempt to cast away any doubt, he wrote:

'Not the case, though, you can trust me'

'but that might be ur trick, men have tricks'

'no tricks'

'Meet up. Get to know each other. Three times catch up together. Kiss . . .'

'True, third date is special, but you're overthinking, I was happy just to be with you, and why did we catch up then? Were you really trying to recruit me?'

'I liked talking with u . . . I knew Relex had already found someone by the time we met again'

'so, there you are then, so we were already on a course without realising it'

'and why did u agree to catch up?'

'because I enjoyed being with you'

'or maybe you just say yes because you were bored'

'no, not bored, I had lots to do'

'like going to the zoo alone . . . haha'

'for research, pandas are rare!'

'maybe u met me for research too, to have a China girl'

'no'

'hah so u love pandas'

'don't love pandas, but curious to see them'

A photo popped into Colin's feed. It was a picture of a cuddly toy rabbit and a panda sitting side by side. Below it Lin had typed:

'Well, that's on top of my bed, did u see?'

'haha, yes'

'once I was told that I should put a pair of dolls there to help with my romance. But I don't have dolls, so I put the panda and rabbit there instead. The rabbit is my birth year animal'

'hah, and I guess pandas are less spooky'

'on the vacant side of my bed'

'oh'

'and u keep talking about pandas, maybe u are the real panda'

'Oh, didn't realise'

'it seems like there are just so many coincidences, it was a lady who did the divination who told me, from the Chinese book of changes'

'but that's crazy, they are true coincidences, everything seems to match'

'or maybe we search for coincidences'

'no, because I wasn't thinking at all about the panda thing' 'just trying to rationalize . . . sorry . . . and true, I guess no man has ever talked to me about pandas when dating haha'

'also, I didn't decide to write a book set in China before meeting up with you again, so you were not my research subject'

'so we are truly close . . .'

'Yes'

'it's too overwhelming . . . I better let you go . . . call me when you arrive at the airport'

'ok, in about an hour, panda hugs and kisses'

'haha, miss u'

Colin then sat back in the cab as it reached the clusters of giant sentinels of high-rise apartment buildings on the outskirts of the megalopolis.

26

Ten minutes later, as he was traveling through flat open country, sparkling under a thin crust of snow, he got to thinking about his future.

In three years' time, his children would both be at university, and his ex-wife would have remarried, he was sure. Where would that leave him? Friendless, without a family, and alone. And yet, he had found someone. Maybe this was what had steered his steps to China in the first place. Perhaps it was indeed a window of opportunity. Could he afford to miss it? There must be something up there, something in the cosmos that compelled him to meet his soulmate, mustn't there?

Bang in the middle of his soul-searching, there came a loud screech, and he was jerked forward. His wallet and plane ticket were dashed to the floor under the front passenger seat. The pull of his seat belt took the wind out of him as his brain struggled to process the situation.

From his stays in China, Colin had come to note that the lack of old cars on Chinese roads and highways was a testimony to China's thriving economy of recent years. But it also showed that drivers had not gone through the driving rites of passage as in older first world countries. As a consequence, perhaps, Chinese driving skills left something to be desired. However, in keeping with the Chinese mind-set of preferring to go around obstacles rather than through them, Colin had noticed, too, that road rage seemed far less common. In fact, he had not witnessed any at all in the months he had stayed in the world's most populated capital city — except, of course, when travelling in one of the yellow-striped bone-shaking taxis. When he had mentioned this observation to Max, the Russian had cynically told him it was because the Chinese feared the penalty. 'And if you knock someone over and kill them, then it's death!' he had said. Colin later checked and found out that it was just Max-talk, which consisted of telling unverifiable lies on the spot just to lead the conversation or win the argument. Anyhow, now Colin was about to put his theory to the test.

From what he had quickly gathered, the driver of the exec cab in which Colin was travelling had narrowly escaped hitting a car that had pulled into his lane — the slow lane where Colin's driver had a tendency to overtake on the inside. Consequently, the car pulling in did not notice Colin's driver racing up on the inside lane.

Colin's driver had slammed on the brakes, narrowly avoiding a collision. But an instant later, Colin heard another screech of brakes as what he instinctively feared came to pass. There was a loud bang from behind, and again his seat belt restrained him sharply after the car behind knocked into the rear bumper. After a quick glance to make sure his passenger was still intact, Colin's driver raised his arms to denote his exasperation and then slowed to a halt, apparently without thinking of pulling over to the hard shoulder. Colin recovered his ticket and wallet under the passenger seat and climbed out sharpish to escape any further danger. The two drivers met and had a brief and subdued discussion; then, as far as Colin could make out, they set about exchanging each other's insurance credentials, still parked as they had halted, in the inside lane.

Before they could finish their exchange, the police came and put down warning bollards. Colin wondered why they did not just direct the two cars to the hard shoulder. But again, he realised it was ingrained into the collective instinct for drivers to go around an obstacle, and it had probably been like this since the time of Confucius. If the same situation had arisen in any Western country, there would certainly have been annoyed drivers yelling and honking at them to pull over, or even worse, there would probably have been a pile-up.

But, standing on the snow-crisp edge of the hard shoulder, Colin was no longer worrying about traffic. Besides the fact that he was freezing, his thoughts now turned to getting to the warm airport in time for a hot latte before boarding. Thankfully, Max had planned for any unlikely mishap, such as a knock on the motorway followed by policemen slowing down the process of exchanging insurance credentials. No less than an hour later, at last he was able to climb back into the cab.

They say patience is a virtue, he thought to himself, looking at the time on his phone; they also say time waits for no man, and neither would his plane.

Half an hour later, he was dropped off at the departure terminal. He scurried to the entrance where travellers and baggage were being screened before they entered the building.

Time was short, but there was no need to panic, he told himself. Besides, there was hardly a soul inside the terminal building. Colin showed his wrist to the guard for a temperature check. Then he heaved his bags onto trays on the rollers along with his phone and wallet. He passed through the metal detector, then went to collect his gear at the other end.

His bag, however, had been directed to the roller conveyor on the inside. For the second time that morning, he was in the wrong lane, he thought to himself. A minute later, clad in white coveralls and a mask, the customs official asked him in a conversational tone if he had packed his luggage himself. Colin replied in the affirmative: *'Dui, dui,'* he said in a vain attempt to show he was not just a tourist, but his lack of vocabulary prevented him from proving his point. The officer asked him if he could open the brown one. Again, *'Dui, dui,'* said Colin before slipping his hand into his jeans pocket. But the padlock key was not there. Alarming thoughts of the key slipping onto the taxi seat instantly assailed him. He searched through his other pockets to no avail. There was only one other place it could be, he thought, unless it had slipped onto the cab seat. But he quickly discarded the alarming thought as he distinctly recalled scanning the seat before closing the cab door. So he felt the inside pouch of his laptop backpack.

Five minutes later, he had half-emptied the contents of his computer bag onto the counter when he felt two keys embedded in the seam of an inside pouch. With visible relief, he handed them to the agent and then looked at the time on his phone. It must be boarding time already, he thought. Were the forces of the universe plotting against him? Or was his reluctance to leave the same time zone as Lin influencing this series of delays? They couldn't be, he told himself, for he had not caused the cab to brake and a car behind to bump into it.

The agent handed him back the keys, having unsuccessfully tried to insert them both into the padlock. Colin placed the key to the mouth of the lock himself, only to quickly realise that these must be the keys he had lost four weeks earlier on his arrival.

Again he searched the pockets and compartments of his laptop bag before the sight of his wallet in the roller conveyor tray jogged his memory. He halted his search as he recalled placing the keys in the coin pouch of his wallet and zipping it up before jumping into the cab.

'Here!' he said, at last pulling out Lin's pair of keys that would now ironically unlock his passage toward the plane that would take him far away from her.

With the luggage opened, the official put in a hand and pulled out a black oblong object. 'What is this?' he said.

'It's a mobile charger,' returned Colin without irony.

The official scrutinized the label, had the object checked, then gave it back to Colin and politely told him he could go.

Colin bundled his effects sprawled over the counter into his computer bag, then hurried away, wheeling his leather luggage bag behind him. He went straight to the usual BA check-in desk. He was both relieved and alarmed to see no queue.

'Ni hao,' he said to the stewardess, then handed over his passport. The look on her face was not encouraging.

'Sir,' she said, in a conciliatory tone of voice, 'your flight has been postponed.'

'That's lucky,' returned Colin, trying to feel relieved. 'I was afraid I was going to miss it. How long for?'

'You don't understand. No more planes leaving Beijing to London. All British Airways flights suspended, sir.'

'Until when?'

'Until further notice, sir. It is because of coronavirus.'

27

It was the first day of the suspension of British Airways flights to and from China. Colin sat down to take stock of the situation; then he typed a message on his phone.

'Hey, Max, there's no plane. BA flights stopped from Beijing.'

A few moments later, the answer came back.

'Hey man, WTF, let me check.'

'All stopped because of the virus. What do I do? Go back to the service apartment?'

'Wait a moment. We have to book first. I will call you a taxi, where are you exactly?'

'At the airport departure terminal, but I can get one on Didi.'

'Ok, go to the service apartment. I will get admin to book you in. Let me know if you have a problem.'

*

Fifteen minutes later, Colin was travelling back to where he had started. He thought to himself, maybe the powers above were not playing tricks on him after all. Had they not kept him from leaving China? Then he thought that Max and his team could have at least checked the flights. There again, it was the spring break; they were on holiday, after all. Never mind, he thought, putting it down to the mysticism of these Eastern lands and Max's notorious lack of empathy.

Feeling fatigued from his failure to leave China, but consoled by the fact that it was the land of his soulmate, he fell into a languid slumber.

*

He was awoken when the driver pressed the brakes hard enough to make him lurch forward. After coming back to his senses, he took up his phone and typed.

'Hey, Miss U . . .'

'Hey, still in China?'

'Yeah, and guess what . . . no more BA flights out!'

'Oh, how come?'

'Virus'

'Oh, yes, it's getting really bad . . . They say cases are doubling every couple of days now'

'Wow, frightening'

'Where are you now?'

'In a taxi, going back to service apartment . . . Where are you?'

'Taking my mum shopping . . . she loves to go shopping. So I'm getting her some shoes'

'Nice, I'd better let you get on.'

'It's ok . . . Anyway, can't say I'm sad your flight's been cancelled though'

'Postponed, so might get a few more days in Beijing'

'Not so sure, just checked, it says BA flights will be grounded for more than a couple of days . . . until March at least, and you probably won't get a seat on an Air China flight now'

'Oh, right'

'So you relax and just get back to your apartment'

'Ok. Feeling better already'

'Me too!'

Still holding his phone, Colin contemplated how he would spend more time with Lin. There was no one waiting for him in England other than his children. He would Zoom call them that night and explain that the flight had been cancelled. He would also have to explain to their mother.

'Mothers,' he thought to himself as he scrolled back

through the WeChat exchange with Lin, 'how important they are.' It pleased him that Lin had a good relationship with hers. Be it fact or just wishful thinking, he had noticed that women who had good relationships with their mothers seemed more relaxed in their relationships with their partners. For they always had their mothers to turn to. His ex-wife had not had such a backup plan; her relationship with hers was stretched to say the least. This meant his wife's only dumping ground for life's frustrations was her husband — both her hopes and expectations pinned on his shoulders — expectations he had not always been able to live up to. It had been a constant strain on their marriage. He had often wished she had someone to tell her woes to, to tell her that men were far from perfect, someone like a mother to relativize situations so she would know when to take a step back and just let the world keep turning.

Yes, Colin was reassured and charmed when a woman spoke endearingly of her mother. It was a good sign, he told himself as he got to thinking back to a previous conversation with Lin. It had come about after their first morning of lovemaking. They had taken no precautions, perhaps as if by not doing so, they were entrusting each other with their lives. 'What if you fell pregnant?' Colin had asked her as she lay with her head upon his chest. She had asked him if he would be mad if she were. He had joked that he wouldn't mind so much if it was a girl.

Now, sitting in the taxi, he suddenly wondered why he was thinking of mothers, daughters, and babies. He had already gone through the stages of fatherhood a number of times; there was no need to go through them again, was there? And heck, how come it even entered his mind at this stage in his embryonic relationship with Lin? Yet, it seemed self-evident. But then he thought: don't they say love makes you blind?

The ringtone of his phone suddenly plucked him back into the present. He put the phone to his ear. 'Hey, man, they've closed the service apartment to new arrivals,' said the voice of Max.

'Oh.'

'It's OK . . .'

'It's not OK,' said Colin, slightly flustered and mentally blaming Max for something that Colin himself had failed to check. 'What would have happened if I hadn't booked out?'

'Then you could have stayed, but now that you checked out, you can't go back.'

'Oh.'

'But let it go, man; there's nothing we can do.'

In a more level-headed tone of voice, Colin said: 'OK, so now what?'

'We managed to book you into another place . . . lucky. The only one nearby the office still open to foreigners. There might be some restrictions, though.'

'Oh?'

'Nothing drastic. Now pass me to the driver so I can brief him.'

Colin caught the driver's attention. 'Here you are,' he said to Max, then put on the loudspeaker. The exchange in Chinese was brief. Then Max was gone.

One good thing about working for video game companies in the West was that they usually treated you well, thought Colin as for the second time today, he approached the clusters of grey tower blocks on the outskirts of the city. He fondly recalled OneSoft, always putting him up in more than adequate accommodation, be it in a luxurious suite in a service apartment in Toronto or in a comfortable condo in Singapore. But ever since his winter visit to a company in Ukraine, he had become wary. That place in Kharkov was what in the West would equate to a slum. A bedsitter with no bed in a building that looked like an inspiration for *Call of Duty* after the bombs had hit. There were times when, with a nighttime temperature of minus 8°C, the heating would cut out, leaving him with the only option to sleep fully clothed, wrapped in his mountain parka beneath the thin quilt on the bed settee. So when Max had implied that the new accommodation was not quite as good as the usual address, an alarm bell went off in the back of his brain.

Half an hour later, he found the alarm had rung true when the driver left him at a lugubrious-looking compound. Three guardians stood chatting in a temporary sentry tent. It also housed an open-air heater and a table upon which Colin took to be the registry of entrants. One of the three guardians called the receptionist to the compound gate via walkie-talkie. Two minutes later, Colin was following the slender masked woman in her mid-twenties. They strode across the darkening and frosty courtyard into the lobby which at best Colin could describe as functional. He noticed the cheerless elevator had cocktail sticks pushed into some foam that was taped to the inside wall. The receptionist took a stick and prodded the button for the second floor, then placed it in a little tray for disposal. He followed her down a dingy corridor that was missing one light bulb in two. She pushed the door into a mildew-ridden, wallpaper-torn room with rudimentary furniture: a double bed, a wobbly chair and sun-faded desk, and a cigarette-stained bedside table. The sink and stove flanked the entrance passage that opened onto the sleeping area. The shower room with damp-eaten plinths was on the other side. It would have been a close rival to the Kharkov bedsitter if it weren't for the presence of a double bed. It was evident to Colin that this must be a student room.

But even this temporary discomfort might have been offset by the prospect of being able to spend extra time with Lin. And as long as he had a chair and a table to work on, he could live virtually anywhere, couldn't he?

But then came the bombshell. The receptionist told him, partly through her rudimentary high-school English, partly though her translation app, that after registering at the local police station, he would have to go into quarantine for fourteen days. It was the rule for any foreigner moving in, she explained.

'But I've been in China a month already,' he tried to explain through his mask.

The receptionist gave an enigmatic smile with her eyes and came back with the verbal coup de grace: 'I am sorry, but it is law,' she said. In China, when it was law, there was nothing more to be said. You just had to hunker down and do as the Chinese do: you had to go round it, or so he thought.

'OK,' said Colin, who then spoke into the mike of his phone for the app to translate: 'I can go to the shops, right?'

'No, sorry, it is law,' said the receptionist, who had quickly figured out which phrase to use to chase away any hint of remonstrance. Colin was on the brink of conceding; after all, it was law. Moreover, fourteen days wasn't so long, and he would have no choice but to get in some serious writing. The confinement could even prove beneficial.

'How far can I go then? Don't tell me, as far as the compound court?' he said, thinking back to the freezing courtyard with its bare trees and lone vending machine sheltered against the wall. But at least he could give his legs a shake.

'No,' said the girl with her smiling eyes that gave nothing away of her true feelings. 'You must only stay in your room. It's . . .'

'OK, it's law,' said Colin, looking dejectedly around him at the depressing grey net curtains and eighties interior design. 'But someone can at least come and see me, right?' he continued, thinking of the consolation of days of writing and lovemaking to help him swallow the bitter pill of isolation.

'No. A delivery man will put food and drink outside your door,' said the girl, while his logical self told him: *Of course, anything else would be defeating the object.*

That took the biscuit, though. His patience crumbled. The isolation would be worse than being in a Turkish prison because it would be in total seclusion — solitary confinement reminiscent of a WWII prisoner of war camp. He pictured Steve McQueen in the cooler. How dare they. But: *It is for the common good,* he imagined the girl saying to him. *It is law.* Then the girl really said: 'First, we must register you with local police.'

'No, no, I'm not having this,' said the Westerner, used to thinking that the individual could change the world. *But one individual cannot stop an epidemic*, he imagined the girl answering. There was only one thing left for a true-grit Brit to do, he thought. It was how Britain won the war. He would abide by the British world view of liberty of conscience and freedom of speech. *But what does that have to do with it?* he heard the imaginary voice in his head answer him back. At last, he said for real and with dignity: 'Alright, give me a minute, please. I must call my embassy.' Colin searched online for the number. It was already past closing time, but he hoped that for desperate situations, there would be someone to man the phones. After going through a series of voice menus, he got through to a warm and very English lady's voice. Colin explained his situation.

'We will be putting on charter planes for British nationals in Wuhan, sir, where the virus is more serious,' she said in an informative tone of voice. 'In the meantime, we advise you to follow the rules of the local authorities.'

'But they want to put me in the cooler for fourteen days! It's totally squalid!'

'If that is the law, then we advise that you follow it, sir,' said the woman, her voice pleasantly immutable. It was not the sound of empathy that Colin was craving.

'Hang on, do you realise? I mean, where are you? Are you even in China?'

'No, sir.'

'Ah, right, so you're in London.'

'Yes, sir.'

'Hmmm,' said Colin dubiously, becoming slightly ruffled by the lady's calm sophistication. He imagined her comfortably sitting with her tea and biscuits in a nice warm civil servant office in a posh district of London. *There's nothing I can do other than pass on our recommendations, and I don't care anyway,* he imagined her telling him. So he just said thanks and goodbye in a tone that really meant: *typical, what's the point*, while thinking that Max would not do anything more for him either.

There was only one person in the whole world right now he knew would help him, because she was his soulmate, the very reason the cosmos had drawn him to Beijing and kept him there. He punched in his SOS: 'Lin, I'm stuck, they're trying to confine me to a single squalid room.'

Then he asked the young lady to give him ten minutes so he could get himself organised. He would join her at the reception area. The girl smiled behind her mask, bowed her head, and quite contentedly left the irate Westerner to his woes and frustrations until they blew over. Colin's phone rang as she went out into the dingy corridor.

'Lin,' said Colin as if her voice were a lifeline. 'I've been sent to a terrible place, and they're forcing me into isolation . . .' He then briefed her on his situation.

‘Oh, yes, I heard there might be new restrictions, but you’ve been here over a month already.’

‘That’s exactly what I told them. Anyway, I can’t stay here: it’s a bloody rat hole,’ said Colin, failing to keep a stiff upper lip.

‘I see. Have you asked the company or called the Russian guy?’

‘He’s the one who sent me here in the first place!’

‘Oh, all right, let me think then . . . Maybe you can just stay at a hotel. They have different regulations for foreigners, and you won’t need to be declared at the police station because they have a special licence to take care of all that.’

‘Yes, good idea,’ said Colin in a tone of relief, ‘even if it costs more, that’s fine, yes, yes.’

‘Let me call around and check. I will call you back.’

It was a simple solution. Why didn’t the embassy lady think of it? he wondered. Then the voice in his head told him: *because she didn’t care. Lin does.*

Before leaving the room, he had the presence of mind to take photo shots of the dilapidated state of the room that he could send to HR to uphold his point, in case they quibbled over the price of a hotel room. He then shouldered his backpack, took up his luggage bag, and strode out of the room. Down the dingy corridor he plodded to the cheerless lift where he used a cocktail stick to press the ground-floor button. Then he went through the lobby and out across the courtyard where tufts of frozen grass poked through the cracks in the paving, and passed the near-empty vending machine that now glowed in the cold darkness. He could picture himself being forgotten in that room, and left to catch mice and cockroaches for his supper.

A guard at the gate let out puffs of fog as he said something in Chinese, probably with reference to Colin having to isolate. Colin looked at him, shrugged his shoulders, and pointed toward the reception area further along the side of the building. The man insisted, but Colin did as they do in China: ignoring the obstacle, he walked around him and pressed on. The guard glanced over to his colleague, who looked the other way as Colin trundled his luggage bag behind him along to the reception area, forty yards further along the sidewalk.

'Ni hao,' he said as he entered the bleak and chilly room. He continued to the desk, behind which the girl was playing *League of Legions* on her mobile phone.

'My friend is finding me another place to stay at,' he said, perhaps a little smugly, 'a hotel'. Then, realising he still needed an ally until he had the all-clear from Lin, he spoke into his phone for it to translate his words. 'Thank you, but I will have to leave,' he said, giving a slight bow. 'Can I wait here?' he continued, pointing to the armchairs placed around a low table on the other side of the chilly room. It was better than standing out in the freezing cold.

The young woman smiled back, no doubt relieved that the awkward foreigner would soon be out of her life. The obstacle would be gone. *'Dui, dui,'* she said with a note of enthusiasm. 'Sorry about this,' she added, her relief translating into a desire to be nice.

Before he could answer, his phone went off. He nodded

to the receptionist to end their exchange and carried himself and his effects to the vacant armchairs while answering Lin.

'Hey,' said Lin's voice. 'How are you now? Calmed down a bit?' Colin had not been aware that he had been anything but calm while hoping she had good news, but what if she hadn't?

'Hah, fine,' he said.

Lin continued: 'I found a room at the Holiday Inn.'

'Oh, great!'

'It costs 675 RMB per night.'

'That's fine; I should be able to get it reimbursed. I took photos of the room before I left to prove it wasn't worthy to stay in.'

'Good. Where are you now?'

'In the reception area with my luggage.'

'They let you out? Well done!'

'They didn't prevent me, at least. And I didn't give them much of a choice.'

'I suppose they are not so stringent yet then,' said Lin, which between the words let Colin know that he could have been detained. And that perhaps the guards were kindly avoiding any confrontation as he did not speak Chinese and so was a dumb foreigner who required indulgence.

'Yeah, luckily for me,' said Colin, changing his tone from the bragging winner to the one they let get away.

'I will call you a taxi,' said Lin, indulgently.

'Great, thanks,' said Colin, thinking that with Lin, life was so easy.

'Shall I come, too, by the way?' she said sweetly.

'I would love you to, but you're with your family.'

'It's OK. We've had the New Year. I can tell them I have some urgent business to attend to before I get locked out of Beijing. My sister is here anyway, so it's OK.'

'Great.'

More businesslike, Lin said: 'I will send you the number plate of the taxi and will catch the next plane back.'

28

Colin stood before the hotel room window in beige chinos and a blue T-shirt, counting the cars on the distant ring road that ran before the Olympic stadium.

Seven, he counted, where normally there would be an endless stream of vehicles at this time of the evening. Casting his gaze over the stadium all lit up for no one, he got to wondering how come such a hugely populated country could not muster a decent football team — football, that is, in the British sense of the word. After all, this was a country whose culture was founded on community spirit rather than the individual. He had watched players on video juggling a ball without it touching the ground up the 999 steps of the stairway to Heaven's Gate on Tianmen Mountain — the highest naturally formed arch in the world. And yet, on a perfectly flat playing field against a moving adversary, they became unimaginative and fluffed it.

Could it be that their education left no space for creativity? he wondered. After all, it not only takes skill and dexterity to win at football but also individual creative thinking. It was true that, judging from what he had learned so far from working in the Chinese mobile games industry, it did seem that their education system left little space for out-of-the-box thinking. And if ideas did not come, then they just dived into the Internet for 'inspiration.' Yet, their capacity to build a one-thousand-bed hospital in just over a week was simply awe-inspiring. It seemed to Colin that what they lacked in creativity they gained in obedience, obedience to follow rules and premade plans so they could exist more as a community rather than as individuals. That was why, he thought, Beijing was able to switch from the world's biggest bustling capital city to a ghost town overnight.

Colin then turned to Lin on the bed. Clothed in a pink hoodie and snug-fitting designer jeans that showed off her shapely hips, she was stirring from her power nap. He mused over her fine traits — her precise nostrils, her fleshy pink lips, and her finely defined eyebrows — as he padded up on all fours beside her. 'I was thinking,' he said, gently kissing her ear, 'did you know that when God made Chinese women, he was short of skin?'

'You silly Englishman,' said Lin groggily, although enjoying the sound of his whispering.

'It's true . . . So you know what he did?'

'How would I know?' she said with a laugh in her voice, while slipping her fingers through his abundant fringe that he usually wore brushed back.

Colin continued. 'Well, he stretched their skin tighter over their flesh! The upside was it made them firm to the touch, their cheeks tight, and they did not get a sagging gullet and a double chin.'

'That's true, I haven't . . .' said Lin as she felt him brush his lips softly under her jaw. 'You're so silly . . . but very nice . . .'

They had spent the past couple of weeks together in the hotel room. It was composed of a sleeping area and a lounge that made it as spacious as his usual service apartment. Their living together had come about naturally. When she first turned up on the morning after Colin's arrival, she presented herself as the lady who had booked the room. By consequence, the receptionist took her to be Colin's partner, which took the headache out of communicating with the foreigner. For even at the Holiday Inn, spoken English was pretty elementary. Likewise, when the neighbourhood community manager called Colin's room to obtain information about the foreigner, as though reading from a script, he said: 'You can pass me your wife?'

Time had passed easily. In the mornings, they took a Chinese buffet breakfast downstairs before ten, and lived on delivered dishes noon and evening. Lin ordered Chinese and Japanese specialties he had never properly tried before, such as Sichuan boiled beef, kabayaki eel, or the must-taste crispy-skinned Peking duck made in Peking, washed down with Tsingtao beer. The rest of the time, they watched movies on the large TV, made love in the king-size bed, and dipped into their laptops for a few hours of the day. The world outside could turn ghostly, the streets could become deserted, the city air could be fraught with cold fear. It did not matter for two people locked in a hotel room in love.

As he laid his head on Lin's ample bosom, there came two

notification pings on Lin's phone. One hand still tugging Colin's hair, with her other hand she reached for her phone on the bedside table. 'Oh, the delivery man's been,' she said, pulling her phone above her to distance it to suit her eyesight.

'I'll get it,' said Colin, whose appetite was now primed to receive nourishment at six in the evening. Then he rolled off the bed, leaving Lin to swipe open the second message that intrigued her.

'Don't forget your mask this time,' she said as he slipped on his ankle boots. 'And be nice to the receptionist.'

'I was only mad because they wouldn't let me back in,' he said, tucking his laces into the sides of his boots.

'He told me he didn't hear you knocking.'

'Hmm . . . all right,' conceded Colin, then blew her a kiss and stepped out of the door.

She was referring to an incident that had made Colin lose his composure. But once he had cooled down, a pang of guilt replaced the rush of anger as he realised that the receptionist had not meant any harm, and that he probably had other things on his mind. But Colin was a counterpuncher, and one who found it impossible to back down when overcome by a feeling of injustice. He was the type of person who would boldly stand before an advancing tank when in that frame of mind. So when the receptionist did not understand his fury, he had gotten unnecessarily hot under the collar. He insisted on knowing what the receptionist was saying to his colleague, wrongly guessing the meaning of their tone of voice and body language, as had often been the case when he had first joined his team.

Only one floor of the hotel was being used, mainly for returning Beijingers desirous to self-isolate for fear of taking the deadly virus to their homes. Colin was the only foreigner. He had since realised to what extent it must be daunting for the staff to come into work in the knowledge that any one of these guests could be a carrier. So was it any wonder that they too had little desire to be conciliating when they would rather be in the safety of their own homes? After all, this mediocre-paying job could cause them to bring death to their households, where often three generations lived. Indeed, this was one reason why PlayZone HR had asked all employees to work remotely for the time being.

Colin gave the receptionist a cordial nod of the head as he walked past the counter to the table near the entrance. It was where the delivery guys left takeaway meals ordered by hotel guests.

As soon as he had gone out of the door, Lin had gone to the bathroom where she pulled up the message on her phone, that message that had aroused her curiosity. It was from Wei, the blind date who had only entered her mind twice since their meal together. She had wondered what had happened to him. He had not given any sign of life even though he had told her he would get back to her, going as far as telling Lin's friend Yuping the same. It had not bothered her, though, busy as she was with falling in love with her Englishman. But even so, it was strange.

She read Wei's message. He apologised for not getting back to her earlier; his mother had been down with the coronavirus. She had thankfully recovered, though. He hoped Lin was keeping well and that they could meet again soon. A straight, factual message, Lin thought, no frills, no emoji, no sweet-sounding words. She nevertheless began to punch in her answer with a pinch of excitement. After all, she now had a lover and a potential suitor, the latter being overqualified, over intelligent, of a good family, and with pots of money. It almost felt like red-packet day.

But hadn't she found love? A stronger, stranger, more exciting love than ever she had known? But how long would it last? How deep was this addiction? She read back her message to herself: *Sorry to hear about your mother. I hope she is fully recovered. Keep well.* Then she hit the send button.

A return message popped up in an instant. Wei thanked her and would call her once the situation became clearer regarding the virus. Lin left the thread at that and pulled up the day's news. Two minutes later, Colin knocked at the door. She called out for him to hang on a moment before pressing the flush button and giving herself the once-over in the mirror.

They spread the hot dishes over the low table in front of the comfortable sofa. Was she happy? she wondered as she gazed at Colin opening the plastic containers. She felt a warmth radiate from her heart that she had never known before, as she smiled at him now sliding onto the sofa beside her. 'They've officially made quarantine an obligation for anyone coming from outside Beijing,' she said.

'Do you think it'll get as bad as Wuhan?' answered Colin, snapping apart his jointed wooden chopsticks.

'Maybe not, because they've been able to act quickly here,

quicker than in Wuhan anyway.' Lin pulled out a piece of chicken and ginger. 'Try this,' she said, raising the morsel toward Colin's mouth.

'Good,' he said, 'what's the figures today?' It had become a daily ritual to check the figures of the infected and deceased in Beijing.

'Three new cases, still seven deaths, I think,' she said, helping herself to a chunk of gong bao chicken. 'And three hundred and seventy-five cases in total in Beijing province. So I think they are being cautious. They don't want Beijing to end up like Wuhan; it wouldn't look good.'

'Makes no difference to us, though, does it? We're both working remotely anyway.'

'No,' said Lin, holding the chicken chunk before her mouth. 'But I should go back to my place tonight.' She popped in the morsel and reached for another.

'Really?'

'Yes, I need some clothes, and I will ask the guard for an entry card so you can enter my compound. Otherwise, they won't let you in. Best do it now.'

'That's OK,' said Colin. 'But can't we just stay here?'

He had been grounded at the hotel since he had arrived there but allowed to wander as far as the little convenience store downstairs. Now, having spent two weeks in isolation, they could envisage going further, and Lin had planned to spend the following weekend at her place. But he had grown into this new habitat, had taken its rules into his stride, and he enjoyed the daily walk downstairs in the bitter cold. He was not in any particular rush to change his routine.

'And we need to go out and get some air and exercise,' said Lin, picking up her phone in her free hand and thumbing to a picture. 'Otherwise we'll end up like this!' She showed him her phone screen that showed two photos side by side, one titled *David* portraying Michelangelo's famous statue, and next to it the same statue having put on twenty pounds and titled *Covid*. So the montage of the juxtaposed photos read: *David—Covid*. Colin laughed. Lin continued: 'I will go home tonight and do some cleaning tomorrow. On Sunday we can go somewhere.'

'All right, where?'

'Don't know because everything's closed down. But maybe just for a walk.' Colin agreed. And a day's break from living together would allow him to gather his thoughts too. After their meal, Lin packed up her effects into her small, pink- blossom luggage bag. Colin accompanied her downstairs. Then he waved her off as her Benz powered through the icy road, toward the exit barrier three hundred yards further down.

Lin felt like she was dangerously abandoning herself to her emotions. It was lovely but quite scary. Was there any future in this relationship? she wondered as she travelled along the deserted ring road to her compound. It was not at all like her to abandon herself like this into the abyss of love. Then a little voice reminded her of what someone had once told her. *You have been too hard on yourself.* She had indeed allowed herself to have some fun, some love, and it was all becoming so addictive. 'Just go with it and enjoy,' that girl at the Chinese New Year party had told her. But didn't that mean placing herself in the arms of danger?

29

The following morning Lin lay in her bed, mulling over the recent memories and feelings she had never before known.

But was it at all reasonable? He was an older man, he had been married, he had children, and he was a foreigner. She pulled up profiles on her phone of mixed couples, and of children of mixed race. They were so cute, she said to herself.

As she was browsing, a message came up. It was from Wei Leng. He regretted the stricter measures imposed by the government but found them necessary. He was hoping they could dine together once things got back to some kind of normality. Lin agreed that these new measures were necessary, and left it at that. He mentioned that the curve was flattening, which meant the authorities were gaining the upper hand. He would call her when they lifted the lockdown.

A part of Lin was relieved. It meant putting off an awkward decision. But wasn't she guilty of betraying Colin? She tried to put it to the side of her mind. After all, she had not committed to Wei. She was in love with Colin. There again, didn't love make you blind?

Nevertheless, curiosity about this Wei Leng drove her to call Yuping under the pretext of finding out how her children were faring. After the niceties and learning that school was closed, Yuping did as Lin had hoped. She asked: 'What about Wei Leng?'

'What about him?' said Lin, lounging, propped up on her pillows and playing it aloof.

'He thought you were very reserved but dignified when you dined together,' said Yuping encouragingly. Lin could hear children giggling together in the background.

'Well, I told you, I found him icy,' she riposted from her bed, 'cold as the Yongding River in Major Cold!'

'Ha ha, that's just his upbringing. He likes you. Has he called since last time?'

'Actually, he messaged me. He wants us to dine again after this lockdown period is over.'

'Wow, girl! You've got a foot in!'

Lin had said nothing of Colin to anyone. Maybe she had half expected it to be a short fling, and after a first argument, having discovered that their cultures and personalities did not match, they would snap apart like disposable chopsticks. But not only were they perfect lovers, even their birth animals matched. In fact, it all matched, and this virus period had given her the perfect alibi to explore this love without alerting her friends.

'Well, we shall see,' she said. 'I was already in a relationship with Wong Li, remember? And maybe I've been wrong to aim for these money-makers with their cold, calculating hearts.'

'Honey, what's happened? Am I speaking to Lin?' said Yuping, half-preoccupied, half in jest. Lin laughed out loud. 'I mean, he has real prospects, has real money, comes from a good family. Honey, he ticks all the boxes!'

'Sure, except he acts like he's got a bundle of chopsticks pushed up his arse! And why did his wife leave him?'

'They didn't get on,' reasoned Yuping as her children now were making squealing noises in the background.

'Did she find someone else?'

'She did actually.'

'Any children?'

'Yes, a boy.'

'You see? Sounds like she escaped from Qincheng Prison!'

'Or maybe he couldn't father children?'

'Oh my God,' said Lin, aghast, 'that's even worse!'

'Ha ha, he might ask why you haven't even been married.'

'True.'

'I would just keep your options open, honey. Best policy. I mean, you could always divorce later.'

'True.'

Lin changed subjects, which wasn't difficult; she just had to ask Yuping about her kids and what she was doing with them while the schools were closed.

The call gave away no secrets and gave Lin the benefit of projecting her thoughts. If ever she had a choice, which way would she go? she wondered. Both these men offered some degree of uncertainty. Looking back on her past, she said to herself: *But wasn't there greater uncertainty when there was no love?* And how could she love a cold-hearted man after being with Colin? Had her relationship with him spoilt her judgement? Or had it opened her eyes? For if there was one thing she was certain of now, it was that true love binds.

Sliding her feet into her slippers while sitting on the edge of the bed, she sent Colin a message, telling him she had managed to get him an entry pass to her compound.

*

The following Sunday, they ventured out to get some air and to experience Beijing during what was now being declared a pandemic.

Horrible scenes of the wet market of Wuhan circulated on WeChat: dogs tied up to be slaughtered; corpses of bats, pangolins, and other exotic creatures amassed in haphazard heaps for market buyers to pick up. Until then, Colin had only read about the national state of emergency. Now, as they pushed the winter curtain into the deserted downtown mall where officials at the door took their temperature, it became stunningly real. Starbucks was only serving takeaways; a table had been placed at the entrance to prevent public entry. Even the karaoke booth, where lovers would daringly sing out repressed emotion, was not taking any payment. It occurred to Colin after the pair of them had sat inside the booth, drawn the curtain, and sneaked a kiss, that it could be a prime hotbed for any virus to develop. He doused his hands in hand sanitizer squeezed from a miniature bottle that he carried in his pocket. Lin did likewise. Only the street-facing boutiques were open, but they were empty of clients. Beijingers were visibly heeding government recommendations, especially as it had emerged that the virus could fell not just the elderly and fragile, but anyone from two to eighty.

Colin agreed to spend the next weekend at Lin's place too; it was more spacious, and they could cook. On Friday evening, Lin having spent another Thursday night at her place so she could receive a delivery in the morning of fresh seafood from home, she announced she would soon be on her way to pick him up. So, masked and wrapped up in Lin's scarf and his mountain parka, he took a stroll to the barrier where she would have to pass. After an exchange of glances with the solitary guard who sat in his cubicle playing online poker, Colin continued past the barrier along the fourth ring road as the night encroached. He felt a vivifying sensation as the glacial air chilled his lungs.

On passing the underground entrance that was deserted, save for a guard stamping his feet and holding a thermometer, he noticed a few solitary joggers — joggers taking advantage of the absence of other bipeds and vehicles to pound down the flat and empty side road. It occurred to Colin that this must be one of the rare times in Beijing's recent history that joggers could run without poisoning their lungs. After pacing for twenty minutes, he headed back to meet Lin. On reaching the barrier, he saw her Benz speeding by in the street lamp light and being waved through without her having to stop. She looked like she was concentrating; Colin hailed her, but she did not see.

He jogged the rest of the way down the gloomy street to join her. To his surprise, she was still sitting in her car, her face lit up by the glow of her phone. He tapped on the passenger window. She gave a little start and put down the phone as he jumped in beside her. They laughed and kissed.

'Busy?' he said in jest.

'Not really, just chatting with my friend Yuping,' she returned, a little evasively. She actually had nothing to hide, although she did secretly wish Yuping wouldn't keep bringing up the subject of Wei Leng.

30

From Lin's apartment the following afternoon, they headed out toward Tiananmen Square.

It was a cold and glorious sunny day, but access was restricted, and the National Museum was closed, so they parked behind the Forbidden City grounds and picked up a couple of hire bikes near the Gate of Thriving Imperial Clan. They went freewheeling joyfully through the recently renovated *hutong*, with its impeccable grey bricks and its straight lanes now virtually empty. The little traditional souvenir and art and craft shops were closed where they usually would be bustling with Chinese tourists and a few Westerners. Shop windows still showed lucky paper lanterns from the Chinese New Year, and others even Christmas decorations, as a testimony to the beginnings of the turmoil caused by the tiniest of enemies that perhaps the great dragon had ever encountered in its three-thousand-year history.

The Chinese government was being slammed by Western media for its apparent slowness in coming to grips with the virus and letting the demon out of the box in the first place. Colin wondered if the Brits would do any better, given their long history of organisational skills and people management from the days of the empire. And would the Americans lead the world in their confident stance against all invaders? Despite the outrage and criticism from Western powers, Colin was seeing all around him how the dragon could sleep through it all in its usual self-sufficient way. The dragon and the phoenix could chase away the Hun. The people's army could force back invaders from the east. But could China destroy this tiniest of scourges that had slowed its beating heart and brought its capital to a standstill?

They got off their bikes to view the Tongzi River, the moat that surrounds the Forbidden City. It was partially iced over as though Beijing were in hibernation. There were just a handful of couples and lone strollers taking the fresh, sun-filled air. On their way out, Lin had indicated to him a traditional Chinese clinic that had prompted him to pull up info on his phone about the SARS of 2003 and how it was stamped out. He had read that China had been victim to many such bacterial attacks in the past. These plagues had even been an integral part of its culture. Despite the huge remonstrance in Wuhan, the common people seemed to know what to do in case of viral attack and played along to mask-wearing in the streets. From the Western Han Dynasty to the end of the Qing Dynasty, there had been 321 such plagues. Each time, Chinese medicine had helped battle against distempers, successfully containing the spread of epidemics. Colin learnt that in China, there had never been tragedies to the extent of the Black Death or the Spanish flu that killed millions in Europe. Plague, cholera, SARS, flu . . . every time, the great dragon had brought out its secret weapon: the medicine of the ancients — medicine based on three thousand years of wise men's observations. And today, Chinese medicine was filling the gap between traditional wisdom and modern bacteriology to treat the victims of the present attack. The great dragon would lick its wounds and rise again.

One good thing during this great slumber was that the air of Beijing had become more breathable. The foothills to the north, that usually trapped the offending clouds of pollution, were visible again like in the days when the fastest mode of winter transport was skating up the river.

As they gazed over the sun setting behind the dragons on the roofs of the Forbidden City, Colin's mind turned from the causes and effects of this pandemic when Lin said: 'Come on, it's getting cold.' He gazed at her, heroically resisting planting his lips onto hers so she would not feel the embarrassment of a public display of passion. But her return gaze and illuminating smile told him the feeling was mutual.

He was wondering and perhaps hoping how Lin would turn him into something better, something he had aspired to become. Lin had once said to him: 'My mother says a woman has to know how to make a man. Only if his wife believes in him will he reach his full potential.' She was encouraging, proactive, and had suggested he take advantage of people being grounded at home by increasing his marketing budget to reach more readers. And it was working.

After a whole afternoon of freewheeling through the heart of the city, they parked their cycles and headed back to the Gate of the Thriving Imperial Clan, where Lin had parked the car.

They had been living virtually together almost a month already, thought Lin to herself as she threaded her hand through the loop of Colin's arm. Was it even possible to carry on in the like manner without any disputes? And how did she, the headstrong trailblazer, become so enthralled to the point of feeling like a chess pawn in his hand and yet also like a princess? How was it possible after so many years to stumble upon such a man from a different world? But how would her parents feel about a mixed-blood relationship? Not to mention a mixed-race child? Especially in China, where Hong Kong Chinese and American Chinese were sneered at and yet at the same time envied. As they approached Lin's Benz, Colin broke away to pay the car park guardian. '*Wu kuai'* snapped the small, leathery-faced man, showing a number five on a small square of paper.

Lin left Colin to sort out the WeChat payment while she proceeded to the parking space. She caught herself thinking that she would change her car if they had a child . . . But then she heard her name being called out in Chinese behind her: '*Hēi Lin!*' Stunned, she turned, the feeling of panic dumping her back into reality, wiping away all romantic thoughts.

'Wei,' she said. *What the heck are you doing here?* she thought.

'I was just taking my mother for a drive. She wanted to get out and enjoy the blue sky.'

'Nice,' said Lin, viewing Colin over Wei's shoulder. Was there time to get out of the two men meeting face-to-face? 'Yes, it's a beautiful day, getting cold now, though,' she said, half smiling. She could see Colin already swiping the QR code. 'Ideal for sightseeing. I was showing a foreign friend a few sights,' she continued, thinking on her feet in case the two should meet. 'Well then, I wish your mother good health. Give her my regards,' she said, half turning toward her car.

But Wei Leng continued: 'Yes, I will,' he said. 'She still needs to catch her breath, but at least the air is better now. We were about to head out to our country residence when they locked down the province. So we shall stay in Beijing for the time being.'

'Yes, that's good,' said Lin, perhaps a little too eagerly as Colin was making his way toward them. Wei did not miss her glance and the slight tension in her voice. He turned as Lin's foreigner friend came strolling up toward them.

'Well, perhaps we can have tea sometime if the restaurants remain closed,' he said in Chinese to Lin. Then, in a perfect American accent, he said: 'I will call you.' He turned and headed back to his sleek black Mercedes S Class as Colin gave a discreet nod, not knowing whether this man was an acquaintance or a colleague.

In the twinkling of an eye, Lin beheld the two men vying for her heart. One dressed in neat slacks, sensible shoes, and an expensive overcoat and scarf. The other dressed in jeans, ankle books, and a parka. She told herself she would have put an end to Wei's hopes, but this was not the moment.

She suddenly saw life with him in a golden prison where never again would it be appropriate to sleep in the nude. She saw restrained emotion and a sexless life, a metronomed existence that lacked panache and adventure, locked in the fear of living up to expectations. But true love should bind not breed fear, should it not? Then she recalled a quote which said: 'There is no fear in love. But perfect love drives out fear.' It was from John 4:18, a quote she had remembered from the times she went to the Christian church in her undying search for an answer.

'Who was that?' said Colin as she started the car.

'Oh, just an acquaintance,' said Lin, evasively and visibly making much of manoeuvring the car out of the cramped car park, guided by the commanding shouts of the little parking lot guardian.

'Why did he say he would call you?' It had not even occurred to Colin that Lin had until very recently been a free agent. She had friends and acquaintances that, in their bubble of love, he had never thought about, let alone met.

Switching the car to forward drive mode, she said: 'OK, Wei was an acquaintance I once met before we got together.'

'And?'

'And that's all,' she said nonchalantly.

'Hmm. I think I've just realised something,' said Colin.

A flash of doubt shot across Lin's face. 'What?' she said.

'Well,' said Colin, slowly. 'That . . .'

'That what?'

'That I will . . .'

'Oh come on, get it out,' said Lin, now playing along.

'That I will have to . . .'

'What, what?'

'That I will have to learn Chinese!'

Lin gave a shrill musical laugh. 'Oh, you are worried I can say things to people without you understanding!'

'Oui, oui,' said Colin, who then strung together a few words in French: *'Sinon, je ne vais jamais savoir ce que tu dis sur moi à tes connaissances; qui peuvent très bien être des anciens amours!'*

'Ha ha, we will find you some lessons,' laughed Lin, who did not need to understand what he was saying to get the point.

'Everywhere will be closed, though.'

'But you can have lessons online.'

'Yeah, I suppose so. Where would I be without you?'

'Either in a slum or in quarantine, ha ha!'

'Bah, I would have found a way out.'

'Sure you would,' laughed Lin as her right trainer hit the accelerator and they zoomed off out of the car park.

31

The following week, they tried to put up an imaginary glass partition between the low table before the sofa and the desk that ran along the wall.

But with exaggerated pantomime, Colin kept knocking at her imaginary door and entering her office space, so they did not get much done. Lin ended up working from her apartment during the day, then returning to the hotel in the evening.

During breakfast together on Thursday, she pointed out some trolleys full of lunchboxes being pushed by attendants spookily dressed to confront the COVID-19 enemy. The pair of them went to inquire at the reception desk where a young woman, who seemed frightened out of her wits, would only say they were expecting new guests. Sensing the extreme fragility of the girl who told Lin she had just been recruited to replace staff in quarantine, Lin did not push any further. As per their newly established morning ritual, Colin then accompanied Lin to her car and waved her off.

It was not so bad living at the Holiday Inn, thought

Colin once back at his desk. The room was spacious enough, and most importantly, the desk space, though not very deep, ran along the wall for over three metres, allowing him to spread out his paper rolls of timeliness. The only inconvenience was the mirror that ran above it and which lured him into staring at his fat mole that sat ungraciously under his left nostril.

The whole team of fifty souls was working remotely. He seemed to spend more time in DingTalk threads than actually moving the game narrative forward. *What do you think of this background set? What about this small map? How about this character design?* How in the world did they expect one English guy to represent the entire Western mobile gaming population? He didn't even usually play phone games, previously considering them as mere time-wasters compared to console games. But he had since come to see the potential of exploiting a full narrative experience even on such a small device as a mobile phone. He now got pleasure out of it, and imaged a fully dialogued version with proper voice actors. It was while he was in the middle of casting voices in his mind's ear that the hotel telephone on the bedside table snapped him from his ponderings.

'Hello?'

'Hello, sir,' said the wavering female voice on the other end. 'You must leave your room, sir.'

'I beg your pardon?' said Colin, taken aback.

'You must leave your room, sir. Immediately.'

Colin churned over in his mind what wrong he could have committed. The young woman did not ask for his 'wife.' Had she and her colleagues cottoned on to the fact that he and Lin were lovers? After all, they did not share the same surname.

'But why?' said Colin in consternation.

'I cannot say, sorry. You must check out immediately.'

'But can you at least tell me if there's another hotel nearby?'

'Sorry, I cannot help you, sir. Goodbye.'

*

Within the hour, Lin had arrived back at the hotel.

Colin had packed his bags after she had called reception. After Colin had called her for help, she had spoken to a more senior receptionist. Then she had phoned Colin to let him know that the hotel was in fact being requisitioned by the government to use as a quarantine centre.

On reaching the lobby with his baggage trundled behind him, Colin saw a drastic change in mood and attire. All the reception staff members were clad in hazmat suits, visors, and masks. A white-clad woman was ticking a register as a group of quarantined guests passed through the main doors and were ushered onto the elevator that would take them to their rooms. It all suddenly took on a sinister air. And there he was, standing like a tourist teleported into some dystopian video game.

He met Lin a few minutes later, and they went to check out at the reception desk. 'Do you mean these new guests could potentially be infected?' said Lin to the girl behind the counter while checking out.

The girl desperately said: 'I don't know.' She had fear in her eyes and, standing next to Lin, Colin wondered if the poor girl had seen the effects of the virus first-hand. She turned imploringly to her male colleague for help.

In a calm and measured voice, he told Lin in Chinese: 'We have been careful to put them on a different floor and on the opposite side of the hotel. They are not infected as far as we know, but they have been in close proximity with someone who is. In any case, there is no risk for you, but you must leave immediately for your own good or you will be asked to stay here and quarantine, bearing in mind that the rules are stricter now. You will not be allowed out of your room.'

Lin turned to translate for Colin.

'But where do we go?' he said a few minutes later once checkout was completed. Lin suggested they go to her place. But was he ready for total dependence? 'Thanks,' he said, 'but everyone at work would know that I must be staying in someone's flat. There would be questions.'

He did not need to explain any further for Lin to grasp his feelings. And perhaps neither was she quite ready to have a live-in lover. It could create unnecessary tension when each of them needed to be alone. She knew he enjoyed being alone sometimes from one of those pillow-talk questions she had previously asked him, such as: *Do you like being alone? How many times a week would be ideal for you to make love? Do you miss your children?* Questions that helped her plumb his depths, questions which, after answering, he turned back on her — *ni na?* — and you? It was straight-talking, no hesitation, and no dressing up the facts. He had said: *Yes, I enjoy being alone sometimes, maybe more than the average biped. Twice a week at least so my yin keeps cool with my yang . . . Yes, I love my children; they are part of me, my greatest creation.* Their answers had matched. Neither could Lin aspire to living without loving her child. And she would not be prepared to let it be brought up by her parents, as so many women had opted to do to be able to continue their careers in Beijing.

So when he said he needed a place of his own, she did not take offence. Moreover, before meeting Colin, she had never taken a man back to her apartment, let alone lived with one.

After a few calls, she turned to Colin, seated next to her in a lobby armchair. 'No hotels are accepting foreigners near your office, so I called another Holiday Inn. But it's in Sanlitun, same district as the Mexican restaurant we went to, remember?'

'Oh, a bit far from the office, though, isn't it?' said Colin, sitting with his elbow on his knee while rubbing the bristles on his chin.

'It's OK,' said Lin reassuringly, clasping his forearm. 'When the time comes to go back to work, you can take a taxi. Without traffic, it will only take twenty-five minutes. It's about the same distance as from here to the office. I know because I've booked candidates into there before.'

Funnily enough, Colin had never felt happier as they headed, totally unhampered by traffic, for a new abode, a new adventure, a new district. Then Lin said: 'This is so eerie; it's really quite frightening now . . . All that's missing are your zombies!'

32

The room was half the size as the one Colin had vacated, with just a gueridon table and a small surface on which to work.

This was the Holiday Inn Express, where every room was identical. His room looked onto the main street at the front, where morning and evening, he viewed the Peking Duck restaurant surviving on its delivery service. Next door to the restaurant, Colin could view the comings and goings at the entrance of a guarded compound courtyard. A bleak area, it seemed, under the leaden late February sky. But with March came more clement days of clear blue weather. The cherry trees that lined the street began to bourgeon.

It had become routine to leave for Lin's place on Friday evenings. But yesterday, Colin had remained at the hotel and now waited for her to pick him up. After weeks of living between four walls in a high-rise hotel, he was looking forward to a foray into the Fragrant Hills northwest of Beijing. He had popped down to Happiness Street opposite the hotel, an expat district that included a Western-style supermarket where they only spoke Chinese, a French restaurant, and a bakery where he had picked up a couple of French baguette sandwiches for their day trip.

Being locked down on the tenth floor was making him feel disconnected from the world. But news from Italy brought him back down to earth momentarily; it would surely only be a matter of time before this virus spread to the rest of Europe, he thought. There again, surely they had a well-plotted road map inspired from the Chinese case study; surely they only had to apply the previous lessons learnt. They just had to lock down, wear masks when about town, and avoid travel between regions, didn't they? Surely they would come to grips with the virus more swiftly than the Chinese and stamp it out before it spread to the proportions of Wuhan, wouldn't they? After all, they knew it was on the way. But once back in front of the hotel where Lin pulled up, it all seemed so far away again, floating as he was in the perfume of love.

Keeping one's feet on the ground is known as *jie diqi*; it is associated with being connected to the earth's energy. A trip to those Fragrant Hills was sorely needed to reconnect with the energy of nature. The long lung-defying climb was worth their while, and the view from the top south-eastward over Beijing certainly put the sprawling city into perspective, but it was a different reality that would properly bring him back down to earth.

After the knee-wobbling descent down the steep granite steps, they stopped off at a coffee shop where tourists were lacking, and where cats were snugly napping on the seats usually occupied by Beijingers out for a bowl of fresh air. As Colin sat opposite Lin, each spooning a piece of the other's cake, his phone buzzed. Now at the bottom of the foothills, a voice message had come through. He dialled the number and listened to the worried voice of his ex-wife.

'Colin, the virus is getting bad here now; I don't know why Boris fucking Johnson doesn't shut everything down. We haven't even got any masks, nothing, everything's out of stock, and people are emptying the supermarkets. Call me.'

Lin, seeing the look of sudden alarm on Colin's face, asked him what the matter was.

'My ex-wife,' he said, holding his chin as the chilling news hit home. 'She says the virus is spreading rapidly in England. She says they lack masks.'

'God. You'd better send her some,' said Lin, snapping into planner mode. 'Tell her to stay indoors.'

'Yes.'

'And get some hand sanitizer.'

'Yes.'

'Soon as we get back.'

'Yes.'

Then they both sat there in silence for a short while, knowing that this was the bugle call that sounded his return to the UK.

33

From Colin's hotel window, the bleak compound opposite was slowly coming back to life, like the rustlings from a hedgerow after hibernation.

Toddlers with young mothers could be seen playing in the courtyard; old men stood smoking cigarettes, slowly nodding their heads; and a tiny green delivery vehicle, small enough to park among the blanketed mopeds where cars were forbidden, began its daily comings and goings. The portly Peking Duck restaurant owner sat outside watching people pass, at first few and far between, but from late March customers were returning in greater numbers. The traffic, though still light, was steadily increasing in volume, even the used-cardboard collectors could be seen once again balancing gigantic piles on their tricycles.

After hunting down masks on eBay and buying vials and the ingredients to make a hand sanitizer, Colin had pulled up Opodo to check outbound flights. But China was still closed. There was no way back home.

Italy had been badly hit. The whole country had gone

into lockdown in a desperate bid to take control of the spread. In France, it was proliferating, too, and the UK announced its first deaths. Yet, to Colin's consternation, experts were not advocating the use of the mask. The World Health Organisation said that ordinary people did not need to wear face masks when they went about their daily business. Colin also pulled up a BBC article that read: *Professor Jonathan Van Tam said he does not believe healthy people wearing them would reduce the spread of the disease.* Was this an attempt to keep people from stockpiling? But why then did they not buy masks from China? Did it not stand to reason that wearing them could only be beneficial? The virus was so small that it could pass through any textile barrier like through a sieve, said the specialists. But, thought Colin, what about the prevention of hand-to-face contamination? And didn't they learn at school that coughs and sneezes spread diseases?

News soon came that they were closing schools in the UK. It was a relief for Colin and his ex-wife, who had been worried sick. All Colin could do was to send the protective gear, Zoom call his children, and make sure they listened to their mother, whose French restaurant also went into lockdown.

In Beijing, on the other hand, restaurants were beginning to open. During the first days of its reopening to sitting customers, the Peking Duck allowed families in if they sat at separate tables, but then relaxed the rule to sitting a metre apart at the same table.

By the end of March, Colin was allowed back to work where barely a handful of coworkers were present, probably those who, like him, were going stir-crazy in their tiny living quarters. But he had no working relationships with them, and so he continued threading the narrative with his usual workmates remotely. Little Dragon and Yang, who were still in their hometown, refused to return until Beijing lifted the obligation of incomers to go into quarantine. So Colin was able to message Lin freely, his working day rhythmed to the appearances of the guard who took employees' temperature three times a day, checked the windows were left ajar to let in the cold spring air — the air con having been turned off — and made sure those present were wearing their face masks. The company provided three surgical masks for indoor usage and one N95 mask per day, along with latex gloves.

The taxi ride across town was easy and fluid as a consequence of millions of commuters still working from home. And where previously his view through the cab window was full of greyness, now every day, the journey was growing in colour. Soon there began to emerge an uninterrupted blur of tender greens.

Springtime happens quickly in Beijing as summer begins in May. One thing that surprised Colin was the number of trees, and at no time were they more beautiful, vibrant, and visible than on coming out of the bleak spells of winter into the spell of the Awakening of Insects. The willows and poplars along the rivers, lilac, peach, and cherry blossoms in the parks where Chinese pines stood with their straight stems, and the sweet-smelling acacias, all burst into an explosion of leaf and flower.

Colin had observed on his first stay that one of Beijing's greatest achievements over the years of modern urban development must be the thought given to planting these trees. If the *hutong* districts of one-storey dwellings of grey brick had been its heart and soul, the trees were surely its lungs. He had since found out that the origin of closely spacing trees along Beijing's avenues and boulevards goes back to the times of Kublai Khan in the thirteenth century. Back in the day, trees were required by law to be planted two paces apart along public roads, not just to create shade during the long hot summers, but also to act as road markers during the snowy winters.

Nowadays, electric mopeds had been introduced, and trucks were banished from the once imperial city, but it still remained one of the most polluted capitals on the planet. The wall of mountains in the west and north that kept the invader out also trapped in the factory pollution blown from the east. So the oxygen-exuding trees were all the more given pride of place along all of Beijing's new highways, avenues, and boulevards.

With the abatement of infections, the parks were becoming peopled again. But instances of bourgeoning cherry blossoms captured on a million cell phones were not all that was spreading across the WeChat stratosphere. With the reversal of situations between China and the outside world that was now battling with the virus in its turn, the fear of the foreigner was also disseminating across WeChat.

One gathering of young Westerners picnicking in Chaoyang Park further stoked the fire of xenophobia. For none of them was wearing a mask, no doubt believing the nonsense expounded by Western experts and politicians at the beginning of the pandemic.

Notices forbidding foreigners from entering premises began to appear. The underlying distrust of the foreigner began to rear its ugly head where usually it kept doggo. Colin was well aware of it, although he had learnt to do as they generally did for most hindrances in China: he ignored it. Only once was he victim to overt racism, or maybe an excess of precaution.

It happened when he had been asked not to enter the Peking Duck when on his own one Thursday evening, Lin having called him to say she needed to stay at her place to wash some clothes. After some remonstrance, he realised he would not get in, so he turned away and fetched some cheese and a pot of noodles from the Western supermarket on Happiness Street. The following evening, he went to Peking Duck with Lin, who put in a word, and all became fine again, which told him that the best policy was to go with a local, and in his case with Lin.

They took a table on the first floor that overlooked the avenue. While pulling off strips of flesh from a large succulent trout with their chopsticks, Lin said: 'By the way, the clinic is open again. I messaged the doctor, who said he can do it next week if you like.'

'Do what?' said Colin, topping up their glasses with white wine while their neighbours at the next table were loudly sucking up noodles.

'Your thing . . . the mole,' said Lin, touching the base of

her own left nostril to jog his memory.

'Really?'

'Yes. Once you have gotten rid of it, it will also remove the barrier to peace and prosperity.' Lin had brought up the subject of its removal the previous week, and he had not shown any resistance to the idea. She continued in the tone of wisdom. 'Now is the best time, because no one will ever notice,' she said.

'Oh,' said Colin, after another sip of wine, 'you mean because the mask will hide the aftermath of the operation, right?'

'Don't sound so dramatic,' said Li, gently mocking while helping herself with dexterity to more fish, 'but yes, although there won't be much to see anyway, and then they will remove the suture. He can do it after Tomb Sweeping Day,' she said, delicately placing the morsel of fish on her tongue.

*

A week after the lockdown was lifted in Wuhan, Colin had taken the day off and was due to go under the knife.

While seated in the empty waiting area, it occurred to Lin that going into a clinic without understanding the lingo might be quite daunting. 'Nervous?' she asked him a little later as he fed his naked arm through the gap of an admin counter to have his blood taken. Lin had previously joked that they did not usually take blood over the admin counter; it was a precautionary measure against COVID-19. It was so that there was a screen between the nurse and himself.

'Nervous to have a blood test?' he replied, glad to talk his way through the point where the needle syphoned his blood.

'No,' said Lin, 'to have a surgical intervention without knowing what's being said around you.'

'Well, you're my ears!'

'Yes, I'm glad you trust me.'

'Relationships are based on trust, aren't they?' Colin continued, suddenly realising that he might be perceived as a pushover. 'I trust you. You trust the doctor. We spoke to him last week, so why should I feel nervous?'

'Good,' said Lin, satisfied, 'I'm glad.'

'Trust is something precious,' he pursued philosophically, perhaps to hide the fact that he hadn't actually thought about it. 'It's something you can't buy or sell,' he continued while following the nurse's invitation to press a piece of cotton wool on his vein.

'True, although the best crooks know how to use it too!'

'You're not trying to tell me you're about to have my organs cut out and sell my heart, are you?'

'Of course not,' said Lin, in her musical laugh.

Colin retrieved his arm, and they went back to the empty waiting area. A few moments later, a masked, doe-eyed assistant with textured fingernails came along and led them into an antechamber. It led into a corridor; on the other side of it, there were a series of operating rooms, the first one visibly deeper than the others, so forming one side of the corridor into an L shape. 'Please, put your coat there,' said the assistant to Colin, pointing to the bed in the antechamber. 'And this too,' she continued, pinching her top under her white coat while pointing at Colin's pullover with her other hand.

Colin did as he was asked as the assistant exchanged a few words in Chinese with Lin. They both gave each other a knowing nod. Then Lin turned to Colin, who had put on the gown over his shirt and was now putting on the blue disposable shoe covers. In a voice she modulated to sound reassuring, she said: 'I'm not allowed in, but you'll be all right: the nurses know a little English. And I'll be here if you call.'

Then a matronly lady burst through the PVC strip curtain from the corridor. 'You can come,' she said to Colin, her smiling eyes exuding a hypnotic assurance. He was beginning to feel like an old dog about to be put down. It suddenly occurred to him that he did not know what to expect, and that no one outside these walls even knew he was there.

'Don't worry,' said Lin. 'It won't hurt.'

God, thought Colin at the mere mention of pain, something else he had not contemplated. But as the matron led him to the corridor and the assistant pushed him gently in the back from behind, Lin kept up the chat. 'They will test your eyesight first,' she said before he disappeared through the double security door.

Halfway down the corridor, after giving his arm a friendly stroke, the matron said: 'Stand here; you do not move.' Then she paced back so she was level with the largest operating room that offered a little wall space opposite Colin.

'Now look,' she said, turning around to face him and pointing to a vision chart on the wall.

'I can't read Chinese,' he said helplessly.

'OK,' said the matron, 'put hand on left eye and tell me what way signs going.'

'I can't read it. Don't know Chinese,' insisted Colin.

'OK, OK, only tell me which way,' said the matronly nurse.

Colin could feel a ball of frustration surging up in his chest. There was only one thing for it. He called out: 'Lin? Lin?' Then, making an effort to keep his composure, in a lower voice, he said to the lady: 'Could you please ask my friend to come?'

The doe-eyed assistant standing behind her hurried to the antechamber where Lin had been asked to wait. But Lin had poked her head around the door before the assistant got there.

Colin called out: 'Can you explain to tell them I don't speak Chinese?'

'I think they already know,' said Lin, with a smile in her voice.

'So why do they want me to read the eyechart?'

'You don't have to read it, just point which way the lines are pointing, up, down, left, right . . .'

'But I don't . . .' interrupted Colin, who then suddenly felt ridiculous for his momentary loss of composure on realising that these were not Chinese characters at all: they were simple symbols formed of straight lines. 'Oh, right,' he said, now seeing the ingenuity of the chart which did not require the viewer to know how to read at all, be it an illiterate peasant or an illiterate foreigner.

The nurse exchanged a few words with Lin, who then said in English: 'It's OK, you don't need to do it.'

'I can, I can do it,' insisted Colin.

Leaving Colin to be led to the operating room, Lin slipped back to the antechamber. She pulled out her phone and continued her chat with Yuping to pass the time. She read:

> 'He wasn't happy about seeing you with a foreigner, which means he must be keen.'

She was referring to Lin's bumping into Wei at the car park. Lin felt she was betraying Colin to let him just be labelled a foreigner — Colin who had blindly placed his trust in her. She typed, biting her lip. She paused a moment, then continued to let her index finger hopscotch over the phone keyboard:

> 'Actually, Colin is much more to me than a foreigner'
>
> 'Oh? You mean . . .'
>
> 'Yes, we've been seeing each other since January'
>
> 'Serious? Or just a fling?'

Again Lin bit her lip, then she wrote:

> 'We are very close'

'Oh dear, a foreigner, what would your mum and dad say? Is he rich?'

'Neither rich nor poor'

'Oh my God, you'd throw over Wei Leng for a common foreigner? Come on, Lin, this is not the 1990s, my girl! What about your future?'

Lin punched in her reply without a second thought:

'What about love?'

'It will be gone in the twinkle of an eye, and before you know it he'll be working late every night!'

Did Lin detect in Yuping's phrasing an inkling of disillusionment? But how could she be disillusioned? Yuping had got what she wanted, a nice house, children, wealth. But did she have true love? Lin wrote back:

'I somehow don't think so. I've had boyfriends before, remember? But it's never been like this'

'Oh my God, honey, that's even worse!'

Lin told Yuping to keep it to herself for the time being, especially not to tell her mum; she wasn't ready to let the world know yet.

'Then it's just a fancy lover. It will pass, but take my advice, darling, don't slam the door on Wei Leng!'

*

Colin, on the other side of the corridor, after the excruciating pain of aesthetic needles going into his flesh under his nose, now lay calmly having his mole cut away and the incision closed with sutures.

Twenty minutes later, Lin looked up to find him following the nurse back into the room as she signed off with Yuping. The nurse gave instructions to Lin as Colin removed his gown and disposable slippers, and then dressed for the outdoors. The whole operation had lasted thirty-five minutes. As they entered the car, Lin's phone buzzed.

'You can answer it if you like,' said Colin, his left index dabbing the plaster under his nose. 'I'm not in any hurry.'

'Oh, it's OK, it's only my mum,' she said, secretly thinking to herself how uncanny it was that her mother should call so soon after Lin's conversation with Yuping about Colin. 'I'll call her later.'

34

Colin noticed a strange phenomenon that coincided with the removal of the mole: his books were beginning to sell.

Lin, who had a good head for business, told him to double down on his ads. By the end of April, he was selling hundreds of books a day, a trend he put down to the increasing lockdowns now all over the world, to Lin's encouragements, and of course, to the removal of the mole. Its removal was also a manifestation of the blind trust he felt for Lin. Their mutual trust nourished their love, feeding into their virtuous circle of unity. But exterior forces could threaten any relationship, and little could they imagine as they visited local landmarks and markets, that *mogwai* the demon was never far away, lurking in the shadows, waiting to smother any bourgeoning happiness.

Lin's mother had gotten wind of the relationship with the foreigner. One day, as Lin was working on her laptop from home, her mum called to say: 'Look, Lin-Lin, darling, I'm not against a foreigner in the family, but this one's been divorced. He already has kids!'

'It's OK, and so does Nicholas Tse. Didn't stop him from going out with Faye Wong.'

'You can't compare your foreigner to Nicholas Tse and Faye Wong,' declared her mother, quite amused. 'She's a famous singer! Now look, Lin-Lin, this is what I want you to do; then you are as free as a swallow in the spring to choose, and I will forever hold my tongue.' Lin pulled the phone from her ear while her mother went on. 'I just want you to dine with Wei Leng one more time. You never know what the future might hold, my girl. What if your foreigner doesn't come back? What if he dies? What if . . .'

'Stop, stop,' said Lin, flattening the phone back against her ear. 'All right, Ma, I will dine with Wei Leng just one more time, and you will forever hold your peace over my choice afterwards. Agreed?'

'Yes, daughter. And I needn't remind you that it's not every day a girl of your age gets another crack of the whip at getting a man! In fact, it turns out that this foreigner is a good thing really because he's whipped up Wei's sense of competition. You must be on a lucky streak, and you know what men are like in China. They usually only want young chicks so they can do what they want with them . . .' By now, Lin had put on the loudspeaker and had placed the phone on her desk so that she could continue typing her report, punctuating her mother's monologue with appropriate grunts. 'And if you're not careful,' continued her mother, 'you'll end up having your frozen eggs fertilized by a complete stranger. Then what? You wouldn't even know who he was, what he was, or where he was from. He could be from a long line of gamblers or drinkers or worse: from a line of lazy, good-for-nothing barbarians from the south! I mean, what respectable man would give his sperm to a clinic?'

Scandalized, Lin stopped typing and snatched up the phone. 'Mother!' she said in a low, chiding voice.

'One who needs the cash, that's what!' continued Mrs Cheng.

'All right, Ma, I said I will do it . . . if only to save you from lecturing me for the rest of your days!'

*

With the epidemic now under control, Colin was at last able to go back to his service apartment, where Lin had arranged to pick him up the following Saturday.

From there they would drive northward to visit a section of the Great Wall. This arrangement would allow her to fulfil her promise to her mother and dine with Wei on the evening before. She would take the car this time, and she would not be drinking alcohol; she would just go there to get it over and done with. 'I might have to dine with Yuping, my old uni friend,' she had told Colin. Saying *might* would not be betraying his trust because she equally *might* decide against it.

Wei met her outside at the agreed address and escorted her into a chic Western-style restaurant located near the Winter Palace. Lin, scarfed and gloved and dressed under her woollen coat in a beige suit and a black polar neck pullover, noticed he had made an effort to dress in a more casual outfit: thick woollen jersey and blazer, cotton trousers and casual town shoes. The low tables were widely spaced apart; the candlelit ambiance was trendy and cosy amid a soundscape of mellow jazz. As Lin perused the menu, she almost made a comment about the extravagant prices. Retaining her composure, she managed to keep it to herself, but all the same, three hundred dollars for a meal, she thought while touching one of her lobes pierced with a silver stud. She turned the pages nonchalantly to the drinks page just to appease her curiosity: $500 for a bottle of champagne!

They were seated in soft-leather dining armchairs near a large window that looked onto the subtly designed decking enclosure, now glowing with discreet sophistication. It was not difficult for Lin to imagine herself in a prized European location two thousand miles away from the pollution of Beijing. She nevertheless kept up her guard and replied with aloof composure to Wei's small talk. He was definitely putting himself out tonight, she thought to herself.

Adjusting his spectacles, he said: 'Did you find the restaurant all right?'

'Of course, I have a satnav,' she returned, forcing a smile.

With a sweeping glance around, he said affably: 'I hope it's to your liking here.'

'It is pretty,' said Lin politely.

Wei leant forward and said: 'Would you like some champagne now?'

'At the beginning of a meal?' said Lin, patting the area between her collar bones as though shocked at his lack of refinement. 'I will just take hot water, thank you very much.'

'Fine,' said Wei; then leaning back, he said: 'My mother sends her regards, by the way. She thanks you for your concern.'

'Oh, but I haven't met your mother, have I?' replied Lin.

'No, but she saw you from the car the other Sunday when we met.'

'Oh.'

'I believe our mothers knew each other when they were young. My mother has much esteem for yours.'

'Thank you. I wasn't aware they knew each other.'

'In the past, for a brief time, I believe. Mother knows everyone who is anyone.'

'Nice. Have you chosen?' said Lin, smiling with discreet impatience. Now that she did not care what he thought, she could not stop herself from being her usual assertive self. She had nothing to lose, nothing to gain, nothing to hide, and had decided to go through the meal as efficiently as the bounds of good manners allowed her to. But her curt replies and forward behaviour did not have the desired effect. Indeed, the curter she became, the more Wei opened wide his beady eyes, which brought a hint of a smile to his lips. It had a surprising effect, like a sunny day in the spell of winter solstice.

He asked questions about her likes, then drilled down further. He asked her opinion on topics related to her profession, such as how to attract top Western talent to China and retain it. This was a subject close to Lin's heart, and he listened to her discuss how to remedy the retention problem by offering candidates more cultural support, such as lessons in Chinese language and culture. In this way, she explained, their job would not be the only reason they stayed in China. Then she talked about her ideas on how to make foreigners fall in love with the culture, the history and wealth of Chinese traditions. Wei listened attentively; his phone was nowhere in sight, and he punctuated her reasoning with observations of his own. Before she knew it, she was in a head-to-head with this top Harvard graduate and intellectual. She did not find it so unpleasant.

'I suppose many foreigners stay because they find a local girl. But I guess these are mainly younger candidates, are they not?' he said, pushing back the centre of his spectacles onto the bridge of his nose.

'Not only, and not just men. We have also recruited women, although they tend to come over with their partners.'

'What about your foreign friend?' said Wei without irony.

'Oh,' said Lin, unable to hide a sudden nervousness at the corner of her mouth, 'he is here to take part in a project.'

Wei feigned not to notice her slight discomfort and said: 'Is he in business?'

'No, no, he works in games,' said Lin, regaining her composure.

'A programmer?'

'No, no, he is a narrative, a very good one; he has worked on some leading Western video games and is here to work on a mobile game.'

'Ah, so he makes up stories.'

'Actually, he builds the narrative into the game, and manages the voice casting and such.'

'Interesting,' said Wei flatly. 'Or should I say, entertaining. Do you play mobile games?'

'Hardly, at my age,' said Lin spontaneously, but she could have cursed herself for saying so. Wei continued delicately cutting his meat with his knife and fork.

'Do you like the beef?'

'Yes, it is tender.'

'I believe it comes from a race in France they call the Limousine . . . like the car, funny, isn't it?' Lin returned a mock laugh, still piqued at the snub about the occupation of her *foreign friend* that visibly interested him less than his slice of French beef. A moment later, excusing herself, she stood up and asked the waiter for the ladies' room. Once there, she checked her phone. There were no messages from Colin.

When she returned to the table, Wei said light-heartedly: 'Getting back to the real world, I have ordered the champagne. I believe you meant that the French drink it with their dessert, don't they?'

'Yes,' said Lin, trying to find a suitable quip. 'And the Americans drink it at any time!'

'You are quite right. We should do as they do in France where it comes from,' said Wei thoughtfully as the sommelier arrived with a bottle, while the dessert waiter placed a vanilla crème brûlée *à l'orange* at seventy-five yuan the mouthful in front of each of them.

'I cannot; I have brought my car,' said Lin, glancing at the brandished bottle of Dom Pérignon.

'Then I will order a driver to drive it back for you,' said Wei winningly. Wei gave the nod to the sommelier.

'Oh, oh,' exclaimed Lin, lost for words as the wine waiter popped the cork of the $500 bottle of bubbly. Nevertheless, she was curious to know what made it so special.

By the time her second glass was topped up again, the tiny bubbles were popping in her brain and, in the filtered ambiance of the gorgeous setting, she was feeling like someone special. Then Wei reached into his pocket.

'Excuse me,' he said, with a little pantomime.

'Go ahead,' said Lin, almost thankful he had not forgotten his precious phone that had played the role of a third guest during their previous meal together. But it was not his phone that he brought out.

He said: 'My mother suggested this would look beautiful on your long ivory neck.'

'Oh my goodness!' said Lin, putting down her glass and catching her breath. The long velvet case he had opened was glimmering with a gold necklace and a moon pendant that dazzled in the candlelight.

'Needless to say, they are diamonds,' said Wei, pointing to the dazzling stones.

'Oh, Wei, it's beautiful,' she said, again patting the area between her collar bones, 'but I can't accept it.'

'Please, my mother would be upset if you did not.'

In a flash of sobriety, Lin realised that this man was a master of manipulation. For he knew she would not accept such a gift from him, not from anyone on just a second date. But to upset his mother who knew her mother, it would make waves. Nevertheless, after some slightly tipsy remonstrance, she managed to stick to her guns, remembering that this man's mother did not matter, that this man, though charming as he was becoming, was not her heart's desire, and that she had only agreed to meet him to put an end to his hopes.

'I am sorry, Wei,' she said a little ruefully, 'but what respectable girl would accept such a gift, such a wonderful gift, after just two meetings? It's too much.'

'Then it will be for another time,' said Wei without vexation as the dark oblong case disappeared into his blazer pocket. 'I won't tell my mother.'

A short time after, despite his insistence, Lin chose to call a driver herself. As she sat in the back of her Benz, she reflected that it had nonetheless been a pleasant evening, drunk as she was on the champagne and the splendour. Wei had shown that he could turn on the charm when he wanted to. She looked at her phone. Still nothing from Colin; he must be writing, she thought. Then a message popped up.

'Well? How did it go?'

Lin was not in the mood to answer her mother. Another message popped up.

'So where did he take you?'

But it was her mother after all. So she punched in her reply.

'To a posh western restaurant near the Winter Palace . . .'

'That's nice . . . and?'

'And that's all.'

'Good.'

Lin knew full well what her mother meant by *good.* She knew by Lin's answer that Lin had not turned him down. But how could she when he was so surprising, when he was making such clumsy efforts to overcome his geekiness? Even to the point of offering her a gift his mother had chosen.

'Oh God,' thought Lin, now sobering from the influence of the surroundings and the champagne. Then she switched profiles and punched in another message.

'What are you doing?'

The answer came back from Colin some minutes later.

'Hey, baobei, thought you wanted to be left alone tonight so I've been on a writing spurt.'

'Oh, not really, but I'm glad you got some writing done. That's great'

'9 o'clock tomorrow, right?'

'Yes, I will pick you up in front.'

'Ok, I'll get the paninis and diet coke from June's café.'

'Good.'

Then, still holding her phone in her hand, Lin dozed off.

35

Colin had spent a good evening writing and felt liberated for their visit to one of the Seven Wonders of the World.

As Lin rolled up in front of June's Garden Café, he smiled to himself on recalling what Max once said when he first mentioned how keen he was to visit the Great Wall. 'What do you wanna go there for, man? They're just stone steps, nothing spectacular about them, man. And they are so badly made you need giant legs to walk up them!'

The drive out was pleasant, the April sky clement. The pink blossoms that left the streets downtown smelling of perfume were also in spectacular abundance in the hills northwest of Beijing. The forests offered an explosion of colour as they cruised along the new mountain roads to the sound of Lin's new playlist: it was the playlist of their love affair.

Lin, though slightly subdued and a little late for their drive out, had soon forgotten the previous night's champagne and came back to herself, her true self, no façade, no pretending, just happy to be going out on a day trip with

Colin like a couple of lovebirds. It compared to nothing else, not even to a diamond-studded necklace. Her only regret was not closing the door definitively on Wei Leng. Was it a trait of her personality to be so easily wooed? But she had not been seduced, just charmed, she told herself and felt better.

The restaurants around the entrance of the wall, renovated with taste, were closed. Where the wall would be crowded with tourists, today there was just a trickle of visitors. It occurred to Colin that perhaps there was no better time to visit these places than during a pandemic. The wall snaked along the peaks and crests of the wooded mountain range beyond the section open to the public. And indeed, Max was not wrong when he had said it took giant strides to climb up the stone steps. There again, this was a defensive wall, and the irregular height and tread would certainly make an invasion all the more arduous, he thought.

Pausing from time to time, they took silly selfies sprawled out on the giant steps and at the various stopping points. These offered seats and an incredible view of the surrounding nature while they rested and enjoyed their sandwich and drink. Once at the top, they sneaked a French kiss on camera, in an alcove out of the public eye to the side of the souvenir shop.

'The toughest part is yet to come,' he said, nodding to the young women clutching their boyfriends' arms for dear life as they descended the alarmingly steep and irregular steps.

'Oh,' said Lin, dubiously.

'It's OK. What we need is rhythm.'

'What?'

'We need to trot down with rhythm, in time. Look, I'll show you.'

Colin tried on a section of a dozen steps first, counting in Chinese to four — *yi, er, san, si* — to a singsong rhythm. Sure enough, the rhythm allowed him to fearlessly bound down the steps, kicking out his feet in time to his count.

He climbed back up to take Lin by the hand, and together, they bounded down those perilous steps, stepping in time to each other's paces like Gene Kelly and Debbie Reynolds, both singing to four, then starting over again: *yi, er, san, si, yi, er, san, si . . .*

She felt intrepid, braced to affront the world. To her, it seemed like together, nothing could stop them as they went joyfully trotting down the steps of the Great Wall of China, leaving the fearful in their wake. She could not imagine for one second Wei taking a firm grasp of her hand and leading her fearlessly along the steps of life. True, he would probably have taken a helicopter and flown over them, her inner voice told her.

*

On the way back through the breathtaking landscape of north Beijing province, they stopped off at a Brand Village for some cake and coffee.

Colin had conceded to browsing around the plethora of top-brand shops from around the world that displayed goods supposedly at knock-down prices. Being the only Westerner in sight, he was becoming slightly irate at the eyes glaring at him. With the virus running wild around the world, it was as though the Chinese had found a good reason to become overtly suspicious of Westerners.

'You can get it all cheaper online,' said Colin as they were sitting on the terrace of a first-floor café.

'Yes, but there are many fakes online. Here at least, everything is genuine, so you don't need to take your trainers to a shoe inspector to get them tested.'

'Really? You take your trainers to a shoe inspector? Hah.'

'Yes, if you buy online, how else will you know if they're fake?'

'Well, as long as they do the job, right?'

'No! Because they might have the same look but not the same quality.'

'True,' conceded Colin, lazily admiring the giant screen in the atrium below, 'and I suppose at least it gives someone a job: shoe inspector, never thought of that one, ha!'

Fatigued from the steep climb and overdosed on oxygen, Colin let his eyelids fall while Lin fell busy to answering messages on her phone. She had resisted answering so far, just enjoying the moment, and besides, she had been driving, and she could hardly answer with Colin sitting beside her. She read the message from Yuping.

> 'He's keen, he finds you incredibly strong and he likes strong women.'

Lin replied:

'He likes his mother!'

In another thread Lin's mum wrote:

'He's very successful, I knew his mother before she married. Married well, so well, strong woman. It would be so nice to catch up with her after all these years.'

Lin replied:

'Mother, no!'

'I thought it went well.'

'I didn't say that.'

'But you didn't reject him either.'

'I couldn't'

'Wise daughter.'

On the other thread, Yuping replied:

'He thought you divine to refuse the necklace, it cost a fortune.'

'I wasn't aware it was a test.'

'It wasn't, and if it was you must have passed it because he wants to take you out again.'

'I can't'

'Because of your foreigner?'

'I could never love Wei Leng even if I lived to a hundred!'

'Maybe you're just too ambitious when it comes to relationships, darling . . .'

'You've been reading Eileen Chang again!'

'So what. She's right about one thing: a good wife can make a man'

'True but Wei is already made. His mother's seen to that'

'No, he has so much more potential with the right woman behind him. Anyway, I have to go fetch the kids. Think about it, darling . . .'

Lin switched to the thread with her mother, who had replied:

'If you didn't throw him over last night then there must be a spark'

'No spark. But I will end it.'

'Lin-Lin, think carefully. This is your future, and he wants children.'

'Is he man enough? His children will be weak.'

'You're too selective for someone of thirty-five with blocked tubes, my girl.'

'I have to go, Ma, talk later.'

Lin slipped her phone into her bag as Colin opened his eyes.

'You all right?' he said to her. 'You must be exhausted.

Pity I'm not allowed to drive.'

'It's OK. Shall we go?'

They descended the stairway into a mix of false European architecture and back through the lanes of the Brand Village. As they strolled hand in hand, Colin sensed more eyes upon him than usual, reproachful eyes. Then, feeling a cool breeze on his nostril where the mark from the mole was still slightly itchy, he stopped dead. 'Damn it!' he said, his hand feeling his face, 'I've left my mask on the table.'

'Oh, I haven't a spare on me either, but it's all right.'

'But people will stare. Wait here; I'll nip back and fetch it,' he said, before taking off in the direction of the café.

A minute later, he was striding up the stairway to the first floor, two steps at a time. From the top balustrade, he could see the outdoor table where they had been sitting. A cleaning lady had already parked her trolley next to it and was disinfecting the table, something she had not done before he and Lin had taken it after having stood in line for another couple to vacate it. But he was a foreigner, and the mask was gone, probably picked up with her giant wooden pincers and dropped into her bin.

While she waited, Lin had found a vacant street seat between the shop façades of the world's greatest brands: Gucci, Louis Vuitton, Calvin Klein . . . all treasures of the commercial world. She was contemplating her reply to Wei, who had messaged her asking if she would be free next Saturday. What a coincidence he should get in touch just after her mother, she thought to herself. But how should she deal with this third meeting? Use it as a backup plan just in case? Or tell him by text overtly that she was no longer available? But then he was bound to ask her why she was turning him down, and she would have to tell him straight and face further insistence. Or should she just ignore him for now? She was about to send her reply when she looked up as Colin approached, saying: 'They were already cleaning the table. The mask was gone so I'll just have to face the world nude from the neck up!'

'Unmasked and moleless,' quipped Lin as she closed her phone and slipped it back into her bag.

Sitting beside her, Colin said: 'Must admit, it's uncomfortable without a mask. Old people keep staring at me.'

'It's OK, they won't say anything. They'll just think you're a silly foreigner!'

'That's true!' conceded Colin.

Lin wanted to visit just a few more shops to check whether their prices were worth going back for. After another stop, she concluded they were not, at least not for those who needed to count their yuan. It would take a marriage with someone like Wei Leng to be able to shop here without any remorse, she thought to herself.

The sun sets rapidly in Beijing as it sinks first behind the mountains to the west. There was a chill in the air by the time they jumped into the car.

36

The chill from waiting outside the shops because he had no face mask had caught up with him by the following day.

He took a flu tablet as per his habit whenever the first signs of a cold tickled his nose. But come Friday, when Lin picked him up from work, though the door staff had detected no abnormal temperature that morning, he still felt lethargic and a little under the weather. After dinner at Lin's, they put on a film, most of which Colin spent asleep, his head cradled on her lap.

Looking back, Lin wished she had sent a negative reply to Wei when she had the chance at the Brand Village. However, with the encouragements of her mother and her best friend, who only wanted what was good for her, she had ended up conceding to another date. It was the third one, and she recalled Colin mentioning once that the third date was special. But Lin had resolved to settle the accounts, not to cash in. It was only right to do it face-to-face, and it would give her peace of mind.

The next morning, having first ground the beans, Colin

made fresh coffee while Lin prepared eggs on toast. It had become their little couple's quirk of the weekend.

'Coffee tastes awful, doesn't it?' said Colin, reaching for the tissue box on the table.

'Tastes the same as usual,' said Lin, sitting opposite him in her soft pyjamas. 'But you don't look so good, though.'

'Just a cold from last weekend, can't seem to shake it off, and I've run out of flu tablets.'

'You don't think you've caught . . .'

'COVID? Nah, hah, just need to sweat it out in bed a while.'

But his little power nap lasted the whole day. Lin did not want to put off the dinner with Wei. So, after getting ready and putting on a little makeup, she brought Colin another mug of hot tea. Sitting on the edge of the bed, she said: 'Remember, I just have to go out to meet a friend. You just stay here; I've ordered some food.'

'Lin,' said Colin, sliding his mug under the lamp on the bedside table next to him, 'you're going to see that Wei guy, aren't you?' Lin could not answer at first. 'Aren't you?' insisted Colin.

'It's not what you think,' said Lin, brushing any wrong notion away with an indulgent laugh while pressing her hand down on his thigh.

'And what is it that I think?' replied Colin, ignoring her touch and clasping his hands together behind his aching neck.

'Actually,' said Lin, still with a smile in her voice, 'I don't know, but whatever you think, know that it's just to tell him that I don't want to meet him anymore.'

'Anymore? You mean you've met him before?'

'I told you I met him before our first kiss, before we became close . . . then I met him again to please my mother, that's all.'

'I thought we agreed to be frank with each other.'

'We are. That's why I'm telling you. Besides, I've nothing to hide.'

'Except that you met him again.'

'I didn't hide it.'

'You just didn't tell me.'

'No. And I wish I hadn't gone.'

'Well, so do I,' said Colin, raising his voice, and then propped himself up with a groan.

'Really, there's nothing to worry about,' said Lin in her calming way.

'Look, do you want me to go back to my place?' said Colin, levelling his eyes at her and becoming irate. But Lin remained calm and soothing while keeping her aplomb.

'No. I want you here. You can trust me, and there's no reason why you shouldn't!'

'I'm just a bit annoyed, that's all,' conceded Colin, calming down a notch. 'Of course I trust you.'

'Then kiss me. You have no choice, because this is our first argument,' she said, leaning closer toward him with a playful smile. 'It's in our relationship agreement.'

She was right, of course, and it was not in the nature of their relationship to fall into dispute, neither did he want any ill feeling to escalate. She brushed his hair back over his ear.

It induced instant sedation, reminding him just how truly close they were.

'OK,' said Colin, diverting his lips from her approaching mouth to kiss her neck. 'But I don't want you to catch my cold . . .' Then she kissed his face, his cheeks, his eyelids. A few moments later, coming back to himself, he said: 'But tell me, what has he got that I haven't?'

'Well,' said Lin, and counted the points on her fingers: 'he's Chinese, he's wealthy, I mean like stinky rich wealthy, he's overqualified, and his mother knows my mother.'

'OK, OK,' said Colin, holding out his palms to stop the onslaught, 'what hasn't he got then?'

'Well, he's a geek, he's incapable of emotion, he's not very handsome, and he bores me to tears . . . and he looks like the type who wears pyjamas in bed come what may. And he probably hasn't got a good sperm count.'

'Oh,' said Colin, letting her hands slowly crawl up his torso under his T-shirt.

'And most of all, I don't love him. I love you.' She touched the tip of his nose with her finger delicately, like a button.

Colin was won over; his anger melted away as she started kissing his collarbone. His firm body became relaxed. But now released from tension, he turned his head away before falling into a bout of coughing.

37

'I hope you don't mind coming to the same place as last time,' said Wei Leng, as they were ushered to the same table as the last time they met. 'I am a beast of habit, hah . . .'

'It's a lovely location,' said Lin, shedding her coat to the waiter to reveal her black blazer and matching flared trousers. She sat down in the comfortable armchair, drawing her hair over her dainty ears, adorned this time with gold earrings.

'Yes, actually, my family are sleeping partners,' said Wei, sitting down after her.

'Oh, good for them.'

'Yes, my mother likes us to make an appearance from time to time to let them know we're still here.'

'How is she now?'

'Getting better, she'll be spending time during the May break at our house in the country.'

'Nice for her to get some fresh air.'

'She likes to get back to her roots, she says. She was from the country herself, of humble stock, you know; that's how our mothers know each other.'

'Oh, really?' said Lin, her wry grin taking any question of complicity out of the remark. 'Well, I'm not sure my mother would agree to you saying she is of humble stock: her father was a respectable civil servant, and she and my father have been very successful, and they are self-made.'

'Please forgive me; I didn't mean it like that,' said Wei in earnest. Then with a coy smile, he said: 'Mother says my social skills often fail me.' Lin granted him a forgiving smile as the sommelier approached, holding out a fine bottle. Wei continued: 'But come, let us toast to the grit of the people! I've taken the liberty of ordering champagne at the start, like they sometimes do in California.' He gave a nod to the wine waiter, who proceeded in uncorking the bottle.

'Actually,' said Lin, 'I'd rather not, if you don't mind.'

'Please, I insist,' said Wei, again nodding to the waiter, who this time delicately poured the sparkling liquid into Lin's crystal champagne flute before filling Wei's. Raising his glass, Wei said: 'To the blood and grit of the people who made us, and to those who made themselves!'

Lin was on the fence as to whether his toast was patronising or not. But deciding to give him the benefit of the doubt, she put the glass to her lips in a show of good will.

'I've taken the liberty of ordering a house specialty: lamb and truffle.'

'Oh, all right, happy to try it,' said Lin, unable to find a reason to refuse.

'My favourite when I was a boy, lamb.'

'Nice,' said Lin, remaining nonchalantly polite.

'I seem to get on with anyone who likes it, actually.

Funny, really, when you think about it. I was born in the Year of the Sheep after all. And you, the Year of the Rabbit, I believe . . .'

'No, actually, in the Year of the Tiger,' lied Lin, thinking to herself that he had planted the whole lamb thing just to place his line.

'Oh, my mother told me it was the Year of the Rabbit,' said Wei, pushing back his spectacles to the bridge of his nose as per his habit.

'Well, I suppose I ought to know my birth animal,' laughed Lin, adamantly sticking to her lie, knowing full well that in Chinese tradition, the tiger and the sheep did not make a good match. Suspecting their mothers had conferred, she pictured his mother showing her mother how wealthy she had become, and her mother putting on false airs and graces to show that she was no pauper either. But how dare he try to correct her! Even though she knew he was right, it was ill-mannered of him to allow her to lose face, especially on a date. But Lin tried to relax. After all, as Wei had said himself, he was not known for his social skills.

They continued to exchange niceties and family tales, with Wei punctuating her thoughts with *hen hao* — very good. At first, she thought he was making a lame effort at being friendly and encouraging. However, when she said: 'Actually, I do like the dish; I used to have lamb on Sundays when I stayed with a family in Paris.'

'Very good, very good,' he reiterated, and she realised that he was not being complaisant at all: he was scoring her answers in his head.

She decided to try out her theory. She said: 'I think one should remain humble in wealth.'

'Very good,' said Wei, bowing his head slightly.

'The poor have no need to envy the rich, for everyone has a role to play in society . . . from the delivery man to the company head.'

'Very good.'

Having apparently won his approval, she decided to try something else. Once she had steered the conversation to serve her purpose, she said: 'In fact, I do think it's more character-building if a child is left to stay with the grandparents as much as possible during the holidays.'

'Good,' said Wei, nodding his head just once.

'And all the more so if they are of humble stock.'

'Quite,' said Wei, fidgeting in his seat. 'Although I should think it would depend on the child's agenda. There are many things for a child to do and see in the world if he is to grow into a responsible adult capable of running a business.'

'Yes, but you cannot substitute the love of a child's kin. It is what forms the character and moral fibre of a girl or boy. Otherwise, they become exclusively the property of the parents, which would deprive them of being shown about life through different lenses, wouldn't it?'

'Quite,' said Wei ambivalently, his polite smile at odds with his unyielding eyes. It was clear to Lin he was fighting off the desire to say something.

To counter the reflex of reaching for her glass of champagne, Lin called for a glass of water, as she had learnt they do in France, so as not to overindulge in the alcohol through having nothing else to hand. But Wei prompted her to drink up, and so she raised her glass and touched the rim of it with her lips.

As far as Wei Leng was concerned, the dinner was going swimmingly. He had been sensitive to her arguments, had agreed with her a lot, and had shown a side of his personality that displayed his love of family. When they were served the dessert, Wei again said: 'You've hardly touched your champagne. Don't you like it?'

'I do; it's very good,' said Lin, thinking to herself that every sip was worth fifty kai. 'But I must have caught a chill the other day. I took some medicine before leaving, and I don't want the champagne to go to my head.'

'Very good,' said Wei approvingly. Now with a few glasses of bubbly inside him, he was feeling that the time was ripe to reach for the lure. A third date was after all a confirmation of a mutual appreciation of being together, wasn't it? At least, that was what his mother had told him.

After another swig of bubbly alcohol, placing his glass with exaggerated attention on the table, he said: 'Well, I hope . . .' Here he paused for effect while reaching into his blazer pocket. Lin was preparing herself for a repeat of the necklace act, and said to herself that the moment had come to put an end to this courtship. But to her surprise he brought out a crushed velvet ring box. 'Well, I do hope this will go to your head!' he said, upon opening the box to reveal a beautiful diamond ring. He had rehearsed his move just before coming out, but now, with the champagne blunting his thoughts and feeling sure he would win over the girl with diamonds, he forgot to start his line before opening the box. This allowed Lin time to jump in before having to make him lose any face.

'No, no, Wei, I cannot accept that, I really cannot.'

'But I want you to have it. In fact, I want to ask you . . .'

In that instant, a life of fabulous wealth reeled through Lin's mind, but it was replaced by a vision of pompous children who resembled Wei, and a life without love. She found the strength to quickly say: 'No Wei, stop. Actually, I've come to say that we cannot meet anymore.' There, it was out, and she felt a weight suddenly lift from her chest. She continued as Wei sat opposite her, wordless. 'We are too different, Wei; it would not work. We come from different worlds . . .'

'Oh,' said Wei, staring intensely at his glass. Then he glanced up at her with a smile and said: 'But that's precisely what makes us complementary. Look at my mother and father: she made him into an even better version of himself.'

'No, Wei, I have no intention of replacing your mother,' said Lin frankly.

'Please, don't say anything yet. Just think on it.'

This left Lin no choice but to give it to him straight. She said: 'Wei, I'm sorry, but I am in a relationship.'

'Oh. Yes,' said Wei, interlocking his fingers as though about to enter negotiation mode. 'With the foreigner friend?' Lin gave a nod. 'Now, we are both grown-ups. At the age you are, I would have been surprised if you hadn't tried a number of relationships. It is not so bad, and I am divorced myself. So please, just think of what it would mean for our families, to you, to me too . . .'

'I could not love a man who places a price tag on love.'

'I was not thinking of love, Lin. I was thinking of a partnership. Like a sort of joint venture. Your mother told my mother about your medical issue which, on the contrary, would suit me fine. We could create a child in vitro. So please, give yourself time to consider my offer.'

Nervously swirling her glass of champagne, she was wondering whether or not to throw the rest of its contents in his face. Then she thought about the lifelong consequence of conversations with her mother and the shame it would bring to her family. They would be labelled as incapable of carrying themselves properly in a fine restaurant. So, for the grace and face of her mother, she set the glass on the table, pressed her fingers against her temples, then stood up and said: 'I have to go now . . . Please take me to my car.'

Her show of authority had the desired effect. He scootered around to her side of the table and escorted her out, only stopping along the way to receive their coats and for him to tell the waiter to put the meal on his account. On the way through the stylish, glowing decking and to the nearby side street, Lin imagined a life whipping this man into submission and him enjoying the feeling of being dominated, a feeling inculcated no doubt by his mother. She saw herself obtaining everything she desired. Everything, that is, except what she hungered for most, what her affair with Colin had made her appreciate. In a word: love. She realised too that the Lin of old, the trail-blazing, strong-headed filly, who thought she knew what she wanted in this world, had perhaps been wrong in her approach to finding a partner. She had overlooked love's power: the oneness that sex in love procured and which she and Colin had mutually attained in each other's arms.

But there again, would it last forever? Would it last as long as that diamond ring she had just turned down? And true, Wei was perhaps not so handsome, sweet, and charming, but he would undoubtedly appreciate her all the more. Indeed, she was sure now that she knew how to make him revere her. Wasn't that something every woman sought in a man, undying devotion?

An hour later, she pushed the door into her apartment. Lamplight emanated from the bedroom, but there came no reply when she called out.

No sound, no greeting. Had Colin gone? She did not stop to wash her hands or even go to the bathroom. She went directly to the bedroom. Suddenly panicked, she paused on the threshold on seeing an inert mound under the covers. 'Colin?' she said softly as she approached the bed. Then more playfully, she said: *'Baobei?'*

There was still no answer. Slightly anxious, she pulled back the cover. Colin hardly stirred. She touched his forehead. He was burning up.

38

Lin knew from her mother, who got it from her mother, that traditional Chinese medicine acted on strengthening the body's qi or vital energy.

She knew that Colin's high temperature must be to do with the heart and his coughing to do with the lungs. But most of all, she knew that he could have contracted the dreaded virus. She tried to coax him into seeing a doctor. But too tired, he refused to get up. 'It will pass,' he said sluggishly, turning his face away to cough. So Lin made him drink warm water and placed an ice bag on his forehead to bring down his temperature. Letting his head sink back into his pillow, he said: 'Don't worry, I'll be better in the morning.' Then he turned his mouth from her masked face to cough again.

'But there's a chance you've caught the virus,' insisted Lin fretfully. 'We will need to take the test.'

'But I don't see how,' said Colin; then reading the anxiety in her eyes, he added: 'But I'll go tomorrow then.' He then let his eyes close, comforted by Lin's presence while breathing like a buffalo through his half-open mouth.

The next morning, he still would not budge, saying it would soon pass. Lin did not want to use the readily available test kits on the market in case they were fake, so she drove to Peking University Third Hospital, one of many hospitals in the Chinese capital equipped to test and treat potential COVID-19 cases. There were only a few cases in Beijing now, so obtaining her test ticket was as simple as walking to the screened counter. From there, she went to the test cubicle where a nitrile-gloved and hazmat-clad nurse plunged a cotton bud deep into her throat to take a swab. With Colin in mind, after replacing her face mask, Lin said to the young nurse casually: 'What is the preferred traditional medicine for flu and coronavirus symptoms?'

'You must ask a doctor, but for the virus, it is said the *Qingfei Paidu* decoction is helpful,' replied the nurse complaisantly. Lin had read about it on WeChat. Based on a third-century Chinese treaty, this lung-cleansing and detoxifying decoction was composed of twenty-one herbal components and designed to counter the effects of fever, cough, and fatigue. 'You would need a prescription, though,' continued the nurse. 'But you can get capsules or granules of *Lianhua Qingwen* for the flu. It was also used against SARS, and now it is used against the coronavirus.' Lin thanked her for the information. The nurse continued in a graver tone of voice: 'If you are tested positive, you will receive a message and will be taken to the hospital without delay in order to isolate. In the meantime, if you have any symptoms at all, you must imperatively stay at home.'

Later in the day, Lin received a delivery of *Lianhua Qingwen* granules composed to attenuate the effects of the flu virus and to prevent pneumonia from developing in the lungs. She had to take it three times a day by adding water to the granules contained in a sachet.

Feeling a need to evacuate her anxiety in her mother tongue, Lin called Yuping to tell her that she might have contracted the flu.

With real concern for her friend, Yuping said: 'Are you sure it's not the coronavirus?'

'I don't see how I could have caught it,' returned Lin, 'but don't worry, I've taken the test anyway.'

'Oh my God, does your mother know, darling?'

'No, and there's no need to worry her either; I'm fine,' replied Lin, 'and I have some medicine. I just have to sit it out, so keep it to yourself. Otherwise, she's capable of taking the next flight to Beijing.' Lin refrained from mentioning that as she spoke, Colin was lying in her bed as nude as an earthworm and with a fever. Shortly after her call, standing by the bed and brandishing a glass of dark brown liquid, she said to Colin: 'You really need to take the medicine too.'

Colin shook his head with a snarl of distaste. 'Western man no like Chinese coffee, make him sick!' he said, feebly trying to lightheartedly downplay his condition.

'Oh, come on,' said Lin, slightly put out as if he were not playing by the rules. 'It's made of honeysuckle and almond and all kinds of plants . . .'

'Yeah, and it looks like the digested consequence of a Saturday night curry,' he quipped. Even with Lin's insistence, he still refused to take the draught.

By the evening, Lin began to feel rough herself. Wearing just an oversized T-shirt, she fell asleep bare-faced, lying next to Colin on the king-size bed that was big enough to lodge an entire family. 'We have to stay isolated until it passes. You never know,' she said in his ear when she woke, 'and we have to take the medicine three times a day.'

'I'll take the first part, but I'll pass on the second,' he replied, turning over to face Lin, who had been clutching him from behind. She had not wanted either of them to sleep in the spare bedroom; she did not want to leave his side.

'But you really should start taking it,' she insisted a few minutes later as she unsteadily heaved herself up and swung her legs out of the bed. 'It will stop the symptoms from getting worse,' she continued, pushing back her shock of dark hair. Wrapped in her dressing gown and holding her aching forehead, she dragged herself to the kitchen, where she prepared the evening dose of medicine. She emptied the sachet of *Lianhua Qingwen* into a glass, poured boiling water onto the granules until they dissolved, and then topped up the glass with cold water. She took the beverage in to Colin, but again he refused. 'Are you being stubborn?' she said a few moments later as she sat up in the bed before drinking down the bitter brown draught herself.

'Yes,' he returned in a faint voice so as not to provoke another bout of coughing, 'told you, don't drink Chinese coffee!' Then he turned over, curled up, and fell asleep.

During the night, he broke into a cold sweat: his fever was high. Colin had experienced a bad case of the flu before and still would not budge except to move from his sopping patch of sheet. The fever would break, he told her croakily. Lin had not the strength to counter his remonstrance, so she agreed to see the night through before making a move. Moreover, even if they had contracted the new virus, neither of them was in the age group at risk, she thought to herself, and neither had any underlying ailments or conditions.

But in the small hours, Colin's breathing became erratic. Lin awoke. 'Can't catch my breath,' he said to her all in one beat, feeling like the air either escaped his gasps or that he was trying to swallow it down in solid lumps. But at last he fell back into slumber under Lin's soothing touch on his temple.

At some point during his restless sleep, Colin pictured his children when young, playing in the garden of what was once his home. The next moment, he found himself transported to the kitchen, his ex-wife telling him: 'I get angry because I love you.' Colin saw himself uptight and furious after finding she had been rummaging through his study and going through his emails again.

'That is not love!' he found himself snapping. 'That is suspicion, possessiveness!'

'You can't understand,' returned his ex-wife in his dream.

But Colin wasn't listening. He was saying: 'You just want me to love you on your own terms, the way you want me to be!'

'A loving husband holds his wife's hand when they go out. Why won't you hold mine?'

Becoming more irate, he shouted: 'Your bloody parents don't!'

'That's beside the point!' she countered.

'That's precisely the point!' he said, letting out his words in short puffs. 'You become exasperated when I run ahead with the kids, and yet you walk ten paces behind.'

'That's because I'm tired from working on Saturdays.'

'Not my fault!'

'Where's your support when I need it? You forget how I helped you when you started your company!'

'It failed!'

'But I helped!'

'Yeah, and you'll never let me forget it, will you! But the truth is, we've lost our togetherness, and without it how can there be love? That's why I can't hold your hand. And that's why you walk ten paces behind. Because it's gone, gone, gone . . .'

Lin awoke brusquely. Colin was becoming delirious, snorting for breath, mumbling in his sleep, a restless sleep. She cupped his head with her two hands and turned his face to her. 'Colin, Colin,' she said softly. He opened his eyes.

'Lin,' he said at last in half a breath. He placed his hot palm on her smooth face. 'So glad you're here, *baobei.*'

Despite lying there both at their worst, Lin felt strangely appeased. It was suddenly clear to her what she wanted and what she did not. Despite the fever, she felt wrapped in happiness, lying there as she was, physically diminished, but with her soulmate. She felt so good, she could die there in their mutual state of perfect oneness. She smiled, her white teeth gleaming between her pink lips on the glowing surround of her face. She gazed at his lips which she knew, according to traditional Chinese medicine, to be the window of a person's wellbeing. Then she touched the space above them where his mole had been.

'Trust,' she said softly.

'Love,' he returned, touching the tip of her dainty nose.

Staring into one another's eyes, they lay there until the goddess of sleep carried them away through the rest of the night. Meanwhile, on her bedside table, her phone continued to blink.

*

Lin did not know what time it was when the next day, a voice calling out her name came to her through the fog of sleep. Then she heard the front door being closed.

Cracking open an eye, she instinctively snatched up her blinking phone from the bedside table. The first of a series of messages told her she had tested positive for COVID-19, that she must not leave her home, and that she would be taken to the hospital. Stunned, she heard the voice, now nearer, cry out in an exclamation of fright: 'Daughter!' Lying in her bed, Lin craned her neck and perceived the postmenopausal silhouette of her mother, wearing a gold necklace over an ample red floral cardigan, a pink silk scarf, and black trousers, and the tall, elegant figure of Yuping in designer jeans and a baggy cashmere sweater. Both of them were standing gloved, masked, and surprised at the bedroom door.

Lin opened her eyes wider, then intuitively followed their gaze and turned her head to Colin, who was lying without a sound next to her. Frantically, she clawed down the cover from his face, and saw his lips had turned blue. She knew now he too had contracted the deadly virus and, suddenly stricken with fear, she let out a high-pitched visceral wail that her mother had never heard before. 'Colin! Colin! *Baobei*!' she cried out.

Her mother and Yuping hurried to the bed where Lin, out of her mind, was now holding Colin's head in her hands, kissing his lips as if doing so would revive him. At that instant, any thoughts of Lin marrying Wei Leng left Yuping's and Lin's mother's minds forever. For neither had ever seen the face of a woman so desperately trying to keep hold of her love.

'Let me see!' said Mrs Cheng, taking charge as Yuping tried to control Lin's agitation, stroking her hair. 'He's alive, daughter!' said Mrs Cheng. 'He's alive!' she repeated, knowing these were the only words that could keep her daughter from folly. 'But he needs treatment!'

'I have,' said Lin between short breaths, still gasping and terrified. 'In the fridge, but he refused it . . .'

Turning to Yuping, Mrs Cheng said: 'Go fetch it, Yuping!' Then to her daughter, she said: 'We'll see if he refuses your mother!' Next, she drew back the cover and shook Colin by the bare shoulders, her jade and gold bracelets jangling with every shake; then she slapped his cheeks smartly while Yuping rushed to the kitchen to make up a glass of lukewarm draught. At length, Colin awoke as though coming up from the bottom of a deep black sea of sleep. It was a matronly lady in late middle age who was commanding him in Chinese to take the draught while Lin held up his head. Calmer and with tears of relief, Lin said: 'Colin, this is my mum. She says the medicine will protect your lungs and keep out the pneumonia. Please, you must take it now.' He searched in her angst-stricken face and gave a solemn nod of the head.

A short while later, it was a frail and startled-looking Colin who was sitting up in the bed with his hands on his knees, trying to take deep breaths. There came the sound of marching footsteps in the corridor outside the front door. Upon the insistent knocking, Yuping went and answered the door. In the immediate shock of seeing three men and two women in hazmat suits, her hand darted to her chest as she let them march past her into the apartment.

They quickly found their way to the bedroom. Lin knew what they had come for before one of the women broke into speech. 'You have COVID-19,' she said to Lin in a compassionate voice, which contrasted with the impersonal protective suit she was wearing. Then, with a sweeping gaze to all present, the woman continued: 'We must accompany you all to the hospital. You will all need to receive treatment in isolation.'

In the renewed privacy of the bedroom, Lin, still shaking with fear, had time to explain to Colin that they had come for his own good. They would take him to the hospital to be cared for. Still feeble, in an effort to give her some comfort, Colin held her as tight to his body as his dwindling force allowed him to, knowing they would later be isolated in separate rooms. After they both pulled on some clothes, he did not cry out for civil rights when two of the hazmat suited, gloved, and masked health agents helped him into a wheelchair. He was then wheeled down the corridor, into the elevator, and out to one of two waiting ambulances.

The only protest came from Mrs Cheng, who complained vehemently about having to isolate. She was wearing a face mask, she insisted; she could not possibly be infected. But it was the law, it was very serious, and it was for her own good. 'Oh my, why did I have to come?' she lamented as the ambulance doors were closed behind her, Lin, and Yuping.

'Mrs Cheng, you insisted on coming to make sure your daughter was all right,' said Yuping, seated on the bench beside her.

'And you possibly saved Colin's life!' said Lin, frailly raising her head from her lying-down position, visibly fatigued now that her extreme anxiety was spent.

'In that case, that's all good then,' said Mrs Cheng, suddenly appeased and not without a sense of pride, now that the Englishman quite possibly owed her not only her daughter but also his life. Meanwhile, Colin, rather shaken and lying in the second vehicle, also felt relieved to breathe more deeply into the oxygen mask as the ambulance whisked him away to Peking University Third Hospital.

*

In isolation, you are alone with your best friend or your worst enemy. But the good thing is that you get to choose, and Colin chose the former.

After all, he had a particularly good reason to boast a

friendship with himself, for not everyone finds their soulmate in their lifetime, let alone in such a faraway land. And in the light of Lin's love, he now saw a gleam of hope for the future. And most of all, he needed all his combined qi to kick out the virus that had been surreptitiously trying to steal the very breath from his lungs.

As soon as it was officially diagnosed that he had contracted coronavirus, he was given oxygen therapy. Still in shock and not really understanding what was going on, he followed the instructions translated to him by a nurse, and he religiously took his daily doses of "Chinese coffee". He was told this was the notorious *Qingfei Paidu* decoction that prevented pneumonia from setting in. Used in conjunction with Western medicine, it worked to prevent dark spots from developing on his lungs and so to stop his blood from turning dark through a lack of oxygen. Brought down to earth at the real prospect of an early death, Colin reacted well to the treatment, and after a few days, he was on the road to a full recovery. In this way, traditional medicine once again helped curb the spread of another terrible plague in China, even before any vaccine was approved.

As soon as Yang and Little Dragon got wind of his hospitalisation, they sent him get-well-quick messages and funny pictures, one of which from Little Dragon gave Colin cause to smile askew. It was one taken of Colin in a somewhat compromising posture, albeit fully clothed, with a karaoke girl one night. He would have to come clean and show it to Lin, he told himself, before the little dragon found out about Colin's relationship with her. Then there came a

WeChat message from Max which read:

'Hey, WTF! Where you been hanging out, man? Where did you catch it?'

It was typical Max, thought Colin. No fluff. No fanfare, straight to the point. Colin wrote:

'Hey, Max! They traced it back to a cleaning lady at a brand village outside Beijing.'

'Why would you go to a brand village in the middle of a pandemic, man?'

'Went with a friend.'

'You mean with a Chinese girl, that Lin girl! Told you she would bring trouble, man.'

Colin did not reply; instead, he let Max continue:

'Now we're gonna have to sort out all the insurance shit! But you just keep breathing, man! Otherwise all this shit's gonna hit the fan big time!'

Lin, diagnosed with a mild case, desperately insisted she be allowed to phone Colin once his condition permitted. Her eyes welled with relief and joy when at last she saw his face on her phone screen. She made him promise never to make her fear for his life again. He promised to do his best.

Having by now amply established they were meant for one another — one in need of a family of her own, the other in need of a new future — they passed the time in insolation talking in detail about their prospects together: their work, their aspirations, and where they would live. Then, early one morning towards the end of their convalescence, knowing Lin would soon be reaching for her phone in her isolation room, Colin copied the message he had prepared and pasted it into his WeChat feed. It read:

> 'Looking back so far at this tragic year of the rat and the virus, although it's already been such a horrible one for so many, I realise now that for me it's been life changing in the best possible way. It started under the mind-quaking realisation that I had met someone very special. And four months later, the two of us having lived together, sounded each other out, exchanged secrets and laid together in the midst of a deadly virus, my feeling is stronger than ever. I love you completely, lock, stock and barrel, my lovely, sweet and beautiful Lin. I love you mind, body and soul! As we come out of isolation, I'd like this to be a new phase in our journey, of

letting our love grow in all its
splendour, like the cherry blossoms
of Beijing in springtime. So I
solemnly ask you, baobei, do you
still want to join me on this journey?'

Half a minute later, a message came back. It read:

> 'hah you're being romantic again! Love it, love you, sweet, beautiful you. Of course, I do, silly Englishman!'

Chuckling out loud, Colin wondered what Max would think of it all. Then he had an idea.

*

It wasn't long after their release from hospital that a number of flights resumed from Shanghai to London. He had to get back to see his kids, but he promised Lin he would be back to meet her parents in her hometown, in a more conventional posture. And he was. He managed to return to Beijing at the end of summer, before the second wave of the deadly virus hit Europe.

Epilogue

Some months later in the spell of December solstice, Colin was sitting alone at his desk in his London flat, thinking back to that past spring in Beijing. It was New Year's Eve.

The winter streets of London were no less deserted at this late hour than they would be the following morning. For London was besieged by a new COVID-19 strain. Christmas and New Year celebrations had been cancelled. Indeed, the Western world had tragically failed to take control of the virus, had not applied lessons learnt from the Chinese case study. Hospitals were overworked. Frontline health workers all over the world were seeing more people die than anyone ever should in one lifetime.

But he was well and thankful, and he was looking forward to being with his kids again despite London being under Tier 4, the maximum level of restriction measures. The boys were safely grounded at their mother's while, during his Christmas leave, he worked remotely with his team in China. What more could he wish for given the circumstances? But there was just one thing missing.

As per his habit around midnight since arriving back in London before China banned flights to the UK, he now typed a message in WeChat. Beijing being eight hours ahead, Lin would be waking and reaching for her phone. He wrote:

'Morning, baobei!'

She replied with a sticker of a panda wearing a Christmas bonnet and poking out its tongue. He hit the video icon, and Lin's face appeared on his screen. She was lying on her belly in bed, her elbows propped up on pillows, having placed her phone on a selfie stick on the bedside table.

'Hey, Happy New Year!' he cheered with a double wave to the webcam.

She blew a two-handed kiss that flew at the speed of light to him across the cosmos. 'Happy New Year!' she said, her smile illuminating her face. Then, pouting, she said sweetly: 'I miss you; when are you coming back? It's been nearly two weeks already.'

'I can't go anywhere at the moment,' said Colin, placing his hands on either side of him like a teapot handle and spout. 'London's like a ghost town. They registered another 964 deaths over here yesterday. Crazy.'

'Yes, I saw, it's horrible. I told you not to go back!'

'Well, I couldn't not be with the boys over Christmas.'

'I know,' said Lin, empathizing. 'And that's why I let you go.'

'I just hope I can get back before we go into another bloody national lockdown.'

'Me too! And when you come back, I won't let go of you anymore!'

'No,' said Colin with a roguish smile, 'because you'll be coming with me, hah!'

'Not before the wedding, though,' said Lin, steadfastly, her chin resting on her hand. 'And I've been thinking, are you sure Max really wants to be best man?'

'Positive. You should have seen his face when I asked him, I swear he had tears in his eyes.'

'Really?'

'Yeah, sure, sure,' said Colin, remembering the scene in the whiskey bar that had made him realise that Max really did have a heart, and that he was just in need of someone to look after it.

Then, in a more gossipy tone of voice, Lin said: 'And you know what? My mum is so excited, and she keeps telling everyone that mixed children are the cutest!'

'Knowing your mum, it wouldn't matter if her grandchild were sky blue with rose-pink fingers as long as she gets to borrow it during the holidays!'

'Hah, that's true; she's so happy. But we will need to find a place to settle eventually.'

'There's no rush yet, though, is there? At least not for the first few years; we can live anywhere as long as I can get back here once in a while for the boys.'

'I thought Francis and Daniel said they would be glad to study in China?'

'Yes, Francis would. But not so sure his mum would let him, not until he's eighteen.'

'Soon passes.'

'True,' said Colin, gazing at her dotingly, mirroring her pose with his unshaven chin resting on his hand.

'And our child must know its brothers.'

'Yes, of course.'

'Oh, oh, I had a terrible thought last night: What if you can't get back for the wedding?'

'I've already thought about that,' said Colin, taking a philosophical posture. 'In that case, we'll have a Zoom wedding!'

Lin burst into a peel of laughter. 'Silly Englishman!' she said. 'And what about our wedding night?'

In all seriousness, Colin said: 'No, the guests can meet at the venue there, but we can be anywhere, can't we?'

Laughing out loud, Lin said playfully: 'Oh, so my family, your family, and all our friends are expected to come to Beijing just to watch us on a screen?' Wagging her finger, she continued: 'No plan B, it will be a white wedding in a real church.'

'Hah, thought white was supposed be unlucky . . .'

'Come on, that's a cliché, and you know it! Every girl in China these days wants a white wedding dress, like in the movies. So we'll have a church wedding before God as we said. And I'll wear a red traditional dress in the evening for good luck.'

'Pity,' returned Colin solemnly, 'I was really getting into the Zoom wedding. It would have been so original.'

Lin laughed and said flatly: 'Sure.' And then, pouting, she said: 'You're making me horny again with your serious face, so you'd better get back quick so we can make my babies!'

'Baby, you mean,' said Colin, sharpening his eyes.

'Babies: a boy and a girl!' said Lin, counting them on her fingers. 'Otherwise, there's only girls in my family!'

Unable to resist her beaming smile, Colin said: 'All right then, babies: a girl and then a boy . . .'

She blew him another kiss and said: 'Done!'

Lin knew she would bring him round in the end. Now she just had to bring him back.

Enjoy this book?
You can make a big difference

Honest reviews of my books help bring them to the attention of other readers. If you've enjoyed this prequel I would be very grateful if you could spend just five minutes leaving a short review on the book's description page.

Thank you very much.

MAY STUART

is out now!

Port-de-Paix, 1691. May Stuart is ready to start a new life with her young daughter. No longer content with her role as an English spy and courtesan, she gains passage on a merchant vessel under a false identity. But her journey to collect her beloved child is thrown off course when ruthless corsairs raid the ship. Former French Lieutenant Didier Ducamp fears he's lost his moral compass. After the deaths of his wife and daughter, he sank to carrying out terrible deeds as a pirate. But when he spares a beautiful hostage from his bloody-minded fellow sailors, he never expected his noble act would become the catalyst for a rich new future.

May Stuart is a standalone novel set in the world of the thrilling Huguenot Chronicles trilogy. If you enjoy unlikely romance, period-authentic details, and rip-roaring tales of redemption, then you'll love this tale on the high seas.

What readers are saying:

"A most enjoyable, uplifting read."

"Great story of a woman with other ideas of her future."

"Entertaining and so well written that the characters come alive with realism."

MAY STUART

Excerpt

ONE

On the day when news of the English declaration of war against France reached Port-de-Paix, Captain Joseph Reners had already set sail to Charles Town.

Standing pensively on the quarterdeck that night, he lowered the flame of his deck lantern so his eyes could become accustomed to the starlight. Whatever anyone might say, he thought to himself, oblivious to the world over the horizon, turning forty was a landmark in a man's life that should not be contemplated alone, so he gazed up at the stars. Both his father and grandfather had drawn their last breath at sixty, which to Joseph meant that he might well be two-thirds through his own life already.

Perhaps it was time to change course, he thought, picking out his old companion, the North Star, as a warm Caribbean wind whistled through the creaking rigging. Anyway, he had quite had his fill of roving from port to port. It was not so much the ports he was jaded by, more the bits in-between, the seafaring bits which were either extremely dangerous or downright tedious. But on this voyage, he had a very important passenger, and he squeezed his hands silently together in anticipation of a coquetry, or even a pursuit of true love, if that was still possible at his time of life.

A strong leader and proud of his person, he had nonetheless made a success of his twenty years of roaming. He had recently purchased a larger vessel to ferry goods and chattel, and he had amassed a fair fortune. His line of business was not likely to flounder either. In fact, he had a notion that it was just the beginning.

But Captain Reners, during those bits between ports, more and more often got to thinking he had no family, no wife, no children. Perhaps it was time to settle down, make a home some place. He could hire a good captain to do the navigating, and besides, what with the hostilities in Europe, he sensed things were about to turn even choppier at sea.

It was two hours after sundown, and a near full moon now shimmered over a slight sea.

Then he heard it.

The creak of a cabin window.

He stealthily stepped to the starboard bulwark of his new merchant ship and leaned over. 'Good Lord,' he murmured, 'she's doing it again!'

He was not referring to his seventy-ton vessel that coasted at an even keel through the Windward Passage into the waters of the Bahamas. She was quite perfect and a beauty to behold—a far cry from his old pink—more navigable on long voyages, and she coursed through the wavelets like a bolt. No, he was referring to Madame Stuart, his very important passenger whose presence kept him well-groomed and smelling of lavender water.

Admittedly, he had been looking forward to his usual stopover at Nassau, until the governor of Saint-Domingue asked him to take aboard his widowed niece. It would be untoward to carry a lady of quality to such a riotous place. He would have to put in elsewhere to water, which was a pity, because of all the lovely ladies he admired in all his ports of call, Betty was the loveliest of them all, and Betty was in Nassau. Soft and reassuring was Betty, motherly almost, and she had the softest bosom a weary gentleman traveller could lay his head upon. The perfect companion to help round the cape of your fortieth birthday.

But this youngish widow would do fine, he thought to himself rascally. He had already noted the worldliness of her glance, and he liked strong-willed women, ones capable of handling themselves.

He looked down the side of the hull again as *La Bella Fortuna* cut through the water. 'How strange,' he said to himself, as below him another dress was thrown out of the cabin window.

He had been considering how it would improve his status in higher circles to marry a governor's widowed niece . . . But was she, though? Was she really who she said she was? He was beginning to wonder . . .

'Cap'n, Sir,' said Mattis, a stocky matelot with a large, bullish head, standing at the foot of the poop-deck steps, 'I managed to pike this . . .' Reners twisted his torso to see the sailor holding up a beautiful crimson silk dress that gleamed in the night, the kind of dress Joseph had seen ladies wear in certain haunts of pleasure. He could barely hide his surprise. Who was Madame Stuart?

*

May Stuart had come a long way since leaving London all those years ago.

Sitting in the relatively comfortable cabin reserved for very important persons, she pulled out another wildly expensive robe from the trunk she had placed beneath the glazed window. She held up the crimson garment of fine silk by the shoulders. 'Pity,' she said to herself, 'shan't be needing you anymore!' Then she pushed open the window and promptly bundled the robe through the dark hole into the star-speckled night.

Pulling out another alluring dress, she inwardly smiled at how easily she had the captain already eating out of the palm of her hand. She well knew the bovine-eyed look of a besotted middle-aged man. Yet, compared to the robe she was now holding up, she was very conservatively clad in a puritan black dress buttoned to the neck, with subtle white frills at the collar and sleeves. It contrasted forbiddingly with her copper blond hair and smooth, light skin. And her ruby-red lips stood out like an exquisite poppy in a field of barley. She did not need a dress to make her beautiful, she knew, but it was always reassuring when her beauty was confirmed. 'You can go too!' she said, and threw the robe she was holding out into the sparkling night.

She was relinquishing her costumes of seduction. And yet, as she swayed gently in time with the pitch of the ship, she had never felt more in command of her life.

The captain would be a fine catch for sure, she thought, if his ship was anything to go by. But May had already told herself she did not need a man to tell her what to do. She had had plenty of those already; none of them had been any good—except for her late husband, perhaps. But there again, she had been blinded by love, and thinking about it with hindsight, he had been no good either. He was the one who had lured her to the thrill of the voyage and the prospect of fortune, only to leave her caught in a never-ending cycle to make ends meet. From the French port of Saint Pierre to Spanish Havana, she had exploited men's pillow talk and lifted their wallets, laced their drinks, and searched their pockets.

She pulled out another low-cut dress and threw it out. She had never intended to be a sinner, though. At least, not until she realised she was in possession of a formidable weapon. Some women were blessed with fabulous wealth from birth, others with a strong sense of motherhood; others still received the gift of caring, and some got nothing but ailments. As for May, the good Lord had provided her with beguiling beauty and irresistible sex appeal. Was it not her God-given right to exploit it for the sake of self-preservation? At least, it was the only way she had been able to navigate these shark-infested waters of man's new world.

'A new life. A new me,' she said to the glorious green dress she was holding up. Then she threw it out through the window.

At thirty-two, May felt like she had lived more lives than a bodega cat. But she had left Havana for good this time, and now she intended to be her true self. She had her little treasure and planned to invest in some land.

Sitting back in her chair, May imagined her new home, and what it would be like to live in four seasons again in the north. She pictured a pretty stone house with a roaring chimney in winter, a flowered garden, outhouses for storage of whatever she decided to invest in, a stable for a wagon and strong workhorses, a fine mare, and an upholstered French carriage with glass windows. But she could not yet picture a man. She would need one, of course, but what he would look like, she knew not. She only knew he would have to be dependable, as clever with his head as with his hands, and not lack etiquette. She would not fall for a fat-fingered merchant or a grubby-nailed tradesman, oh no: she wanted nothing less than a fine gentleman to be her partner through life. And she would spend the rest of it trying to be righteous and mending her soul; that is what she planned to do.

She would start by removing anything that reminded her of her past lives. But throwing away beautiful dresses was not as easy as she thought, and she had been obliged to stop the previous night. She could have sold them, or even given them away, but that would have been betraying her true self, not to mention the dresses. They had been like a second skin to her and had served her well. They had raised her profile and given her a certain standing. But if she was to seek redemption, she would have to part with them, to relegate them to the vault of her memory like past lovers.

She took another sip of rum, braced herself, and then threw out the offending dress.

After leaving Havana in her usual, more . . . uplifting attire, she had changed into something more appropriate once in Port-de-Paix. Here, the governor, in exchange for her intelligence services, had assured her of a passage aboard the merchantman headed north to Charles Town, Carolina, the new port town where she returned twice yearly.

She picked up the last robe but one left in the trunk, her second favourite. This time, after flinging it out, she poked her head through the window and watched the shimmering saffron dress sail away into the night like a phantom of her past. It suddenly occurred to her that someone could have spotted it as it momentarily floated up with the wind in the direction of the ship. But then it did a pirouette and tumbled blindly into the dark sea. Besides, who would be looking out into the night at this late hour? 'There,' she said, sitting back down in the armchair before her trunk, 'all gone, all but one, just in case . . .' and she gave a deep sigh.

This is the end of this excerpt.

ABOUT THE AUTHOR

Paul C. R. Monk is the author of the Huguenot Chronicles historical fiction trilogy and the Marcel Dassaud books. You can connect with Paul on Twitter at @pcrmonk, on Facebook at www.facebook.com/paulcrmonkauthor and you can send him an email at paulmonk@bloomtree.net should the mood take you.

To receive Paul's newsletter, please go to the subscribe page on his website at www.paulcrmonk.com.

BY THE SAME AUTHOR

In The Huguenot Connection trilogy:

Merchants of Virtue

Voyage of Malice

Land of Hope

Also in the Huguenot series:

Before The Storm 1685

May Stuart

Other works:

Strange Metamorphosis

Subterranean Peril